Snow Angel

Badger Jones

ISBN: 978-09879463-1-7

~~~~~

To my dearest L, who thought I should keep the cat.

~~~~~

"Stupid moron."

His voice hits me hard, and pretty much at the same time as my ass hits the pavement.

There I am, gaping way up at this dude. I don't know him, never seen him before, and have no clue why he'd yank me backwards off my feet.

I'd have a perfect view up his nostrils, except he's glaring down at me like I'm something he'd scrape off his shoe. There's no chance to say anything, because a bus rockets past us, pretty much surfing on the curb where I had been standing - so close to me and travelling so fast, there's no time to flinch until after it has passed. All I get is a spray of slush off the tires, and the taste of road salt in my mouth.

"Moron," he says again. But when I look up to thank him or whatever, he's faded into the crowd. Yeah, weird. He should stand out like a grizzly bear in a frickin' kindergarten, but there's nothing.

Stuff like that's been happening all week, maybe all month, to me, like the big guy, like the bus. Well, not just to me, to everybody I know. Unfortunately, the only people I know are winos, crackheads and hookers, and weird things are *always* happening in that crowd. But this is different, somehow. We're all feeling it.

Anyway, it took my mind off how I feel. That's a bonus, because I feel like crap, I mean, real bad. Shakes, worst I've ever had. Definitely need something to drink, and I don't know how much of that I'll be able to keep down.

That's where I'm going, to get my breakfast. Lorenzo's will be open by noon, which isn't that far off. I think so, at least, but I can't find a clock.

The vibe in the city is off. It's like a hum that you can't quite hear, or a subway train rumbling but far enough away that you don't know you can feel it. But whatever it is, it's in the wrong pitch or key or tempo, or something. It's just off.

I've been having disturbing dreams, strange stuff, the voices don't go with the faces, or it's scary, flames, screaming, fangs … Last night, I dreamt I was a deer, which wouldn't have been so bad, except something was chasing me, hungry for my blood. I don't get much sleep lately.

Sucks.

So I round the corner, and there's the liquor store. Yeah, Lorenzo's isn't a diner, sorry.

It's a crappy day to be waiting – cold and damp, with lots of snow on the ground – but I'm not the only one looking for a little wake me up drink. Plenty of people I know are here, like, way, way more than there should be. We all look like hell, more so than usual, as if someone rounded up all the available street people and dragged us around the block.

And I can see it in everybody's eyes, we're all thinking it: "What the hell are they all doing here with me?"

Yes, we are all feeling it, whatever the hell it is. The vibe is just off.

"Y'got any smokes, Alex?" Dingle asks, sidling up next to me. He's looking wild, like at any moment someone is going to say the wrong thing and he'll go running down the street, screaming blue murder. I don't think he's been sleeping much either.

I only have three cigarettes left and really I want to keep them to myself, but I owe Dingle money, so I'm hoping maybe he won't remember that little fact if I make him happy.

"Yeah," I say. "Give me a second." But he's too anxious and he's making it tough for me to give him one on the sly. Then everybody is stumbling my way, wondering if I can spare another cigarette. It looks like a scene from a movie, with the lone surviving human at the center of a shrinking circle of stiff-legged, man-eating zombies. There's desperation written on every face, all looking for whatever fix they can find.

"Gimme a smoke" rumbles one of the zombies. I don't know him, but I've seen him around – likes to yell a lot.

"Fuck you," I reply. Yeah, real witty, but I'm not feeling my best right now.

'Gimme!" he shouts, like a spoiled four-year-old, and he grabs my sleeve and yanks on it. His other hand winds up for a punch.

And then, he's moving away from me in clichéd slow motion. His face is twisted, eyes shut hard, teeth clenched and lips pulled back, feral. Even through his teeth, he lets out a shriek that makes everybody run.

Except for me that is.

I'm staring at the fist that hit him, following the line up the arm, until I'm staring up, up, up into the face of the guy who saved me from being flattened by a bus. For a second or two, he doesn't say anything, just looks at me, searching my face for something.

Then he lets out a sigh, and pinches the bridge of his nose, like he's trying to rub away a headache. "Aw hell," he says. "You can see me."

2

"Okay, first, you're definitely going to need a drink." His voice is all business, and with his sizeable hand on my skinny little shoulder, he doesn't need to put any effort into moving me, since I'm not much interested in being a hero. And, he is pushing me in the direction I was originally headed anyway, so there's not much sense in resisting.

Lorenzo's is still closed. I can see the old man moving around the store, mopping the floor in futile preparation for his customers, so that they can shuffle in and cover it with slushy boot prints. He's like Sisyphus, but old, fat and Italian.

My companion pounds his fist against the security gate, and Lorenzo looks up sharply, glaring. He points at his watch, and then goes back to his mopping.

More pounding on the gate.

Lorenzo takes his time walking over and opens the door an inch. "It's ten minutes to opening. Wait." Just as quickly, his head drops down again, to eye the stringy mop and dingy floor

"My watch says it's noon." He says it calmly enough. Just looking at him provides enough threat.

Lorenzo's forehead is covered with angry creases now, and his bushy eyebrows have collided in a scowl. I can see him weighing the different options. Open ten minutes early, and save himself some hassles, from someone far meaner than the winos he's used to dealing with, or stick with his scheduled hours and be forced to sell booze one-handed, with the other hand under the counter, resting on a baseball bat.

The gate opens reluctantly, gate and owner feeling much the same way about the day, apparently.

"Thanks," says the big guy, who doesn't sound like he means it. Lorenzo pointedly doesn't look at us as we walk in, instead retreating to his cash register, and the security camera monitor beside it.

"So," the big guy says to me, feigning amiability. "What are you buying today?"

"Wine, I guess. I like port usually, if he's got the cheap stuff in stock." His attempt at putting me at ease has the opposite effect – I'm like a mouse waiting for the cat to get bored of playing with me and bite my head off.

These days I know my way around the liquor store pretty well, so we head directly to where I need to go. Despite the fat man's mopping, the floor is mildly sticky under my boots. Little rip, rip, rip noises accompany every step I take. Not my unwanted companion, though. Each step is a sharp click, like the breaking of glass.

I grab the neck of a bottle, and I'm just about to turn, when he shakes his head.

"Better make it two," he says. "Trust me when I say you'll want it."

"Ain't made out of money," I grumble. For once, I actually have the money in my pocket, but screw him if he thinks he can strong-arm a free bottle out of me.

"It isn't for me, dumb-ass. Like I said, you'll want it."

We lock eyes for a second, and I look away first and shrug. "Okay, we buy two."

With my best poker face, I'm talking winning the Oscar for Best Dead-Pan Face, I make like I don't care, but I'm worried that he's right. That's a real bad place to be, to have someone tell you authoritatively that today is a day in which you should be drinking heavily.

Greasy old Lorenzo still refuses to look us in the eye, especially *him*, but instead counts my money with elaborate care, pulling each coin away with a careful finger, and slowly uncrumpling the one bill in the mess on his counter. Okay, sure, it isn't like I have a flight to catch or I'm running late for my television appearance, but it's annoying to wait. Plus, the day is already catching up on me – shakes, chills, general crapitude. I want to sit down somewhere, like now.

Three thousand years later, we're walking down the street, alone – nobody has dared come back yet. The bag in my hand clinks lightly, a boozy little wind chime. Normally that might be a problem, signalling the availability of bottles to this neighbourhood. But, with the big guy beside me, there's no way anybody is coming near.

The thought occurs that I might just have purchased his booze for him, and now I'm carrying it to wherever he plans on drinking it, but it isn't like there's anything I can do about it if he decides to rip me off.

"So, what can I call you?"

"Serapion," he says, looking down the street.

"Interesting name. Russian?"

"No." He doesn't volunteer anything else.

I take the opportunity to sneak a look at him. I've already established that he's big, but it's hard to get across just how big is big. He's tall, he's wide, he's thick, but none of it is fat. A mean, walking refrigerator comes to mind. And, there's the impression of, I don't know what to call it, 'inner bigness' perhaps?

I don't mean some sort of hippy-dippy bull, but more like he's restraining himself, that if he felt like it, he could just let go and be even more huge than he is now. What else, black hair cut short, chin like the front end of a battleship. There's not much more I can make out with his coat buttoned and the collar up. I can't tell if he's wearing a suit or if it's 'Casual Friday' for him. Could be a flasher, for all I know.

There's a place nearby where we can break out the bottles – my own little hobo haunt. It's a little sheltered spot – the front of an alley beside a stairwell. Ain't warm, but it's fairly dry, and out of the wind. I'd prefer to be back at my apartment with the booze, but not with Serapion.

"Drink. First you can drink; later we'll talk." That's all the encouragement I need to take the cap off the first bottle. The day's events have already taken a toll on me and it'll just get worse if I wait much longer with nothing in my belly. So I drink.

"Feeling better," I say. Immediately I wish I hadn't said that, because I get the impression I won't get to say it again for a while.

"No problem. I guess you're curious as to why we're here?" I nod, between pulls at the bottle. "Here it is then: I'm your guardian angel."

I laugh in response, ending with a coughing fit from wine snorted up my nose.

He doesn't say anything, just waits for me to get the coughing and laughing out of my system.

"Wow, that's funny," I say. "Damn, thanks. Nothing has made me laugh for a while – needed that. So, who would want you to keep a lookout for me? My sister?"

"I'm not being metaphorical. I'm an angel. And, I'm here to guard you."

Chapter 3

"Okay, for the eighth time, no, I don't need to have wings or a halo. I do not necessarily dress in white, and I don't know how to play a harp. I do not have to wait for Christmas or Easter before I appear..."

"Yeah, but..." I splutter.

"Don't," he warns, pointing a very fierce, very intimidating finger at me. "The next spew of words out of your mouth had better be a new question."

A pause for thought would be good right about now. For a moment, if we take what he says as true... no, wait, that one can be handled later. Start with the most likely premise, that he's crazy. Okay, that doesn't necessarily have to be a bad thing. Twice already he's saved my ass, plus getting me into Lorenzo's early. So maybe he's delusional but helpful.

Could be problematic later, if he decides to go on a righteous, divine killing spree, but he's useful right now.

There it is then: keep him around until he starts telling me that God wants him to start fires or hurt small animals, and at that point, ditch him.

...But what if he's telling the truth? says a little voice.

"Have you noticed what's been happening around here lately?" His voice cuts through my reverie.

"What do you mean?"

"People. Places. Events. There's been a general turn for the worse over the last several months, with a distinct acceleration in the last month or so."

Another drink. "Hadn't noticed."

He nods, letting me have my little illusion.

For a while, we sit in silence as I drink. Slowly, the shakes subside. Slowly, whatever anxiety I'm feeling gives way to happy warmth and the beginning of a buzz.

Momentarily, I forget my problems, my dreams, the creeping fear. There's just me and the bottle. Just more proof that breakfast is indeed the most important meal of the day.

Drinking like this is a new thing for me. Not drinking itself, I mean. I went to university so it isn't like I've never seen the bottom of a beer mug before. Lately, though, I'll do just about anything to be drunk, high, oblivious, at any time of the day. That's troubling.

I am becoming one of *them*. Okay, so there was a little hubris on my part. No matter where I was on the whole low-life, drug culture spectrum, there was always someone lower down for me to compare myself against. And, it always made me feel, well, not better, but at least I felt some security in knowing that I wasn't as bad as them.

The bottom of the bunch is the mouthwash drinkers - sorriest excuse for a human being, but with the freshest breath. It bothers me that I don't find the idea repellent.

What scares me, though, even more than hitting rock bottom, is how quickly things are spiralling downwards. I feel like I'm losing my grip on the rope.

"Hey," I say. "What was that you were saying about things getting worse?"

But my angel is gone. Nothing here but me and the second half of my second bottle. Looks like he was right about that.

~~~~~ Chapter 4 ~~~~~

The great thing about being unfit to hold a job is that you've got all the time in the world to work on your *project*. You know, that piece of art, whatever medium, that's going to set the world on fire, and enshrine your name in the pantheon of muses, as soon as you finish it. Problem is, there's a *reason* you're unfit to do work – any work. Phrased uncharitably, you're a fuck-up. So, in the great tradition of people who call themselves artists, nothing actually gets done.

The process is pretty much the same each time: set up your workspace and tools of the trade, a few deep breaths to get into the right frame of mind, and then… poke at your work for a bit, rearrange some inconsequential things, maybe, then feel free to let the mind drift to the smell of pot coming from down the hall, and how a hit of that would really fire the creativity. And then, I'm done for the day. It isn't that I don't want to get it done, get it finished, get it out there, but self-sabotage is far easier.

I use an old Underwood manual typewriter, a vanity on my part, because I like the image. The lonely playwright, alone in his garret, typing away like he's Dashiell Hammet or something. All I need is a fedora and a monotone colour scheme and it'd be perfect.

Almost perfect. Perfect would include inspiration, drive, determination.

We are now at the point where normally I realize I've been staring at the same damn blank piece of paper for at least 20 minutes, without typing a single word. Today, though, is different. My fingers fly across the keys, sounding like a room full of tap dancers. The little bell goes off at the end of each line, signalling me to slap the return bar. I haven't been hearing that noise much lately. Today it genuinely surprises me, amazes me that I've filled another line that quickly. Line after line, the pages fill up, and I'm fumbling with a fresh sheet, trying to roll it in the typewriter in a race to get it to the right spot before my fingers dive onto the keys to start typing some more.

Apparently, almost dying, almost being beaten up, getting drunk and meeting your guardian angel is what it takes to leap over a writer's block. Somebody find me a pencil so I can write that down for the next time.

Of course, finding a pencil in my apartment could be a major struggle. My place is, as usual, trashed. Sorry, but it's the maid's year off, and I'm an artist, and artists do not clean things.

This apartment is about the only thing going even marginally right in my life at the moment. I don't have to pay rent, or more specifically, an ex-roommate paid up the rent for a year in advance, and then just as charitably, disappeared. That's a very good thing, because there's no way I could pull together that sort of bread every month.

Then again, considering how much material I'm churning out right now, maybe my personal pendulum is finally on the upswing. Could be things are going my way.

The building is falling apart, and the hallways smell of something rancid, and I have to walk up four floors because the elevator doesn't work, but it's home. At some point in its history, I suspect this building was considered a bit posh. There's a few surviving flourishes here and there that haven't been broken off or painted into obscurity, which hint of past glory.

Those days, sadly, are gone.

Finally, I push myself back from the table. I've written my fill. There's a stack of paper on the left hand side of the typewriter that wasn't there yesterday. Hell, wasn't there two hours ago. I'm feeling good, I'm feeling sated.

And now the eternal question: get some food or get high? Sure, not what everybody else asks themselves, nor how they plan their day, but we all have our own little realities, don't we?

Mine just happens to consist of a daily struggle for survival and the pull between the poles of personal oblivion and getting fed.

Today, though, the belly wins. The warmth of the wine still has a few embers left in me to sustain happiness for a while, and I'm on an adrenaline high from the writing – an honest to god adrenaline high. A quick check says there's still some change in my pocket, and the weirdness of the day continues, because there's a few coins in my old coffee can too.

And just like that, I'm out the door again. Past the peeling paint in the hallway, down four storeys worth of stairs I go, step over an unconscious neighbour, and out into the street. The sun is peeking through the clouds off and on, but it's still that ugly damp cold that seeps through whatever clothes you're wearing. I fucking hate February – there's not a single redeeming feature to the whole month.

Today's eatery of choice, as is just about every day, is the local convenience store. Cheap food and I don't have to wear a tie. And it's close, less than a block from my place, which is a big plus in the winter.

This is a favoured roost among my crowd. The building next to the store, formerly a grand old bank, has been long abandoned so there's no one to chase us off the steps, and it faces to the south so at least the assorted winos and homeless get a bit of warmth from the sun.

I'll join them in a moment, but first, I head into the store. The fluorescent lights inside the store hurt my eyes, even though I've just come in from daylight. They're bright, obnoxiously so, and I think they're giving off this odd tint to it. Greenish, rather than that regular wash-out blue. Is that what happens when they're about to burn out? Maybe so, but every light in the place is doing it, so it has to be something else.

It doesn't take much time to make some selections. Price limits me pretty quickly, and then it's down to taste, and fat content – the first because if I have to choke this shit down, best it be as palatable as possible, and the second because if I looked in a mirror, I could count my ribs as easily as fingers on a hand. Wonder if I'm at risk of developing scurvy?

What I really want is a pack of smokes. I burned through my last three cigarettes during my little writing jag, not even thinking that I didn't have any more. And, I just don't have the money for another

9

pack. Instead, I plunk the essentials down on the counter, and start fishing out my change.

While I struggle with my jeans pocket, I take a look at the guy behind the counter. I think I've seen him a couple times before, but right now he doesn't look so good. In fact, he's a good match for the bad lighting – his skin is off-kilter, somehow. A fish's belly is the closest thing I can compare it to, with the wrong colour, texture, and a lustre you never expect to see on a human being.

He never actually looks at me, just glances at my purchases, and rings them up on the cash register.

"Cold day, eh?" I say. He doesn't answer, doesn't make any indication that he heard me, and I give up with the small talk. There are times when conversation could be just as uncomfortable as silence, and in retrospect I'm glad he didn't respond. Seconds later, I scoop up my food, and head for the door. No, thanks, don't need a bag, and no, I don't need or want you to tell me to have a nice day – not that he does.

I'm almost blind as I step out the door. Between the overly bright lights of the store, and the late afternoon sun sinking in the west, my eyes just can't keep up. Rather than stumble around, I hold my ground in front of the store until I can see again.

The stairs are relatively free right now, so I grab a convenient scrap of cardboard to sit on, and unwrap my meal. Nobody asks if they can have a bite. Nobody so much as looks in my direction. I think word got around about what happened at Lorenzo's.

For a while, I eat in peace.

"Look what the cat threw up," I say as I see Dingle approach.

"I don't get it," he says. I shrug.

Rest assured, the staff of the Smithsonian aren't wearing themselves out to hire the brain trust I hang around with. What little is left of my intellect is wasted on this crowd.

"So earlier," I say, casually. "Back at Lorenzo's... had you seen that guy before?"

"The Yeller? Yeah, but normally he just sits there and shouts threats. Don't think I've ever seen him actually try to hit someone."

I shake my head. "No, not him. The other guy, big guy in a trench coat. Kept the Yeller from punching me out."

"Nope. Soon as I heard a scream, I hightailed it out of there. My nerves just can't take that kind of shit." He sits quietly for a second. "Speaking of nerves, can I have one of your smokes now?"

When I tell him I already smoked my cigarettes, it looks as if some internal structural holding Dingle upright just collapsed – he slumps a little more, but from the inside out.

Poor guy, Dingle, always looks like someone just told him his puppy died. Filmy eyes peering through filmy glasses. He's a little guy too, so between the facial expression, his physicality and his nickname, he gets picked on a lot. Typical story – too fond of his drink, had a bad month or two, and next thing he knows, he found himself living on the street. Stories like his are commonplace, to the point that you rarely bother asking each other how you ended up here, because likely you won't hear anything new.

Typically, my peers fall into two main camps: the mentally ill and the substance abusers. There's plenty of crossover, with each cause feeding into the other. After a while, there's not much difference between them anyway – are you an alcoholic suffering from depression, or a depressive smitten with alcoholism? Does it even matter by that point?

We can subdivide further, if necessary. There's the off-their-meds, the veterans who just couldn't leave it behind, the screamers, the twitchers, the uppers and the downers. It's a full spectrum of mental problems, a veritable cornucopia of crazy. Trust me; I've got all the crazy a man could ever use, all within arm's reach.

Substance abuse is far easier to chart. Are you a wino or a druggie? Did the after-work drinks with your stock exchange buddies do you in, or was it just not possible for the dope to make the world go away anymore?

A lot of the winos here really should be in a mental hospital, but the city has been cutting budgets for years. The ones who aren't going to kill anybody get the boot and end up here. Their minds are halfway gone, and bodies soon to follow. No more family, no possessions. Nothing left to them but their names and whatever time is left to them before they die.

As long as they keep to themselves until that happens, nobody in a professional capacity has to officially notice them. There's a lot of latitude as to what constitutes a 'danger to oneself,' which means that until they start hurting someone, they're considered to be 'integrated into society.'

Yeah, no home, no money, no health, no sanity – sure. But, talking is free, and with no alternative entertainment, that's what we do on our staircase. It drives me crazy, because as I've mentioned, this isn't an intellectual bunch. Current events form most of the topics of conversation, gleaned from whatever newspaper happens our way, or random bit that someone saw on the men's shelter TV. Everybody has an opinion – no actual knowledge to back them up, but hey, that isn't considered to be important.

We all have our ways of getting out of the cold for a while, browsing through bookshops, or wandering through a shopping mall. All-night Laundromats are a good option too. But it's a balancing act – hang around too long in one place and you risk being banned.

Every season has its challenges too. While there's no danger of freezing to death in the summer, there's major competition from slumming teenagers. Everybody just had to hang in long enough for the weather to turn cold, and for all of them to reconcile with their parents and head home. At least, that's the gospel I've been taught. Again, when talking is free, there's a lot of information you can pick up.

I spend a lot of time in my apartment, but the solitude gets to me after a while, and I find I need contact with other people. Unfortunately, the winos are all I get.

The older guys tend to be more traditional in their substance abuse, primarily alcohol. There's a steady flow of crack junkies and meth-heads too, since they tend to have a faster downward spiral and end up on the street that much more quickly. Inevitably, they process out of here just as quickly.

And then, there's guys like me, who will take whatever we can get. You can pick your poison, but for me, meanwhile, I'm open to anything. I'd dunk my head in a toilet if I thought it would get me high.

Oh, and we all smoke.

Although our social interaction doesn't change much from day to day, we're all acutely aware of what day of the week it is. It's important, the difference between survival and, well, not surviving. Monday through Friday, we panhandle the crowds on their way to and from work. Some days are considered more profitable than others, but there's no consensus, which fuels conversation at least.

Sunday means soup kitchen to us. The local church lays out an okay spread, and if it weren't for the sermon at the beginning, it would be perfect. But, it's warm, it's free, and fairly plentiful. I can shrug off the rest.

Saturday is a nothing day for us. For whatever reason, people just aren't willing to share their pocket change. Might be a worthwhile subject for some sociologist, but for us, it just means we strike out.

Someone is shouting, breaking me out of my reverie. For a second, there's the thought that it might be the Yeller again, and I don't see Serapion anywhere. But it isn't him. It's one of the older, mentally-ill, homeless guys, one of the mumbler brigade. One of the ones who should have been in a mental hospital or something. Instead, he's swearing and cursing hard at three young guys standing at the door to the boxing club above the convenience store.

They aren't feeling particularly threatened by him, and it's a good thing he's only raising his voice rather than taking a poke at them – it's three versus one, and the three aren't elderly, long-term alcohol abusers who live on the street. Mostly they just ignore him, and head inside for their workout.

All of us, though, know what we just saw. There's a saying: "there are old pilots, and there are bold pilots, but there are no old, bold pilots." When you see someone out here take a step across that line, abandon that rat-like cunning that enables survival, you know his time is marked. It won't be long before we see him carted out of here, stiff limbed, zipped into a rubber bag and loaded into the coroner's van.

"I give him two weeks," someone sitting behind me says. "Guaranteed dead, no problem."

"Nah," says someone else. "The old guys are always stubborn. He's making it through until the end of March."

It touches off a flurry of rising voices as everybody tries to get in with a competing bet. Somebody gives odds, and the volume goes up a notch as they all try to simultaneously offer their opinion, their bet and what they're wagering. It doesn't matter, since nobody is writing it all down, and none of them would be able to remember it a week from now anyway.

"Why'd he do that?" I ask. I didn't really mean to – it was a little bit of internal musing that slipped out. All conversation stops for a second and everyone turns to look at me. The effect of close scrutiny is not one I enjoy.

And then, like some choreographed number, all heads swivel away from me to face one another. *Yeah*, you can see them think, *why did he do that?*

They all dive onto the new conversational points like it's a free hot lunch, thankfully leaving me alone.

Like I said, weird stuff happening around here.

Winter in the city is miserable. If it isn't pelting with snow and sleet, it's biting cold that leaves you chilled for the whole day. There's a little leak in my boot that gradually lets in the wet and makes my foot ache with the cold. As long as I can dodge slush on the sidewalk, I'm generally okay, but eventually it'll get in, no matter how careful I am.

It's insidious, the cold.

For a while now, as I've been talking with my confreres, I've been feeling a certain anxiety. Yeah, I've been feeling an overall anxiety for months, but right at this particular moment, I'm feeling something different. Looking around, I can see what the problem is. Behind me, not ten feet away, is the Yeller. I don't know how he made it up the steps without me noticing, but that's just what he did. He's standing, leaning against the wall, and staring at me as if he could bore holes into me with just his eyes.

I'm half-convinced that he actually could do just that. It looks like his day hasn't improved at all. There's an ugly bruise on one side of his cheek, and I think the purple splotches are Serapion's knuckle marks. His eyes, though... Man, they burn. There's an inner fire in this guy, a rage that just wants to explode.

He would otherwise look like the rest of us – battered clothes, battered bodies, but whereas we all look pretty much defeated, he looks like he's just getting ready for the fight. A big fight.

Anyway, I know when it's time to split. I've run away from smaller men than him, and I'm not about to stop now. Old pilots and bold pilots, as they say. Time to take my leave.

By the time I abandon the street corner and head home, it's full nighttime dark. Ain't that it's really late; it's just that winter sun. The days really should be getting longer by now, but they don't seem to be. Panhandling is an activity best performed during daylight, I think because people feel less threatened, not having some beggar loom out of the darkness.

What's funny about that, though, is it's like a shift change at a factory. The winos go off to their squats or shelters, or whatever they've found to sleep in. Meanwhile, the hookers come out to work their trade, with the darkness providing the anonymity their clientele prefer. They'll be out on the streets until tomorrow, going home after the end of the morning rush hour and the few customers it brings.

All this is an indicator of how far I've fallen. I used to be on the night shift with the hookers, which is also the domain of creative fringe-dwellers – artists, musicians and assorted hangers-on. Hell, for a little while I had a job driving the escort girls around to the various hotels and restaurants. You might be surprised how many politicians and judges I know by sight alone. *"Evening, your honour. In the mood for a little rough trade tonight?"*

Things change. I prided myself on not seeing the sun for an entire week once, but that's changed. Winter's short days and long nights are starting to prey on me. The nights, that's the worst. I'm not an insomniac – if anything, I'm the opposite. Getting to sleep isn't the problem; it's what happens when I'm asleep.

Christmas, I think, that's when I made the big switch to days. I don't care if you're an adult or not, or if you're the sentimental type, but there are occasions where being alone powerfully sucks. Yes, fine, I will concede that the music is the aural version of a venereal disease, but we all know the words no matter what we think of the songs. Those hooks are dug deep into all of us.

Anyway, I'm on a much lower social stratum now, and the hookers I know won't even look at me, let alone talk to me. Can't really blame them – the guy they knew isn't the guy I am now.

Daylight didn't help much anyway, today. People are not willing to give money. Hell, they're not willing to break stride long enough for the usual cursory "sorry" or "afraid not."

That's fine, I'm fed, topped up with booze and I've had my social contact for the day. Waiting back at my apartment is my typewriter, and by now, the keys have cooled off enough for me to touch.

There's a few extra people in the building's lobby, hoping they can stay somewhere warm for a few hours before the inevitable rousting. A quick glance confirms that I don't know any of them, which is both good and bad. The good part is I don't have to worry about anybody discovering my apartment and trying to cadge a warm place to sleep. The bad part is that I should expect to see at least one familiar face. There are certain barometers that one can find in any community. Among the drunks and junkies, an influx of newcomers says something unpleasant is coming down the chute.

With some nimble footwork, I make it to the staircase without stepping on anyone, and then it's up to the apartment, taking the steps two at a time. Already I'm feeling a little rush of anticipation, gearing up to start writing again.

By the time I make it to my apartment door, I'm shaking with excitement. It's like having the DT's or something – my hands are trembling, and I can't get the stupid key in the lock. On the fourth or fifth try, I finally get the door open, and slam it behind me.

And in a heartbeat, I'm sitting in front of my typewriter. There's a fresh piece of paper all ready to go. To my left sits the pages I did earlier, and to my right is a stack of beautiful, pristine white sheets, ready to be fed into the furnace that is my creative streak.

A deep breath to center myself, and I rest my fingers on the typewriter keys. I ready myself for the wave to hit me again, to be carried along by it and lose myself in my work.

I continue to wait, for hours, in fact.

My hands sit immobile on the keys, like a mannequin's hands. Not a single letter gets marked down on the paper.

I sit there, until I am about to fall asleep in my chair. My legs and ass have long since lost any sensation, and I think my back is starting to do the same thing. And still, not a word comes to me, not a single word.

"Come on, damn you," I yell at my hands, at the typewriter, at the whole fucking world, but there's nothing. Frustration tears at me and I fight back, slapping the typewriter hard, hard enough that the little bell goes 'ding' from the force of impact.

Slowly, like a cripple, I force myself to a standing position and shuffle out of the room, to go and throw myself down on the crappy old green couch. Sleep hits instantly.

~~~~ Chapter 5 ~~~~

I'm beginning to really hate sleep.

Unless I miss my guess, I'm dreaming. As I've been finding out lately, that hasn't been much comfort against the things that I've been seeing. Yes, they are only dreams, but that doesn't change the fear I feel from being anything other than real. The emotional content hits just as hard as it would if I had been really awake. Even on waking, I'm still scared, sometimes for the rest of the day, until sleep comes to claim me and the process starts again.

Does everybody know when they're dreaming? I think I've always been aware of that, on some level, as far back as I can remember. Although most of me is there in the dream, there's always a sliver of my consciousness that stays separate and aloof, looking down on my dreaming self.

The hallway I stand in is pitch black, and I'm only guessing that it's a hallway. If I reach out to the left and right, I can feel the walls. They are cool to the touch, and smooth, but there's nothing to the texture that would give me any further clue to where I might be.

Standing where I am isn't doing anything for me, so slowly I begin to walk, one hand on the wall, the other out in front, groping blindly for obstacles. The hall turns corners often, maze-like. I don't pass doors, and other than the edges when I round a corner, there are no features on the wall. There is also no way to tell how long I've been wandering, or how far I've walked, not that there are such distinctions inside the elastic dimensions of a dream anyway.

So, I continue on, in my shuffling walk, probing ahead with one hand, and my feet searching the floor in case there's some pit waiting for me around the next corner. And then, I realize I see something. Up ahead, there's a source of light, coming from around the next corner. I can't see the source of it, but only where it falls upon the walls, making gentle illumination. It's blue, like cobalt glass.

Eager, I rush toward it, heedless of whatever 'it' might be. My eyes crave light, and I can't stop myself from bolting down the corridor.

Rounding the corner, I immediately know everything I need or want to know about the source of light. It's coming from a sword, a flaming sword, and in my haste I damn near manage to impale myself on it.

In that first moment of animal panic, as I windmill my arms to keep my balance, my eyes drink in everything they can, which isn't much. My eyes hurt against the glare of the blue flames licking their way up the blade, and render everything behind them as inky blackness. I can see the hand holding the sword's hilt, with fingers seemingly too delicate to hold the long, wide blade.

The heat off the flames makes my face tingle unpleasantly, and a few strands of my hair are instantly crisped. I would swear I hear the sweat on my face boiling off.

I fall to the ground in a heap, but at least I haven't fallen on top of the sword. It scares the crap out of me, and not just because I almost ran onto it, but something intrinsic to it, to whatever it represents. Scrambling, hands and feet clawing at the floor for purchase, I turn and run. I can see the hallway corners now, thanks to the flames, but the further I run, the darker it gets. Predictably, I smash into a wall. I think there's blood trickling down from my forehead, but there's no time to wipe a hand over my face to confirm. There's only run, run, run.

While I'm casting about with my hands to find the walls, the sword-wielder catches up, and I'm off running again. Again, I keep slamming into walls and corners, and throw myself forward to get away from the flaming sword.

Even though I'm moving, I can feel the heat of the flames on my back, as if I was standing still next to a campfire. The heat clings to me.

Rounding the next corner, my feet slide out from under me, and I slam into a wall, and then the floor, hard. The impact of my head sends a little burst of stars across my vision, a little meteor shower in the darkness.

My hands wave around in a futile attempt to find something to grab onto. The floor is cool against my back, feeling unnaturally cold in contrast to the heat I felt moments before.

The blue light gathers around me. I can see the hallway, can see the splatter of blood my face left on the wall. The ceiling is still shrouded in darkness, too high even for the flame's light to touch.

And then the sword comes into view above me. I have an excellent opportunity to study it in detail, although it scares the living hell out of me. The blade is long, wide at the base and tapers to a point. The cross guard is plain – just two unadorned bars that stick out to the sides. The flames lick and run up the blade, but don't make a sound.

The hand on the hilt – it holds my attention. Each finger looks impossibly long, and their slenderness looks wrong. The fingers look reedy and weak, and couldn't possibly hold such a long weapon.

But, hold it they do, right above me. Whoever the sword-wielder is, he or she, it, stands right next to my head, but a quick glance to the side confirms that all I can see is blackness. No feet, no nothing.

Back to the sword. I feel the heat intensify, and quickly understand why. The tip is now poised directly above my chest, a few scant inches away. The smell of my burnt chest hair fills the air, and I don't dare move, don't dare to even breathe.

The sword lifts up a bit, then down, then up again, like a pool player gauging his shot, and I'm screaming to myself "wake up wake up wake up wake up," but it doesn't do any good.

Down drops the sword. There's a moment's resistance from my breastbone, and pain, but then the blade drives through, and the bone makes a sound like a handful of twigs breaking over your knee, and I feel every awful inch of the blade slide into my chest. My skin crackles as the flames cook it, but all I can hear is the sound of my voice screaming and pleading for it all to stop.

The pain stops suddenly, like a light switch was flicked off. I realize I'm awake. There's the raw taste of bile in my mouth, and I'm shaking all over, but at least I didn't wet my pants. Small mercies. Yeah. Score one for Alex.

There's a pounding sound, and it takes me a few moments to realize that it's my neighbour, slamming his fist against the wall. Okay, now I know I wasn't just screaming in my dream.

My hands can't help but run up and down my shirt, trying to find the gaping hole that should be there. My chest aches a bit, but I think that's from me clenching my muscles, and thrashing in my sleep. I would swear that I can still smell the burning hair and skin – at least it speaks to the eternal question as to whether people have a sense of smell in their dreams, and the answer is yes.

What the hell is all this about? Paging Dr. Freud. Dr. Freud, to the white courtesy phone please.

The apartment is dark, except for a little city light shining in through the living room window. Middle of the night, I guess. Shakes still ripple up my spine – I'm wired, and there's no way I'm getting back to sleep.

I really, like *really*, hate sleep.

From where I sit, I can see the typewriter in the other room. Stupid, cold, mute hunk of metal. It looks like a big, fat, ugly toad, under the half light from the window. Really, I should just pawn it, get it over with, take the money and go score something.

But, as soon as that happens, I will have to admit that there is no redemption for me, and that I am an absolute fuckup, never to come back from the brink. So instead, I get to sit here and be mocked by an inanimate object.

The typewriter sits in the middle of the apartment's only bedroom. A more religious person might think that there is some sort of shrine mentality to the set-up, and I'm not so sure they'd be wrong. In addition to the typewriter, there's the small desk it sits on, a chair, a pile of paper, and an ashtray crammed to overflowing with cigarette butts smoked right down to their filters. The table is set up exactly in the center of the room, with the chair positioned so that my back is to the door when I'm writing. When I'm trying to write.

My eyes fall on the pile of paper on the other side of the typewriter. The 'done' side. At least I have that to look at and say, yeah, there is potential. If I can get through a few more weeks until this bad stretch ends, maybe when the weather warms up, and there's more sunlight, I might be able to finish my play. Yeah. And then, who knows?

Stand, listen to the groan of the couch springs as I rise, and stumble to the writing room. Flick on the switch, and squint against the wash of light. Shade my eyes with one hand and flip through the pages of my script with the other. And I hate it. Maybe I'm just in a

19

mood, maybe it's the whole lack of sleep thing, but it's terrible. Pages and pages of banal tripe. It reads like the token chunks of plot they throw into a porn movie as a preamble to the next sex scene. It reads like the writer just polished off two bottles of wine – which he did.

I can't even be bothered to throw it in the garbage. I drop it back on the desk.

Well, so much for potential.

Out of the corner of my eye, I catch a glimpse of movement. I don't know what I saw in the dark of the living room, but there was definitely something. There's nothing there now, although I have the distinct impression that it was a cat, walking past the bedroom door, and heading through to the kitchen. It is a measure of just how fucked up I am, that it takes me a second or two to realize I don't own a cat. Which means that one of the neighbourhood's carrion-eaters has managed to sneak into the apartment. I'm not sure how, since there's only three ways in – the front door or the two windows. But, when I go to the kitchen, to kick the stupid thing out the door, it's not there.

I am fucking losing it. The dreams were bad enough, but now I'm hallucinating. Breathe in, Alex, breathe out. You are thinking rationally, you have a brain.

... *And a guardian angel*, says that stupid inner voice.

Really, really losing it.

So, this is what it is like to go crazy. What else can it be? I'm circling the drain, here, spinning round and round, faster, as I get closer to the edge, and the point of no return.

Looking around my apartment, I see it, I mean see it, really notice it for the first time in a while. There's crap everywhere, it smells, probably bugs in there too. Everything of value is gone already, and what's left is garbage. It could be a metaphor for my life.

Got to clear my head, I have got to start thinking about what I'm doing.

Boots on, coat on, dodge the sleeping cattle in the lobby. Outside I go, looking for some cold, crisp air to clear my mind, and to get me away from the vibes in my apartment.

A dusting of snow is coming down, little sparkling crystals on a windless night. It's actually pleasant to be out here in the middle of the night. The streets are empty of people, and traffic is minimal. There's me, and the buildings, and that's it, mostly.

Pretty cool, if you ask me.

The city was profoundly lucky, architecturally speaking. A huge surge of buildings went up in the first half of the last century, back when aesthetics and style were considered essential. I like that I can look at an old building from blocks away, and find it pleasing to the eye, then walk towards it, and the same building has something new to offer. I can play this game right up to the point where I could pretty much smack my face into a wall, and there'd be something to look at.

The newer stuff, modern stuff? Whatever. Bomb it. Bulldoze it. It was designed to suck the will from the people who have to work in them all day, keep them docile. It came as little surprise to me when I was told there is a style of architecture called 'Brutalism.'

I think my eyes are going bad for a few seconds – things are sort of swimming. It takes a lot of blinking and rubbing before I figure out it's the streetlights. The lights are fluttering, but they're all different – some fast, some slow. The more I look, the more variation I'm noticing. It's not just the light I'm standing under; I can see it happening all down the street, in either direction.

Unfortunately, there's nobody around for me to ask if they see the same thing – not that they'd be likely to indulge a derelict like me. I can just imagine: "Hey, do those lights look... different to you?" "No, why? Do the voices in your head tell you they're different?" A little independent confirmation that I'm not going crazy would be nice, though.

Yeah, and I realize I don't just mean right now – I also mean it in a larger sense. My current peers aren't the best choice for a baseline. I need to talk with some sane people for a while, maybe it'll rub off on me and straighten me out a bit. Now if only I knew somebody sane.

My sister. Yeah. Claire.

I talked with her on the phone a couple months ago, wishing her a Merry Christmas. By that time, the nights started getting rough, really rough on me. The conversation was brief – she had guests over, and she didn't want to be an impolite hostess. That, and if I had started manoeuvring for an invite, it would have been uncomfortable for her to refuse me. Cutting the call short got her out of the situation.

But this isn't a social call. And I need more than just a free turkey dinner.

Now if only I had a quarter. Maybe I should just call collect and hope like hell she accepts the charge. Can you still do that with payphones?

Suddenly, I'm on the ground, spread eagled on the sidewalk, hugging it like a lover. One instant I'm standing, the next, face down.

What the hell was that? A burst of light, a crack like fireworks close by, and me diving for safety.

It takes a few seconds to figure it out. The darkness around me is what clues me in - almost directly over my head, one of the wavering streetlights has exploded. Shards of glass lie scattered on the pavement. Have I been cut? Run my hands across my face and my scalp, but there's no blood – some snow from the sidewalk, and a few glass fragments, but otherwise unscathed.

My heart is still pounding hard, and it will be a while longer before it can be convinced there's no need to run like a rabbit. Thanks, but the danger is passed now. All is quiet. C'mon, heart, settle down, do it for me, would'ja? It takes a while.

If I felt like it, I could check my pulse without moving a muscle – the beats are so hard, I swear they're making my coat jump. Of course, not having a watch would make it a challenge, to count the beats and the seconds simultaneously. I muse about such things while I wait, and eventually things slow down to almost normal. Push myself up from where I sit, and brush the snow off my cold ass.

Time to head home. I take a few dozen steps, before the next streetlight blows. Again, almost directly over my head, and just like before, I find myself sprawled on the sidewalk. The glass makes little musical noises as it pings off the pavement.

What the hell is going on? One bulb is within reason. No, I've never heard of one exploding before, but it *could* happen, I guess. Two, though? That's just frickin' insane.

Damn, there's that word again.

And what are the odds that they'll both blow while I'm walking underneath them? It's like I won some sort of perverse lottery, where the prize is the chance to have a piece of glass stuck in your head. Second prize is two pieces of glass.

This is just crazy. *Damn!*

Again, stand up, brush the glass off my coat, a quick check to see if I can find any cuts. A few slivers of glass fall from my hair and down my shirt collar. As I shake out my shirt, I can feel them tickle their way to freedom. Wait for the heartbeat to slow down to a point where I could actually count the beats if I wanted to.

Now I'm standing in an even bigger pool of darkness. Before and behind me, there is light. Around me, nothing but darkness.

Tentatively, I take a step. And then, another. The street light ahead of me looks like a big, baleful eye hanging high. It dares me to take another step, dares me to try and make it home.

Another step. Feeling pretty damn stupid right now, sneaking up on a streetlight. For a moment, I contemplate taking the back way, sneaking through alleys, but I pass on that idea pretty quickly. The darkness there is absolute. The snow is piled pretty high in places, and I'm in no shape to go snowshoeing. They wouldn't find my frozen corpse for a couple of months, I bet.

Another step closer. Is that a waver in the light? A shimmer? I've got myself so psyched out now, I can't tell anymore.

Fight the craziness, Alex, fight! The urge boils up suddenly, volcanic in its urgency. Only crazy people are intimidated by inanimate objects.

I let out a war cry as I run at the streetlight, and its cone of light on the pavement. Just like before, this one explodes too, leaving me blinking away the after-image. And then, all around me, the other lights blast their glass onto the street. It sounds like Chinese New Years, with firecrackers going off all over the place. I keep yelling as I run, and the lights keep exploding. The headlights of the few cars in the street join in the chaos, spraying more glass and adding to the darkness in my wake.

I can barely see now, with the clouds covering the moon, and no other lights around. Doesn't keep me from running though. Yeah, and yelling my fool head off. Suddenly, it stops. The lights don't explode when I run underneath them, cars aren't skidding to a sudden halt on the streets. I'm surrounded by light again, and it's so startling to be able to see again, that I stop running. There's car alarms blaring in the distance, calling out to each other in the dark.

Behind me, the way I came, is nothing but darkness. It swallows up everything. Ahead of me is light, and safety, so I start running for home again.

Back to the apartment building, and just stand in the lobby for a minute or ten, long enough to catch my breath. That's a pleasant way of saying I'm wheezing like a broken accordion. Man I hate running. Hated it when I was a kid in school, hate it even more now that I smoke. Take my time, breathe, then dodge the snoring people in the lobby, up the stairs, and into my home. Home. Safe. Yeah.

The door is locked, my back resting against it, and it feels damn good to have something propping me up. Air seems to be in short supply at the moment, and I'm sucking back as much as I can. Never been much of an athlete, unless there's a sport where they want you to smoke cigarettes. Pain in my chest feels like I strained something. Can you strain your lungs? Probably.

Still wish I had a cigarette.

Can you hallucinate about exploding streetlights? I guess so, I guess you can hallucinate about anything. But I'm sure that really happened – not only were the lights exploding, but they waited until I was standing underneath them.

What the goddamn hell is happening to me?

~~~~~ Chapter 6 ~~~~~

Call Claire. Call Claire. Yeah, that is what I need to do.

Ain't like I can call her here from my apartment – I don't have a phone. Not a working one, at least. I haven't had phone service in months – just couldn't afford it, and eventually there was no one I talked to who had a phone anyway.

If I was in better shape, I could look at it as a positive thing. Get rid of distractions, get rid of unnecessary attachments. Focus on writing, focus on your craft. To a degree, I understand why hermits don't want anybody hanging around. People take it personally when you say, "Hey, I just had this great idea. Shut up for a while so I can get it down on paper." And people surround themselves with these interruptions: telephones, cell phones, pagers, doorbells, *friends*.

The phone – it rings like a fire alarm, unnaturally loud in the quiet of the room. Jangling, brash. It shouldn't be ringing, there's just no way.

But, it's ringing. Yeah. Who are you going to believe – the phone company, or the evidence from your own ears?

I push a magazine and an old pizza box off of it and sit and stare in wonderment at this odd, alien thing, this ringing telephone. It sits all by itself, on an end table that was probably very fashionable in the 60's – Danish teak, I think they call it – but now is battered, and covered in cigarette burns and promotional stickers of a long defunct band.

Who the hell would be calling me in the middle of the night, or any time at all for that matter? And why? My sister? That'd be an odd coincidence, not to mention impossible, since the phone doesn't work.

Doesn't work, yeah.

Eight or nine times, it rings. Loud, shrill. Still I sit there staring at it, head lolling to one side like a confused cocker spaniel.

Suddenly desperate, I scramble to pick it up before it stops. What is it about phones that command our attention so? Why can't we resist answering them when they ring?

No matter. I pick it up and listen, expecting … what? Really, there should be nothing to hear. Maybe the sound of the ocean like when you put a shell against your ear, but that's it.

"Hello?" I say. Again, what is it about phones that command us so, in this case, to social niceties?

To my continued surprise, there's a voice at the other end.

"Mr. Mackie?" says the voice, sounding like wind sweeping dry leaves down the street.

"Yes, this is he," I say, like it's the most normal thing in the world for me to be talking to someone on a disconnected phone in the middle of the night. Yes, I'm a down and out, drunken failure, who seems to be going insane, but I still have my manners. Mom would be so proud.

"I have a job for you," says the voice. "I need a writer. Immediately."

"I'm flattered, but I don't think I'm your man."

"You come highly recommended," the voice continues. "And we would be willing to pay you quite generously for your work."

Money, yeah, that would be good right now. My stomach growls in the affirmative, so do my alcohol shakes, as well as my tobacco jitters, and whatever the hell else I've got right now. Looks like the entire committee votes "aye."

Yes, says my whole body, yes!

But the mind, the rat-cunning mind, chairman of the board, says no. *Why would someone leave a perfectly good piece of cheese just lying out here?* it asks. *Because it's a trap!*

Money, yeah, but nothing about this adds up. Who the hell knows who I am? And why would you choose me when there has to be a thousand other people who they could call, people who aren't rejects? And how is my phone working?

That decides it for me. "Listen, your offer sounds very generous, but I'll have to take a pass on it. Too many things on the go, you see."

"We understand. If you change your mind, come see us – 16 Beasley St. We're the office at the top of the stairs. Please remember there is some urgency to our offer."

The phone line clicks as the voice hangs up. There's no dial tone – it just goes dead in my hand. Hanging up and picking it back up does nothing, likewise mashing all the buttons.

Dead as before, apparently.

I toss the receiver back at the phone. Whatever.

There is nobody, *nobody*, calling me up and offering me money for anything.

Still …

It takes a second for me to track down a pen, and there's an empty cigarette pack handy, so I scrawl down the address while I still remember it – just in case.

There's something moving in the apartment. I don't see it, and in fact I'm not sure what sense tweaked to it, but yeah, I look up in time to *almost* see whatever it was. I'm sure it's a cat, but just like the last time, there's nothing when I go look.

I flick on the lights as I explore. Nope, nothing in the kitchen, or the bathroom, or the writing room, and I'm back to where I started, sitting on my couch and listening to the springs creak.

That's just great. I'm hallucinating, really truly hallucinating. The dreams were bad, but this is a thousand times worse. Lots of normal, balanced people have bad dreams, but there's only one kind of person who hallucinates.

What am I going to do?

I'll write. Yeah, channel my fear into my script, use the edge, use the tension for fuel. Ain't like I'm going to sleep.

Sit at the writing table, adjust the chair to its optimal position. Roll a fresh sheet of paper into the faithful Underwood, flick a corner of the paper with my finger just to show it who the boss is.

And type.

The words come, slowly. They don't race out like they did yesterday, like a firehose. It trickles, but at least there's something. The clacking continues, punctuated occasionally by the little bell at the end of the line.

Finish the page, pull it out and look at it. And all I can see is more evidence that I'm a crazy man. It reads like the first page of a berserk manifesto, the kind they find after some tragic event, that brings neither solace nor understanding to all the grieving families.

This is just great. I'm seeing things, being approached by lunatics who believe they're angels, and I'm imagining phone calls.

I've lost it. I've gone crackers. My little intellectual choo-choo train has just driven off its tracks. Crazier than a shit-house rat, that's me. Hell. What am I going to do?

Call Claire. That's all I've got left. I'll talk to her, and she'll tell me I'm not crazy and things will go forwards from there.

She'll straighten me out. Maybe I'll ask her what she thinks about the job offer. Maybe.

Nah, the whole thing is just stupid and crazy, and I'm neither of those. Still… that money would be really sweet right now. What could it hurt to check it out? I've got some free time – hell, got a bumper crop of that, and not much else. Plus, it's not that far away, so no skin off my nose.

Boots, coat, hallway, stairs, lobby, outside and stop, just beyond the door. Should I just walk out there? What about the streetlights? What if they all explode like before?

It's clear and crisp, still. A few flakes of snow are still falling, but less than before. I stand, shuffle my feet a bit. What's it going to be, Alex?

Boredom wins out. I can either be bored and fidgety in the apartment, or I can try and walk some of it off. At the first sign of weirdness, though, I'll turn around and come back. Yeah, that's my plan. It's good to have a plan.

Walking again, on the cold and quiet streets. Keep a close eye on the streetlights, Alex. One waver, one little shudder to the light, and I'll hop back inside. But nothing. They stay lit just like always. Off to my right, I can see the darkness stretching into the larger black of the night. I don't necessarily have to go that way, so the choice is easy. More than one way to get around. A few streets later, and there I am.

The building is like a thousand others in the city. It's a small office building, shoehorned into a space left over between two larger ones. A few steps lead up to the glass front door, and I can see the steps continue up from where they share a small foyer with an elevator. There's a directory of the offices, on the wall next to the door.

If I cared, I could go and check it out, see who might be listed.

But, I don't care that much, just stand and stare at the building for a while and at the top floor where my mystery caller presumably sits.

Well, that was a fun way to kill 20 minutes, but now to get on with the rest of my life.

I'm about to head off to my next pressing engagement, barely taking two steps, and glancing down I catch a glimpse of metal.

It's a quarter, a beautiful, shining, glorious 25-cent piece. Won't buy you much these days, but there's only one thing I need it for.

Call Claire.

The payphone on the corner is a real survivor. All day, every day, it bears up under the onslaught of the weather, constant sprays of slush off the cars driving by, and the feeble attempts by the vagrants to try and filch a quarter out of it. And despite all that, the damn thing still works. The dial tone hums in my ear as I sandwich the receiver between head and shoulder. The mouthpiece stinks of cigarettes, which makes me think about how long it's been since I last had a smoke. Too long.

Fish the quarter out of my pocket, and pop it into the slot on the top of the phone. The coin is still cold from where it lay in the snow. It makes little musical noises as it bounces around inside the machinery.

I still remember Claire's number, even though I haven't used it more than a half-dozen times in the last few years. Some things just stay with you, even when you wouldn't have noticed if they left or not. Funny.

The sun isn't up yet, and won't be for hours yet. Damn February. And anyway, when it is up, it'll still be hiding by yet another cloudy sky. I've waited as long as I can stand before calling. It's cold out here, enough to make my feet hurt. Hope I don't wake her up, and if I do, I hope I don't put her in a bad mood – not a good idea when you've got a favour to ask.

The phone rings twice before it gets picked up.

"Hello?" says my sister, half greeting, half who the hell is calling this early.

"Hey, Claire, it's me, Alex."

There's silence from the other end of the line. I don't know what I should make of that. Tick, tick, tick, come on, Claire.

"Listen," I jump in. "I know it's early and I'm sorry if I woke anybody."

"No," says my sister. "No, that's fine, Alex. We were already up. The kids were just sitting down to breakfast." I can almost hear her biting her lip. She's expecting the worst, and I guess I don't give her much reason to think otherwise.

"So, uh, yeah…" I trail off. What exactly do I need that she can provide?

"Alex?"

"Yeah."

"Are you in trouble?"

I snort. When am I not in trouble, in one way or another? All a matter of degree, really. "Kind of. It's difficult to explain. I just need some normal people to talk to. Soon."

Claire covers the phone. I guess she's talking with her husband.

"Would you like to come here for supper tonight, then?" Relief washes over me like a flash flood.

"Sure," I say. "That'd be great."

"Are you going to take the bus out to see us or..." She hesitates. "Listen, don't worry about the bus. Harold can swing by to pick you up on his way home from work. Where are you living these days?"

I wince. The words themselves aren't insulting, but the tone in her voice betrays her thoughts. And there's a lot of them. Concern for her brother collides with her Christian conviction that she's failed to save me before, combined with the fervent hope that this might be her big chance at finally getting me to accept Jesus as my personal saviour. And at the end of it all, she's thinking sometimes you have to be drowning before you're willing to ask someone for a life preserver.

Are you homeless? is what she wants to ask. *Just how close are you to dying?*

"Same place as before," I say, and then it occurs to me I have no idea what "before" might mean. Just when was the last time I had to give her my address? "Tell you what, it'll be easier to pick me up on the corner." I give her the street names in front of the convenience store.

"Okay, expect to see him around 5:30."

"Okay, thanks, sis."

"We'll see you tonight then. God bless."

"Yeah." I hang up.

What now? Wander around a bit more, or head back to the apartment. There aren't many options. No money in my pocket now that I've spent my measly quarter, and none of my haunts are open for the day yet. The apartment is warm, but I also haven't eaten anything today, and with no money, there's little prospect of eating anything for several hours.

I might be able to score a little lunch at the perpetually overworked men's shelter, but lunch is a long way off still. My other option is to panhandle for some change and grab a snack at the corner store, like usual. I'm not superstitious, but maybe finding a quarter is a sign my luck is finally changing.

Walk around the corner to one of the main streets, a busier one. Even this early, there's people. Yes, fewer, and they're not usually in a good mood, but I can still panhandle them. All it costs me is time, and I've got plenty of that on my hands.

Find a spot where I won't be exposed to the wind, and start looking for customers. "Spare some change, spare some change, spare some change." It's not a question anymore, delivered with a flat tone. I tried snappy patter for a while, like a carnival barker or something but I gave it up after a while. Too much effort, with little return. Plus, eventually I'd start getting snarky – hard enough to get people to give you money, even more difficult after you've insulted them.

It is quickly apparent that this is way too early in the day. Not only am I not making any money, people are looking at me oddly – like they're confused by me. What's he saying? What is he asking me? They shuffle on with their morning, some of them looking back over their shoulder at me with a questioning look.

I'm feeling the same way about them. They don't look normal, not 100 percent. It's like they're wearing masks, but not really, not literal masks. I see their face, but I also see another face superimposed on that. And while their real face can't figure me out, the extra ones seem very interested in me. Rub my eyes and blink a few times, and remember just how damn tired I am.

It's at the point now where I'm not sure I care anymore. Yeah, yeah, seeing things, whatever. All part of the magical experience of being a street person.

Fine, it's obvious I'm not getting anywhere. I should go to the corner, see who is there.

Walking past a newspaper box, I stop dead in my tracks.

One of the front page blurbs on the newspaper catches my attention. Seems some kids with slingshots or something took out a bunch of streetlights last night. I don't get to read much more, since the rest is hidden below the fold, and I've already blown today's budget by calling Claire. Man, this is one time I really miss not being able to read a newspaper when I want to – not that I often want to, but there are moments.

I don't really understand why most people read them so devoutly anyway, since so little of it actually applies to their own lives. Who cares what war is being fought on the other side of the world? Who understands half the arcane crap in the business section? And for those few people who do, they already know what's going on, and don't need the newspaper to tell them.

Today, though, the newspaper does indeed apply to my otherwise insignificant life. Streetlights, yeah. You'd never notice them unless they weren't working properly, or in my case when they explode and shower you with glass. The sun is already high enough in the sky for them to have shut off, and I barely noticed it happen.

Today, I want a newspaper. I guess guile is what I need. That I can do; it's the life's blood of the junkie. Stand next to the newspaper box, not so close that I'm threatening, not so far that it'll snap shut before I can grab the door.

And I wait. A few people slow, looking like they'll go for the newspaper box, then glance at me, then keep going on their way. Three times it happens before I finally get the hint.

So, when Contestant #4 shows up, I turn away, pretending to be engrossed with something dug out of my pocket. It works. Yay guile. Hear the coins drop down the slot, hear the door open, and I make my move. Turn around, make a lunge for the door before it can snap shut.

It's an awkward moment. I've gone too soon, and the guy is still pulling out a newspaper. There's alarm written over his face, staring at the grubby street person now standing *far* too close.

A polite cough. "Hey, can I get a newspaper?" I ask. "I need to see how my investments are doing." Just maybe, a smile, a friendly tone and a joke will win the day.

"Sure," he says, before very deliberately closing the door. "You just have to pay for it like everyone else."

Fucker. He probably cheats on his taxes, and parks in the handicapped zone, but for one brief, shining moment, he gets to be law-abiding. I hate people.

Fine. Screw it. I didn't want to read it anyway. Go to the corner and find a seat. It's still early, and most of my peers haven't made it out here yet. Soon enough, though – morning rush hour is coming and no panner wants to risk missing it. My luck sucked with the early crowd, but hope springs eternal.

Considering the amount of time I sit here on the corner, and listen to the unending stream of conversation, you would think I would know everything there is to know about the people who sit here. And maybe I do, at least, know everything worth knowing.

The reason this thought occurs to me is sitting less than ten feet away. He's one of the guys who would otherwise be in a mental hospital, if they still had the funding they needed. Thick, black curly hair hangs low over his forehead, making a fringe to conceal his eyes.

Occasionally he has a drawing pad, but usually just a piece of scavenged cardboard. He draws with one of those thick, thick pencils usually reserved for little kids, going over and over the same lines, or filling in a section, until it's black with graphite. His fingers are just as black, from his habit of rubbing the paper. There are notes in the corners, away from the drawings, but it is nonsensical stuff, and he writes over them with more notes, so it becomes an illegible mess pretty quickly.

I don't know his name, or anything about his background, because he never really says anything intelligible to us. He mumbles and laughs, but it's always meant just for him, and maybe whatever invisible nothings that surround him. He whispers to the air, makes vague gesticulations and smiles as if something had been explained solely to him. Every movement is furtive, looking around slyly, or patting a coat pocket to make sure that the contents are still there.

Today, though, he is staring directly at me. Look up, stare, pounce on his paper, scribble, repeat. After the fourth or fifth time, I start feeling the hackles rise on the back of my neck – I don't like crazy people in general, and ones that are obsessing about me, even less so.

Stare, scribble, stare, scribble.

His head snaps up to look at me, fast as a mouse trap, so fast that I flinch.

"Hey," he blurts, which makes everyone look. Nobody here has ever heard him speak up, let alone say anything understandable.

He waits until absolutely everyone is looking at him, before holding up his drawing pad.

ALEX, WE WANT YOU, it says, in big, bold, capital letters. What the hell?

And then he rips the page from the pad and crumples it in his hands, before leaping up and running away, shoulders hunched.

Should I be getting used to this? Like one does with bad weather? Yep, sure is crazy out, better wear my tin foil hat. That's when I'll know when I've finally adapted to it.

I have at least a little sympathy for some of the bums I share the corner with. Not the drunks, or the lunatics, but the ones for whom life just shat upon.

One of the guys used to be a commercial fisherman, worked on all sorts of boats far off the Alaskan coast. Tough work, for sure, and not just because he says it is. Around his neck, he has a thin leather thong, and one of his own severed fingers dangles from it. It was his foot that did him in, though, mangled up in a later accident and leaving him unable to work.

Broken and out of work – well, where else would he end up?

I'm not sure of his name, because everybody settles on one of various nautical nicknames – Captain, or Skipper, stuff like that. He commands a lot of pull on the corner, I suspect because he still has his mind. Yeah, he drinks, but he's fighting real physical pain, not trying to make some internal demon shut up.

He's not a friend of mine – he's too damn grumpy for my tastes, and he's got enough on the ball to know what sort of an asshole I am. Our non-friendship is based on a mutual lack of respect.

So, it's a little surprising when I glance his way, and he nearly jumps out of his skin. He looks scared – a guy who proudly wears a severed body part – and he's looking at me.

"Skipper? Are you okay?" I ask.

"Not when I'm sitting next to one of the loonies," he says. "Right now, I've got all the crazy I can use." Then he moves away, shuffling sideways from me on the steps. I literally don't know what to think of it. Probably some people would get all puffed up at the idea of being able to intimidate someone. I know better, though – there's nothing in me that should provoke anything like that in anybody. All it does is weird me out.

He puts some space between us and sits with his cane across his lap, held with both hands so he can swing it like a club if necessary. Next to him is Dingle, who has been watching all of this. Slowly he gets up, manoeuvres around him and sits next to me. It's good to have someone on your side who can intimidate others.

"Morning," he says.

"Yeah. Did you catch the game on TV last night?"

"Nope. You?"

"Me neither."

Between us and the Skipper is another of our august gathering serving a buffer, a guy using an unstrung guitar like a drum, tapping away with his fingers on the shell of it. I'm not sure if he fancies himself a musician, or if he figures he might get more change as a street-busker than as a panhandler, or maybe it's just a way to pass the time.

Occasionally he sings along with his non-strumming guitar playing, with that high-pitched, tone-deaf quality one gets when wearing earphones. Unfortunately, he's not wearing any.

It's painful to listen. Tune him out, Alex. Think of anything to fill up your mind – multiplication tables or favourite drinks, or women. Yeah.

There's very few women who ever share our corner. Overwhelmingly male here. Maybe women just don't crash like the men do, or maybe it's because they've still got a commodity – sex – that they can sell, so it's only an unfortunate few who end up here.

"Pretty" isn't a job requirement for a whore, but there's definitely a minimum limit. By the time they end up sitting with us, they've fallen about as far as they can go.

One thing I've noticed about them, the ones that hang out with us, is a stereotypical walk. They all walk with their heads canted to one side or the other, sometimes with their mouths lolling open too. It's distinctive enough that I could pick one out at a distance – just a glimpse of the lean of the head, and that particular gangly walk. I don't know why they do it, but I'm certainly not going to ask anyone. Not a damn chance they'd know either.

And I can't ask the women themselves, because I can't score with them. I've nothing to offer, no drugs, booze or money, no food, no status, and for goddamn sure I'm not willing to share my apartment with them. No pull, don't even bother striking up a conversation – it'll just sound like I'm trying to pick them up.

He stops tapping away on his guitar, and you can almost hear the relief from the rest of us. Gets on your nerves, not just the tapping, but the attempt at singing.

"Have you ever noticed how pigeons walk real casual, like they're trying not to attract attention?" he says. "Hey, just one more person going off to his day job. Nothing out of the ordinary here." His comment couldn't have been better timed, falling into a lull in conversation and a gap in street traffic. It pops up, undiluted by other noises.

Everybody stares at the pigeons. And yeah, by and large, they do look like they're trying really hard to blend in with the crowd.

While we're all eyeballing the birds, it looks like they're giving us the exact same treatment, walking back and forth, but always keeping one red eye on the denizens of the steps. Or perhaps just one particular denizen – me. The little feathered rats are all staring at me. An entire stoop full of people, but I swear I'm the only one they're looking at.

I move my head a little, to the left and to the right, and a dozen feathered heads swivel to follow. Left, right, slow or fast.

Get a grip, Alex, you're being an idiot.

From deep within me boils up a rage, and letting it out seems like the sane thing to do. Leap to my feet, throw my arms in the air and yell like a lunatic as I race down the few steps into their midst. The pigeons fly away in an explosion of flapping wings.

Sit my ass back down on the steps next to Dingle. Damn straight, we'll have no more talk of pigeons.

Dingle pretends nothing happened. You can really appreciate that in a friend. All he does is indicate a spot down the street with his thumb. Time to go to work, and not entirely figuratively. Morning rush hour means lots of people, which means lots of opportunities to wheedle a little cash.

We all have our own way of going about it. There's a kinship with fishermen in my mind. Everybody has their own opinion of the best lure, which we resolutely defend for no other reason than it is ours. We're also protective of our favoured fishing spots, convinced that it's only a matter of time before Moby Dick comes our way and drops $20 into a hat.

For instance, is it better to panhandle in a group, or alone? Staunch advocates on both sides will weigh in. I'm a fence-sitter myself – context is everything.

Same with signs. Some of us like them, but most just find it a nuisance to carry the damn thing around all day. There's a younger guy on the steps with us, probably mid-20's, with a piece of cardboard. Somewhere, he managed to find a black marker, and scrawled "I mean you no harm. Spare some change." The fact that he's still sitting with the rest of us, shows that it can't be doing him that much good.

Hell, the fact that he's sitting with us at all means he isn't good, in so many ways. He won't last long – they never do.

Presently, I'm in a group of three. There's Dingle and me, which is typical and Special Ed, which isn't. Ed will cast the line, since he's a mellow dude. That's good, puts people at ease. And if you've given money or smokes to the first guy, it'd be uncharitable not to give some to his buddies too. Plus, three people have much better odds at staking out a prime spot than one. There's strength in numbers.

We take up our positions not that far from the corner. Plenty of street to choose from, and lots of foot traffic to beg from. Nobody has a problem with our spot.

So, we settle in for a morning of begging. Sweep the snow out of the way, throw down some cardboard to sit on, and wait for the fish to swim our way.

For whatever reason, nobody's willing to bite. We have our pet theories as to why one day will be better or worse than the other, but the truth is nobody has the slightest clue. Won't stop us from talking about it, of course.

"Spare some change, spare some change, spare some change." It becomes Ed's mantra, repeated endlessly. One day he'll achieve enlightenment and become the god of begging. His paper coffee cup keeps time with his voice, as he rattles a few coins in the bottom as encouragement.

Anyway, today is shaping up to be one of those no money days.

Good old Special Ed though, he keeps right at it. What a pro. At least an hour goes by with no luck. That's when we notice the change. His chant starts to lose its metronome quality, a little louder, more emotional.

That's... odd. Ed is like the atomic clock of beggars – never angry or perturbed, fast or slow. He's got his rhythm and he keeps to it.

Next thing we know, he's on his feet and yelling "thanks for nothing" at the backs of passers-by. Dingle and I give each other curious looks. I make little walking motions with my fingers. Time to get up and go somewhere else? He shrugs in reply.

Ed makes the decision for us, tailing some poor bastard down the street, haranguing him the whole time for his cheapness. He's got this funny kind of walk, all stiff-legged. Well, usually it's funny, but right now it turns him into Frankenstein's Monster. We can hear him yelling even after he goes around the corner and out of view.

"If he comes back, we leave. Okay?" Dingle nods agreement and we settle back to work. I handle anyone coming from the left, he handles traffic from the right.

Dingle gets a kick out of upsetting people. If he were a bigger, more robust individual, perhaps that frame of mind would manifest in a very nasty way.

But he's not, so really, it's harmless. Anyway, his little thing is to ask passers-by for change, and when they inevitably says something like "Sorry, no," or "Afraid not," he gets this fake concerned look on his face and says in this meek voice "You don't have to be sorry," or "Nothing to be afraid of," like he thinks he's offended them, and that it really matters to him. It flusters people. They sputter, and get embarrassed, and try to explain that it's just a figure of speech. Dingle doesn't care; he's already asking the next guy for change or a cigarette – he just wanted to get a rise out of you. It's a power trip, I guess.

He doesn't get to do his little thing much today, though. Normally there are three reactions from Joe Citizen: he gives up some spare change, he mutters some little apology, or he walks on by without offering the slightest indication that he noticed the panhandler.

Today, and lately, we've rarely had the first, occasionally the second, and an overwhelming collection of the third. People just keep walking – if anything, they speed up.

Dingle keeps his hopes up, looking for that victim who will step into his semantic bear trap. We entertain ourselves any way we can.

He gives me a nudge and points with his chin at the next guy walking along. Expensive overcoat, a haircut that wouldn't dare look mussed, and a stride that says he's got somewhere important to be.

Perfect.

"Spare change?" asks Dingle, with a deft mix of humility and despair.

"Sorry, no," he says, predictably.

I swear that Dingle makes tears well up in the corner of his eyes when he says "Hey, man, you don't have to be sorry." I wish I could applaud his performance.

"Hey," says Mr. Upstanding Citizen. "I was just being polite. I don't really give a damn about your feelings."

"Geez, dude. I was just asking," says Dingle, genuinely surprised.

"And I'm just telling you no." He's getting louder, and closer. Dingle and I both have our hands out, palms making a little virtual barrier. We look like two of the Supremes, about to break into a street rendition of "Stop In the Name of Love".

He slaps Dingle's hand out of the way, and Dingle cowers. What the hell else can he do? But it just makes the Citizen hungrier, leaning right into Dingle's face and shouting.

"Get a job," he yells. "Or go to jail, or I don't care what. Just get the hell out of my city."

"Back the fuck off," I screech. Dingle shoots me a look, begging me not to. It'll just make things worse.

Screw it – go for gold.

"Move away from my friend, asshole."

"Or what?"

"Or I'll kick the living hell out of you. Do you think we can lose a fight in any way that matters? Do you think there's a goddamn thing you can do to us that hasn't been done before? It's two against one, and the two don't care if we get humiliated, or hurt, or get muddy clothes, or spend a night in jail. We just don't care. Ain't like there's a downside to our friends seeing us with a black eye tomorrow. In fact, you're pretty much burying the fucking needle on my don't-give-a-fuck-o-meter."

Every third word or so is punctuated with a poke in his chest and a little move forwards, stealing a bit of his territory each time.

"Take your best shot," I yell, throwing my hands wide and pushing out my chin as a target for his punch. But he's in full retreat, scrambling back away from me.

A lunge forwards from me, with an animal yell, and he turns and runs, throwing a handful of change from his pocket as he does.

The money scatters on the sidewalk, each coin doing its own little dance, letting out its own music. Dingle and I look at each other, eyes wide, poor kids on Christmas morning who've just discovered that Santa is real.

And then, again just like kids, we dive after the money. There's real urgency at work - money is like blood in the water, and we're not up to fighting off sharks. We're within easy sight of the corner, and things could get crowded in a hurry.

"Holy crap, Alex. We're goddamn rich."

Yeah, rich is one of those terms that really depends on context. And in this case, yeah, a couple of bucks makes us rich. Makes us survivors, at least for a little longer.

"Don't-give-a-fuck-o-meter?" Dingle asks, from where he kneels beside me.

I shrug, suddenly sheepish, wondering where the hell my bravado came from. I'm just glad my bluff wasn't called.

"What do you think we should do with it?" asks Dingle, hissing his voice through his teeth. He's looking around like we're trying to hide a stolen painting under our coats.

"Coffee," I say. "Coffee and some place warm to drink it."

Dingle nods vigorously. "Yeah, let's go to Niko's."

"Where's that?"

"A block or two from here. Hot coffee and they won't kick us out before we've had a chance to sit down."

I nod assent. A warm place to sit, with coffee, and with staff who don't give a damn – I'm amazed that I haven't heard of this place before.

Life on the street is a balancing act that way. When you don't have any money, there's very few forms of legal tender left. Companionship, that's a big one; it's always important to have someone to talk to. Backup, that's another. And because I was willing to step in and help Dingle, he's willing to give up a little of the most valuable item of all: information.

Anybody with some smarts, or just animal cunning, plays their cards very close to the vest. You can't predict when something you know will come in handy. Often it can be used several times before it gets disseminated, diluted if you will, and has no more leverage. Conversely, wait too long, and someone else might stumble upon the same tidbit you have.

Information is also the only transferable wealth we have. That Dingle told me about this place is a big thing, since not only has he weakened the value of it by spreading it around, I now have the opportunity to spread it around too.

Make a slip, and tell the wrong thing to the wrong person and watch its value evaporate, possibly right in front of you.

Case in point: there's not too many places that will serve the likes of us. We smell, we're broke, we take up a table for hours at a time if given the opportunity, and many of us are as crazy as a shit-house rat. One or two of those people, barely tolerable. Much more than that, and you can scratch that diner off your list of warm places to wait out the winter.

And just like he said, two blocks walk, and there it is.

I could describe the diner as having seen better days, but what, or who, hasn't? The sign is bold, red background, sweeping white lettering spelling out "Niko's." These days, the sign would have been done in some faux ancient Greek stick figure script in blue and white, instead of its 1950's cursive.

Push open the door, walk in out of the cold wind. Stamp the snow off our boots in the little vestibule. Take the opportunity to scan the place before entering the restaurant proper, look for a good place to sit first instead of just wandering around like the vagrants we are.

It's not a shithole, to be fair, just the inevitable downward progress of life. Floor tiles that show the path of decades of shuffling feet. The formica pattern on the tables has long been rubbed away by the elbows of thousands of patrons. The overstuffed seats wheeze gently through cracked vinyl when we sit. And the walls, knickknacks, gewgaws, tchotchkes, mix with long yellowed newspaper clippings and photographs.

Flip the coffee cups upright, and wait for the waitress. While we sit and talk, my finger finds a convenient cigarette burn, and spends the time tracing its outline, over and over. I'm the type of person who needs that sort of thing – if I had paper, I'd be doodling while we talk. Dingle wipes the condensation off his glasses with a napkin.

"What's up with you, Alex?"

"What do you mean?"

"You look like hell, man. Like seriously bad."

I shrug. "We all do."

He gives me a sour look. "Yeah, we all do, but you look worse."
I shrug again in response.

The waitress wanders past with a carafe full of coffee, does a little double-take when she spots us. Doesn't say anything, just spears us with her eyes, sizing us up.

"What do you want?" she says – half request, half accusation.

"Coffee?" asks Dingle.

"Yeah, coffee," I say. "Please."

She doesn't move to fill our cups, just stands there silently. Then I notice her rubbing thumb and forefinger together. Right. Money first. Into our coat pockets we go, spelunking for change. The coins clatter on the table as we dig them out, then dig some more, just in case.

"How much?" I ask, looking back and forth between waitress and coins. I should know how much a damn cup of coffee costs, but I'm too far gone lately. There's two things every wino on the street knows, and that's the price of a coffee and of a cigarette.

She doesn't say anything in response, just pulls the requisite number of quarters over with the tip of one long painted fingernail and then scoops up the pile. No way is she going to risk contamination by direct contact with the likes of us.

The change goes into a pocket, and coffee gets poured into our cups.

The aroma hits me immediately. Strong, bitter, good. We're lucky – I think this is a fresh pot. Can't see them caring much if the carafe has been bubbling away all day, no matter what the resulting tar smells like. It's hot coffee, so I wouldn't turn it down anyway.

Her face is pinched sharp as she looks down at us.

"You get two free refills. That's it. Yes, I keep count. You can smoke if you have your own, but if I see you ask anyone here for a cigarette, you're out. I'm going to mostly pretend I don't see you, so if you make it so I can't ignore you, you're out. Do we understand each other?"

"Yes ma'am," we chorus. Life on the streets gives one a certain incentive to be polite when you can – hold a door open for someone and maybe they'll give you some change if you ask. Be polite to the waitress to let her know we'll be good boys – not stupid, not crazy.

With the cups filled, and the two of us properly warned, off she goes on her rounds. Fill a cup, fill a cup, fill a cup, like a mobile version of those glass birds that dip their beaks in the water.

Dingle starts pouring sugar in his coffee, and keeps on pouring, while I savour the smell of mine. Warm cup in my hands, held close to my face – a feast for the hands and for the nose. By the time Dingle puts down the sugar dispenser, I think he's got more of a coffee-flavoured syrup than anything else. Bon appetit.

God, I want a cigarette. Is there anything on the planet that gets better than coffee with a cigarette? I could ask the people in the next booth, but that'd get the two of us kicked out in a blink. Sneak a glance at the waitress, and decide no, it isn't worth the risk. Short term pain, long term gain – I want to be able to come back here again.

Dingle points with his chin at some guys sitting across the aisle in another booth.

"See them?" he asks. "Dealers. That's what made the neighbourhood go downhill. Drugs. They started selling their crap, and this…" he takes in the room and the street beyond with a sweep of his arm. "… is what happened. I hate that shit."

"Dingle, I've seen you wrecked plenty of times. What are you talking about?"

He snorts before answering. "Sure. Ain't nothing I wouldn't try, ain't nothing I haven't taken. Doesn't mean I like it. Ain't what I would've chosen for a life, y'know? That shit rots a person, from the inside out."

I study the dealers some more. Every single one of them has a cell phone clapped to the side of his head. This place is driving me nuts – everybody around here is smoking and I can't ask them for a cigarette. Drug dealers sitting less than 10 feet away from me and I don't have any money.

Money, yeah. Why is it that drug dealers all dress like rodeo clowns even though they've got income? C'mon, guys, spend a little and buy yourself something with class. When you get to the point where someone who looks like me, is giving you advice on how to dress, chances are you need to revise your wardrobe.

"Surprised you never heard about this place. You always seem pretty smart and plugged in and stuff."

I don't say anything, just shrug and sip at my coffee. Talking would just spoil the moment.

"I grew up just around the corner," says Dingle. "Lot has changed since I was a kid. Not this place though – it's been here forever. Before I was born, I think. Niko, the old man, he opened this place pretty much as soon as he got off the boat. It's changed since then, but it hasn't changed, y'know?"

"No, actually, I don't know."

Dingle nods as if I agreed with him. "I mean, like, I think the stuff on the walls, or the seats, or the floors has been the same since I

41

was a kid. It doesn't stay the same – it wears out, or gets broken, or maybe just beat up a bit. Even when they replace it, though, it's still the same stuff, y'know?"

Yeah, I guess I do know what he means.

"It's a lot like us," he says. "We're the same people, but we get a bit more worn out each day. Eventually the same damn thing happens."

"What's that?" I ask.

"Death, I guess. They'll close this place down one day, same as them burying one of us. The old man's gone – I hear it's his son who runs the place now. I'm just like Niko's. I used to have a good life, but now I'll do anything for a little money, and I'm waiting around for death."

Death, and then what?

"Hey," I ask. "Do you believe in God?"

Dingle considers it for a moment, like he's drawing on years of education and reflection on said question. In reality, I think it just takes time to filter through the few working sections of his brain. Whether he's a nice guy or not, any intellectual capabilities he once had have been dealt a series of mortal blows from years on the street.

"I guess I don't know much, but maybe, God is like, this cool guy," he says. "And say you've heard about some big party or something, God would call you up and tell you he was going to give you a ride there and back. He'd bring booze for both of you, and you wouldn't have to worry about being busted by the cops, or being rolled or nothing, because he's God, after all."

He falls silent.

"Wow, that's profound," I say, keeping my voice neutral. "Sort of a cross between a deity and a frat boy." Dingle can pick up on the sarcasm if he wants to. He just nods for a bit, looking out the window at the traffic.

He shrugs. "It's as deep as I need it to be, I guess. What the hell is a guy like me going to do with all the thee's and thou's and stuff? I don't need Jesus doing miracles, just a full belly and a warm place to sleep. That's all."

He falls silent again, and I don't say anything either. I see his point though, and it's a good one – any god he would worship had better be pragmatic. Why pray if the only answer you're ever likely to receive is "No"?

"Okay, Alex. Your turn. Do *you* believe in God?"

Yeah, do I? That's a pretty involved question these days. Even when I was a kid, going to church daily, prayers daily, Sunday school, and a home filled with Christian propaganda, I still wasn't sure I truly believed. I'd have my head bowed in prayer, hands clasped together and eyes closed. The words would spill out of my mouth, but my mind was elsewhere.

Once in a while, I'd peek around, just to see if everyone was doing what they were supposed to. If any of them were peeking, I never caught them. That just frustrated me more. If they weren't fidgeting or looking around, were they really praying? What was happening internally? I guess I could've asked someone, but that just felt like a dangerous question, and I had learned a while ago that I didn't like the answers I got back from those.

"Why would God change his plans, just because we pray and ask him?" That one got my ass spanked until it was bruised, and a week where the time between supper and bed was spend on my knees in prayer.

In comparison, asking one of my friends "when you pray do you really pray, or do you just sit there and think about girls until *they* tell you you're finished for the day?" would've probably been worse. The former was a theological thorny bit, and could've been explained away, or an appeal to the infinite and unknowable nature of God might have sufficed. The latter, though, that smacks of apostasy, and even worse, an attempt by me to tempt another member of the congregation into free-thinking and faithlessness. No, best to just shove my questions down deep, and hope one day that I'd finally find what everybody else seemed to have and I lacked.

Is there anything in my life like a supreme being? Was there ever?

My script. Maybe that's my god. In some ways it's like having a high-maintenance girlfriend. It's always demanding my attention, and things suffer if I don't think about it often enough. Depending on the time of day and how things have been going, I either love it or hate it. On the most miserable days, I do both simultaneously. God? Girlfriend? Hard to tell.

But, like many long-term relationships gone sour, there really isn't an easy way to end it. It sounds like it should be simple enough – toss the damn thing in the trash and walk away, but the characters have been with me for a decade at least. Some of the ideas in it have been with me since the beginning of college. There's a lot of mileage gone by.

Frankly, other than family, it's the longest relationship I've ever had. And what little family I have, they mostly are there for me to mooch off, it seems.

The script, though, sometimes I do wonder if it's time for a divorce. Been writing and rewriting the damn thing for so long, I don't think the words consciously register when I read them anymore. Just going through the damn motions. There are days when I just want to boot its ugly ass out the door and be done with it.

In my less deluded moments, I ask myself why the damn script is so important. So what if I get it finished? It's a freaking play, for god's sake. It isn't like there's going to be a line-up of theatre companies at my door, all clamouring for a chance to bid on it.

Theatre groupies – that's what the world needs, women turned on by a guy who can write a script. Hey, baby, watch me block out a scene.

Yeah.

Maybe I could get back into acting. I was in a toothpaste commercial years ago, although now, I guess I'd be the guy they pick for the "before" pictures.

I spend so much time thinking about my answer, that Dingle figures I've mentally wandered off into the woods – typical in our crowd. When I finally begin to speak, he can't figure out what I'm talking about. I guess that's pretty typical too.

"Well," I say. "I don't think I believe in some guy with a long beard and bathrobe, sitting on a cloud, counting how many times you jerk off. I don't know. Maybe the universe is God? And we're all just little cells, little parts of the big machine?"

Dingle nods in agreement, and then says "you don't really believe that, do you?'

"No," I laugh. "Just spouting a theory. I'm not sure what I believe."

"Me neither," he says. "Went to church when I was a kid, but we never talked about it, my folks and me. I don't know."

I don't know – now there's the barometer of religious belief. When you meet someone who says he *does* know, then you can safely assume he's a liar, a lunatic, or he's scared but doesn't want to admit it.

"Maybe I'm what you call one of those no-god types," says Dingle.

"An atheist."

"Yeah, one of those. I've seen a lot of guys on the street who spend their whole day talking about God and praying and all that, but y'know, they're as badly off as the rest of us. For all their talk, they don't look happier than anyone else. If there is a God, he ain't listening."

"Do you think it's possible God is out there?" I ask.

"I've seen some weird shit, Alex, stuff that'd make you crap your pants, but I ain't seen anything that would tell me God is real. I guess it's possible. Who knows?"

"So maybe you're an agnostic?"

"Maybe. If I knew what the word meant, I'd be able to tell you."

It reminds me just where I am, and who I'm talking with. This is not a philosophical discussion at a university coffee house. I'm in a crappy diner, sitting across from a guy who would drink bleach if he thought it would get him half-way stoned.

Oh well, work with what you've got. "An agnostic says that he feels there's probably a god, but isn't much sure about anything after that point."

Dingle sits back and thinks about it for a while, chewing his lip and occasionally sipping his coffee. He nods his head slowly, turning the idea over in his head.

"Maybe that's me," he says. "I only say there may be a god because the world is a damn big place, and there's lots of places to hide. What if I said there's no god, only to find him when I turn the next corner? I'd feel pretty stupid, I guess."

Given a different set of circumstances, Dingle might have been an average guy. I think the raw material is there, but not only did it never get developed, it's been steadily poisoned. At least he knows how to read, which is more than what some of our contemporaries have. He also shouldn't be in a mental ward, again a notable difference.

Life on the street has made his already skinny body into something more like beef jerky, I suspect. I'm not sure of his exact age, but I am sure he looks at least a decade older than he is. So, 40 maybe?

In a fair universe, he should be making a living digging a ditch, or punching out widgets in a factory. Come home at the end of the day, a beer in front of the TV, boff his plain-looking wife once in a while, and eventually die of something unremarkable at the end of a very ordinary life. A life like about another five billion people on the planet. No grand purpose to it, just existence.

"Well then," I say. "Whether or not he exists, do you think people need God? How will we know what good or evil is without God?" Best to pitch him an easy one.

"People who are good just because God is watching them, they're not really good," he says. "They're just being smart. If I want to steal something but don't because a cop is standing next to me, I'm still a thief, just means I'm not an idiot about it."

"So," I ask. "Does that make you a good person? Or at the heart of it are you still bad?"

He shrugs. "Me, I sleep fine. I've got a clear conscience."

I bite my lip, and then decide to ask. "Have you been having dreams lately?"

He shoots me a look, like I've been spying on him or something. "No," he lies. "I don't dream."

"Me neither," I say. "I was just curious." We sit in silence for a while. I go back to tracing the burn in the formica, while he rips a napkin into strips. What is he thinking? He looks as tired as I am, like everybody on the street does. It's a safe bet we're all having the dreams. Are they hallucinating too? I want to know who else has an imaginary cat wandering through their apartment, or a guy who thinks he's a guardian angel.

I want to know, but I know I won't find out. We might talk a lot on the corner, but we don't talk a whole lot about ourselves. There's a definite stigma against crazy people, not because they're rare, but because they're unpredictable and dangerous.

The guy at the next booth finishes up and leaves, but not before tossing his newspaper on the table. I jump at the chance to derail any further conversation.

A quick look around to make sure the waitress isn't watching, in case she decides that I'm after her tip, and I snatch up the newspaper. The crossword puzzle is mostly filled in. Can't finish it anyway, since I don't have a pencil, and that's aggravating. Bad enough if you don't know the word, but far worse if you know it and can't do anything about it. The horoscope makes me laugh though – *"You will realize your dreams through the efforts of a new acquaintance."* Thanks, no. I emphatically do not want to do anything with my dreams other than not have them anymore.

Damn, there goes that urge for a cigarette again – some things just go better with one. The newspaper is just more satisfying, as is coffee, as is beer.

Dingle gets bored. "I have to hit the can. Wait for me, okay?" Yeah, like I'm just going to bolt out the door while he's off at the toilet. He shuffles sideways out of the booth, and ambles off. "I think I'm going crazy," I say to him, but only after he's far enough away that he won't hear me.

When he's out of sight I start reading the rest of the newspaper, specifically the article about the street lights. Seems the cops have no idea what's going on either, blaming it all on unnamed "vandals." Street lights blown out for a full five blocks, and a score of cars with broken headlights.

One of the columnists ties it in with a spike in police calls, fires and admissions to the hospital's emergency department. I don't even bother finishing what he wrote, because I can guarantee you that he got it all wrong.

Toss the paper on the seat next to me and look around the room again.

There's a radio, up on a high shelf behind the lunch counter. It looks like it was part of the original equipment of the diner. Big, clunky, dusty, probably uses vacuum tubes. Works okay, though, with some music creaking out of its ancient speaker.

"Louie, Louie" is playing, and for once, I don't bother trying to decipher the lyrics, just lose myself in the rhythm and the fun of the song. My head bobs slightly, and I close my eyes.

"Alex."

I snap to attention at the sound of my name, but when I look around, there's no-one who would've called me – just one of those weird moments when your brain pulls out what it thinks is a familiar noise from a jumble of other noises. A deep breath, a sip of coffee and I relax.

Again. "Alex." Only this time, I'm not drifting, and I hear exactly where the voice is coming from – my name is being very clearly spoken, in the middle of a song that I've heard 10,000 times. If anyone else heard something odd, they're good at covering up their reaction.

My stomach knots up, and my hands start trembling where they lie on the table. I clutch my coffee cup to try and steady them, but with little success. It just makes the coffee vibrate and threaten to spill over.

"You have something we need," the radio sings, just to me. Oh fuck, I'm like Charlie Manson listening to Helter Skelter. This is stupendously bad. This is how it starts. Next thing you know, the cops will be gunning me down in self-defence.

Nothing else matters at the moment, nothing else exists. The universe consists of me, and that damn radio. All around me is black and silent.

The song ends, and the next one starts, and I brace myself for the voices to start up again, but they don't. Calm down, Alex, it's just a transient thing. You can get past it. Just calm down.

Dingle will be back in a minute, and I don't want to look like one of the crazies we're forced to hang out with. Bad enough that I feel like I'm one of them. Breath in, breath out, nice and slow. Stop looking around like someone's out to get you.

He returns soon enough, automatically scanning the tables. I can see he's looking for what he can scrounge or scam or steal – it's just an instinct – but he won't. Sits down across from me.

There's a sustained blast of cold air coming in from the front door. Lots of people on the way in, and the door never gets the chance to close fully. Looks like the beginning of the lunch rush. I guess technically we could stay at the table, but if things are getting crowded, they're going to want paying customers filling the place.

"Getting crowded," I say. Dingle nods agreement.

"Probably time to move on." Dingle nods again.

Fine by me, frankly. Get outside and let the cold air clear my head.

Gulp down what's left in our cups, do up our coats and make our way out. Everybody sneaks a look at us as we go, curious, or suspicious or whatever. Typical. No, we don't leave a tip, but is anyone really surprised? I don't feel guilty – service sucked anyway. Wish I had the guts to swipe the tip off one of the other tables, as a discourtesy tax.

Back out on the street, back into the cold and the damp. Ah well, it was nice while it lasted.

"Where to next?" asks Dingle.

I shrug noncommittally.

"Back to the corner?"

I shrug again. Dingle starts walking – if I want to go, I'll go. He doesn't feel the need to wait for me. And if I want to do something and don't feel like sharing, that's cool too. That's one reason I like Dingle – it's a no-stress, no-strings friendship.

I wait until he's out of sight before heading back to the apartment. I like Dingle, but I don't like him well enough to tell him about the apartment. Enough, I'm warm now, and I'd like to stay that way if possible.

Do I have any money left? Food, smokes, that'd be good right now. Digging through my pockets comes up with nothing but the scrap of cardboard with an address scrawled on it. Well, nice to know that wasn't a hallucination, or if it is, it's a very consistent one.

The scrap sits in the palm of my hand, and weighs about a thousand pounds. The address isn't far from here, easy walking distance – wouldn't take me more than five minutes.

Nah, don't be stupid, Alex. And yet, I can't make myself throw it away. Back into my pocket it goes.

Head back to the apartment before I get cold. While I walk, I briefly contemplate stopping by the corner, just to hang out, see if Ed made it back, see if he's still a raving loon. When I pop out of my little reverie, I realize, son of a bitch, that I find myself standing in front of the damn office building. Why does this job offer keep drawing me back? Everything about it is weird – not just weird, but impossible. I should take the scrap of cardboard, drop it in the snow and walk away, forget that it ever happened.

But, I don't. Instead, I stand there like a fool, staring at the building and forcing pedestrians to walk around me. The building, of course, does nothing. Just sits there, staring me down with mute patience.

In the end, what have I got to lose? So what if the offer is fishy, or that someone called me on a disconnected phone? I'm tired, hurt and hungry. I want a smoke. I want to get high. There's a list of things I want and standing out here isn't getting any of that for me.

My feet, though, don't do anything. I'm still standing here, and getting colder by the minute. Slush is seeping into my boot, making my toes ache. Still I stand.

There's a pull from the building, almost literally. Subtle, just below tangible, but I swear to God I feel it. Pulling at me, tugging, plucking at every loose thread on my clothes. The scruffy hair on my chin eases forward. I lean forward – further, further, until one of my feet, rebelling from the rest of me, takes a small step forwards. Just one, and the other foot doesn't follow. I am standing there in an awkward stance, one foot forward, one back, and taking up even more room on the sidewalk. People have to give me a wider berth. I don't mind that, but eventually someone is going to trip over me, which will probably spill me onto the ground as well.

My other foot takes a step. Still standing awkwardly, but a little closer to the building.

The pull is stronger now, much stronger. I can feel it, can hear it whispering in my ear urging me to climb the steps.

What is stopping you, Alex? Why aren't you walking? You've never resisted temptation before, so why now all of a sudden? This doesn't fit you very well.

Yeah, why?

Another step, and the whispering becomes more urgent. Time is running out, it hisses at me. Do it. Do it now. Shivers are running up my spine, one after another, making my whole back twitchy. People are looking at me strangely as they pass. Fuck them. Let them stare. I don't care what they think at the best of times, and these are decidedly not the best.

It's more than just looking at me strangely, though. The expressions on their faces, those are troubling. You don't look like that just because some homeless guy was standing still. No, that's a look of impending dread, of nameless apprehension that something very wrong is just about to happen. They don't know what it is, just that it's imminent.

Fuck them. Fuck them all.

Another foot forward, up a step this time. And another, a pause, and then a few more and the front door of the building stands directly in front of me.

The sound, the pull, the urgency backs off, waiting to see what I'll do next. It hovers on the verge of my consciousness. I ignore it. I don't need its opinion.

The door is wood, with a long slim window running vertically along it. Through the window, I can see the lobby is beyond clean, well-lit, and empty. No potted plants, no crappy plastic chairs. The joy of simplicity.

Open the door, Alex, says the voice. The invitation is warm, and sincere, comfortable, cozy even.

Pull on the door handle, but it feels wrong. No, not wrong, just out of place. It isn't the smooth and sleek feel of an office building, but one of a house, one that is incredibly familiar to me.

I'm home, my parent's home, my childhood home. The screen door makes that same old whine when I open it and step inside. The side door of the house opens onto the kitchen, and everything is exactly where it was the last time I visited, just like it was every day I lived here.

The kitchen smells of coffee, from the old glass percolator that sits atop the stove, perking endlessly. On the wall next to me, the cuckoo clock ticks away.

"Don't just stand in the doorway, dear. You're letting in mosquitoes." I know that voice, probably better than I know my own. My mother.

"Sorry, Mom," I say, stepping in and letting the screen door slam shut behind me. Shake off my winter coat and toss it over the bench near the door. My mother lets out a little "tch" – she'll hang it up soon, first chance when she walks by there.

"Have a seat, Alex."

I do, sitting in a chair I haven't seen in years, at a table I haven't sat at in years.

Mom putters, her standard mode of behaviour. Always on the move, straightening, wiping clean, taking something out of the oven, putting something into the wash – she's constantly in perpetual domestic motion. I'm sure she dreams of it too.

I take a look around, though I don't need to. Nothing has changed in this room, forever as far as I can tell.

The wallpaper still looks like something you'd see in grandma's cottage with all the big flower prints and the orange theme. The table is up against the wall, looking out over the window and the alley. Everything is spotless – nothing would dare look dirty or out of place in this house.

Nothing has changed, and nothing ever will.

"So glad you could drop by, Alex. It's been so long since I've seen you," says my mother, as she flits from task to task.

"Yeah," I say. "I've been real busy." My hand glides over a tabletop that bears the memory of every meal ever eaten here, served here for decades. The marks Claire left as a baby, working her first teeth on the edge of the table, imprints left by our pencils as we did our homework – all of it is there, if only one knew how to look for it.

"And what have you been up to, that keeps you from visiting your mother?" she says, setting the coffee pot on the pad on the table. The same old glass percolator that again, my mother has had since the dawn of time. As far as I can tell, the universe started with the Big Bang, and then my mother came along and swept things into neat piles and organized all the galaxies and stuff. An elemental force, that's her.

"Stuff, Mom, just stuff. Been working on my script, as usual, and just ... just having a tough time of it."

She nods sagely as I talk, taking it all in. While she listens, she pours coffee, and then pushes a little plate of cookies at me.

"Thanks, Mom." My mother's coffee – again unchanging since the dawn of time. There has never been a better pot of coffee ever brewed. Way better than the crap I was just served at Niko's.

Yeah, Niko's.

What is wrong with this picture?

Mom breaks me out of my reverie with her hand on top of mine. "You're not looking well, Alex," she says. I shrug. Even people who don't know me could tell at a glance.

"You could always stay here until you're feeling better. Really, dear, you're never too old for your mother to take care of you."

51

It's a pretty sweet offer. Food, laundry, a soft bed, and a chance to get straightened out again. Just my mother and me.

"I'm serious, Alex. I want you to stay with me, at least until you're feeling better."

Why wouldn't I? I feel like shit, and I'm strung out. Staying with my mother would heal me up quick.

So why do I hesitate? Why?

It'd be a real trip to be in my old room again. Wonder how much of my old stuff is there? When I moved out, I took whatever I needed and left the rest. Didn't care, never figured I'd see it again. Now, I don't know. It'd be interesting to see.

I remember summer nights, growing up in my room. The windows were open, because my father was too cheap and fussy to get air-conditioning. There was a train line that ran pretty far away from the house, but on the still nights, I could hear the train whistle. It wasn't harsh or blaring at that distance – sounded more like a musical instrument.

I'd be lying there, awake, wondering where it came from and where it was headed, and would I ride one out of my parents' house, like a hobo. Johnny Cash could've narrated my childhood.

Now things have come full circle. I'm back in my parents' house, and yeah, I'm a hobo. Irony just sucks.

"Eat as much as you want. You're too thin," she says. I think I heard that from her just about every day of my life. She's right, I *am* too thin – and not just now, but in general.

No more encouragement is needed, and I shovel some more cookies from the serving tray onto my little plate. Coffee too – can't get enough of that.

I'm pouring my third cup when it happens. I spill the damn thing all over the crocheted white doily on the center of the table.

"Fuck," I say. "Shit, Mom, I'm sorry."

Shows how long it's been since I was last in my mother's kitchen that I would dare to swear. She wouldn't have said "shit" if she was buried up to her waist in it. Certainly she wouldn't tolerate anything stronger than "geez" in her presence.

But, she just sits there, stirring sugar into her coffee and looking at me with that familiar, benign gaze.

"Mom?" I say. "I spilled my coffee." She makes no move to clean it up, and still no reaction to my swearing.

"Goddamn Jesus Tap-Dancing Christ," I say, experimentally, and instead of the reprimand I should be getting, she says "He won't admit it, but your father will be happy to see you too."

What? Just what the hell? Standing up, I'm suddenly a little dizzy, and there's a buzzing noise in the air. "Mom?"

It's wrong, it's all wrong. Why isn't she cleaning? Why haven't I been reprimanded? It's like the sun is moving backwards in the sky, or gravity doesn't work. She's not there anymore. The room swirls and dissolves, colours fading out from the cheerful oranges of the wallpaper, to grey concrete and marble and dirty snow. The buzz resolves into the sounds of traffic.

I'm standing on the street. I'm on Beasley St. again.

My mother isn't here – she's dead, been dead a couple of years now. No mother, no kitchen, no cookies or coffee. Just me and a street with a few miffed pedestrians having to walk around me, and Serapion standing nearby.

"Welcome back," he says.

"Where was I?"

"Doesn't matter. It's just important that you made the choice to come back."

"What are you talking about? I didn't choose anything. I was here, and … and in my mother's kitchen, and here again."

I look up at the building, but it isn't there. No, I'm facing the same direction, but the space it was in, wedged between two larger buildings, that space isn't there anymore – likewise the building. It's darker out, the sun is setting.

What the hell?

"Yeah," he says, by way of explanation. "There's people who want you to stay safe, so why don't you do them all a favour and stay out of trouble? Why don't you go somewhere where you can be sure you'll be protected?"

Who the hell would care to keep me safe? It's a short list, for sure, and Claire is the only one on it. Yeah, she sent Serapion – that's the only explanation. Makes sense, I guess, though I have no idea where she would've found anyone like him. He's a lot rougher than anybody she'd ever likely meet in a church social.

Did Claire really send someone to look after me? It's the only explanation. Could he be a private detective? Sounds like something out of a movie, but it makes at least a little sense. Okay, not a lot, but still …

In any case, I am not going back to my apartment while he's standing next to me. My hobo haunt, though, is both close, and he's seen it before. And once he's gone, home is a mere block further down the street.

I start walking. He keeps pace beside me. "You know, you really don't have to follow me around," I say.

He rolls his eyes. "Yes, you've shown me that you're such an expert at taking care of yourself."

"So, do you still think you're my guardian angel, or have you moved on from that? Where do you stand on things today?"

"I think what amazes me most about you, Alex, is that you ask a lot of questions, but it seems you never ask the right ones."

"Just what does that mean?"

He just shakes his head in reply, and then turns and starts walking away. "You'll be okay now. Go somewhere safe." I watch him walk until he goes around the corner, before I move on, just to make sure he's not following me.

Back to my apartment building. For all the travelling I've been doing, you'd think I was a courier or something, that I was making money with all of this walking.

Even when the lights are on in my apartment, it never looks lit. Probably I just need to replace the Christmas lights or whatever is in the sockets, with something better but that'd cost money. In any case, more light wouldn't make the place look any better. I think the original paint colour on the walls was a mint green, but that was easily decades ago. Cigarette smoke and general grime have left it more of a mustard colour, really. The floors, grey linoleum that certainly is several shades darker than what it should be.

Home, such as it is.

Thinking of home makes me think of my mother. Despite the coffee and cookies I scarfed down, there's no weight in my belly. Nothing but the memory of it all. Been a long time since I've eaten my mother's food, and the taste stays with me.

All of my clothes are in a pile on top of a duffel bag. The bag used to be for carrying anything that wasn't my typewriter. Now it serves as a marker for the spot where I pile all my dirty laundry.

It's been a while since they were last washed, so it isn't easy deciding what is the least dirty. I sit down hard on the floor. Man, what the hell am I becoming? In one hand, I'm holding a t-shirt with some unidentifiable food stain, in the other a shirt that wouldn't even make a good rag, and they're both looking like viable options.

I've got to turn this around. And I don't think I have much time left to do so. Among my peers, 'hitting bottom' is more than just a phrase; it's a state of being. When you hit bottom, that's it, last stop. Either you're going to seek whatever help is out there, or you die. A lot of them can't build up enough steam before it's too late for them to be helped.

I don't think I'm there yet, but I can see it from where I'm standing and the gap is closing fast. Seek shelter, or die.

A quick shake of my head to clear the cobwebs. Okay, pity-party over, Alex, get back to work. I throw on some clothes, and stuff the rest in the bag. Boots on, coat on, out the door and down to the street corner to wait for my drive.

Living without a clock, or a watch can be tough – I don't really know how close it is to 5:30, and there's nobody around who would tell me. When you look like a homeless junkie, it's pretty much impossible to ask a normal citizen for the time without them expecting you to hit them up for a little spare change too.

I know I'm leaving the apartment early, and maybe even by an hour or two, but there's not much choice in the matter for me. Can't even judge by the sun, since it's pretty much set already. Aren't the days supposed to be getting longer by this point in the year? Seems to me that, if anything, there's even less sunshine than there was a month ago.

Missing sunshine is a bit of a surprise to me, considering that until fairly recently, the day was when I did the majority of my sleeping.

The smart money says it's before 5pm – nobody is heading home from work yet. Might be able to bum a little change, or maybe a cigarette with any luck.

By the time I drag my duffel out to the corner, my peers are leaving, off to the shelters, or hang around the mall. I suspect one or two have a place like mine, but they're as prudent as I am with letting on about something like that. My guess is that today has been, like several before it, a complete washout for panhandling.

"Hey," calls one of the step-dwellers. "Moving?"

"Sister's," I say. "Supper, and thought I'd do some laundry." And then I shut up. Let them talk about that, instead of wondering where I've been keeping my stuff all this time. This crowd endlessly dissects anything that resembles news, so it's in my best interest to give them something to talk about.

And talk they do. Starting with scoring free access to a washing machine, we go through memorable dinners we have had, meals we'd like to have, eventually settling on Christmas and Thanksgiving spent in a church basement. No one takes another glance at my duffel, which is fine by me.

"Here comes the 5:10 express," someone says, and we all laugh a little. It's funny because it's true, and the same joke gets recycled. We see him, twice a day like clockwork. Always has his hands stuffed deep in his pockets, head down like he's walking into a stiff wind, and eyes on the ground. Looks like he's carrying every problem in the world on his shoulders.

And just like clockwork, someone on the steps asks him for money. He's always startled and apologizes because he doesn't have any change. Just like clockwork.

The routine never varies. He's always preoccupied, always startled, never has change. But, he's never actually grumpy – unfailingly polite, and wishes us a good day.

Even though we don't get money out of him, I wish there were a lot more people just like him. He doesn't ignore us or pretend we don't exist. It's a nice change.

There's a balancing point for me in dealing with my fellow street people. You have to understand that I don't like them, first of all. Ain't like there's too much to enjoy. I love the street, though, the weird vibe that all the thousand varieties of people bring to it. It's like the carnival visited the city, and forgot to bring its freak show with it when it moved on. The winos, pimps, whores, junkies, the poets, artists performers, buskers, all contribute the myriad threads of the crazy carpet that makes up this life.

And the guardian angels, says my inner voice.

I think I'm getting a headache.

"Hey, Alex," calls a voice. It takes a second for me to locate it. And then I see the hand waving from the car window and everything clicks. Harold, my brother-in-law. Harold, not Harry – that's the way he likes it. The car is nice, not too old, and about as clean as it can be in February. The trunk unlocks as I come near, so I can throw my duffel inside.

It's a little tricky getting into the car. The snow bank on the curb makes an impromptu obstacle course. I am reminded that agility and living on the street do not go hand in hand, but at least I don't make a complete fool of myself. Into the seat, close the door, and relax in the warmth.

"Good to see you again," I say, holding out my hand for Harold to shake. He doesn't shake it, but not because he's rude, but because he's looking away from me and over his shoulder, hoping for a break in traffic so he can pull out from the curb. My hand hangs in space for a few seconds, until I feel awkward and drop it.

I hear the little motor whir for a fraction of a second – he has rolled his window down a crack. Can't really blame him – I haven't had a shower in, well, in a long time really. There's rarely hot water in my apartment, and cleanliness isn't worth standing in freezing cold water.

The trip is mostly conducted in silence. Both of us try a half-dozen times to start a conversation, nothing controversial, small talk stuff, but it never gets any traction. Yes, it's awkward, but it would have been worse if it was Serapion taking me to see Claire. Does he even have a car?

Out of the downtown core, and into the suburbs. Shorter buildings set back from the sidewalk, more trees… and absolutely nobody who looks like me. No, not surprised, but it's amusing to note the differences.

As we pull into the garage, and the door shudders closed behind us, Harold turns to me, looking at me for the first time in the whole trip. He's not startled, at least, but I can see his eyes scan me up and down, making mental notes. He's not happy.

"Listen," he says. "Claire is a little nervous about having you here. She wants to see you, she misses you, but well …" He trails off. I know what he means. My sister lives her life fretting. She's rarely happy, and when she is, it's because she's found something satisfying to fret over. Often that's me, and my life. Harold should be thrilled I'm around – if it wasn't for me, she'd be fretting over him, and I guarantee nobody in their right mind would invite that into their lives.

She prays for me, I know that, and is terrified that I'll die without salvation. I'm a big enough problem that Harold looks positively faultless in comparison. He should be damn well thanking me. But, things don't work like that. Claire is worried about me, and some of that will bleed out onto him.

"You're a good guy, Alex. I like you. I'm just asking you to be nice, okay? Don't start anything?"

I nod. All I want is to maybe get my head straight, and my belly full. There's no need for fights.

As a brother-in-law, I like him. Good to my sister, which is about all you can ask for. Even if I was doing well, he's not the type of guy I'd have anything to do with, though. Harold is just too damn normal, if you know what I mean. Always pays his bills on time, always returns tools he's borrowed, always votes, always concerned that he's on the same mental wavelength as the neighbours. He likes a circumscribed existence, prefers the self-imposed limitation. He wears colours that won't stand out, has his hair cut short enough that

57

you'd say 'cop' or 'soldier', but he doesn't give off that vibe. A living embodiment of the status quo, just like Claire, which is another reason they like each other so much.

Harold goes through the door to the house, holding it open behind him for me. "We're back," he yells. I join him just as his kids greet him, hugging him around the legs. They're bigger than I would've guessed, but considering that it's been, what, a year or two since I last saw them it isn't surprising. Can't remember their names either. Also not a surprise. Wish I had thought to bring a gift or something for them. Hell, wish I had the money to buy them a gift.

"Say hello to your Uncle Alex," says Harold, and the two of them look at me dubiously, shyly. Neither ventures away from the safety of dad. Can't blame them – I know I look like hell, and aren't grownups supposed to be big on personal hygiene? Honest, kids, I'm not one of those zombies that eats brains, I'm the kind that just wants a hug.

Plus, God only knows what their mother has told them about me.

And as if on cue, Claire comes around the corner.

"Hey sis," I say, as I shrug off my coat.

"Hi, Alex." She hides her shock pretty well, just a burst of blinking eyes, and then gives me a quick once over. I can tell by the way she's biting her lip, she doesn't approve of my present condition. What a surprise.

"Okay if I run a load of laundry while I'm here?" I ask, while holding up the duffel bag. "There's nowhere for me to do it where I live."

Yeah, so it's a cheap trick – if my dirty clothes are already here, she can't really refuse me. But I can see Claire fret inwardly, thinking of what sort of residue will be left in the machine, but she's trying to be a good sister, so a quick nod, and she points to the basement where the laundry room is. That she didn't offer to throw them in the washer herself is telling, but I understand – I wouldn't want to touch my clothes if I wasn't forced to.

So, I stuff the duffel's contents into the machine, follow it up with what I hope is a suitable amount of soap, and then stand there trying to figure out the controls. Man, I think the Space Shuttle has fewer buttons. I turn a knob or two, poke a button, and it obligingly starts making noises and filling up with water. Score one for the degenerate.

Should have thrown the duffel in with the clothes, probably, but that might be too much.

At the top of the stairs, I come face to face with a dog. For a moment I have an impression that I'm hallucinating about dogs now too, along with the cats, but quickly I realize this one is for real. It's staring intently at me. Not growling, but definitely on high alert – ears forward, tail pointing up like a flagpole. I really hate moments like this, because I have no idea what I'm supposed to do. Pet the dog? Talk to it? Shout? The little Mexican standoff continues, and any motion I make is mirrored by the dog.

It curls back its lips, revealing teeth. Still isn't barking or growling, but I feel like it could lunge at me at any moment, and that's not a good feeling when you're standing on a staircase.

Harold comes around the corner though, and the dog slinks away without a sound. It still keeps eyeing me as it retreats, letting me know there's unfinished business.

"Listen," Harold says, ignoring the dog completely. "Supper won't be for a little while. Why don't you grab a shower too while you're here?" The idea sounds so good that I ignore what underlies the suggestion. Yes, I stink. Yes, I'm filthy. No need for me to get defensive about it.

Harold and I head upstairs again, and he points me down the hall. I can guarantee he had absolutely no say in the decorating of this room. What married guy really does get, or want, any input in what gets done with the bathroom? As long as the toilet, shower and sink work, a man is happy. Leave the decoration to someone who cares.

I can ignore the delicate flower print wallpaper, ditto for the display towels and soap that were never intended for actual use. What really bugs me, though, is the big portrait of the Very Caucasian Jesus staring down at me from high on the wall. Nothing better to unnerve a person, than to have someone benevolently ogling you as you drop your pants. Swear that his blue eyes follow me around the room. Hell.

Water on, clothes off. Steam rises up inside the shower enclosure pretty quickly. In I go. The water is really, really hot, surprisingly so. I thought it'd be, I don't know, lukewarm considering the laundry is running too. Or maybe in my current state, I just don't have the capability to judge? I don't know. Feels good, anyway. Who cares?

The dirt swirls down the drain, and it seems there's an endless supply of it. My scalp feels like it's on fire as I grate my fingers through the tangled, greasy hair. Work the dirt out from under my fingernails. The washcloth gets the workout of its life, as I scrub until my skin is sore.

I want to stay under the shower until the hot water runs out, but my stomach reminds me that I haven't eaten anything today.

Grudgingly, I shut off the taps and stand there, letting the water drip off me, breathing the steam deep into my lungs.

It feels good, hell, it feels great. The towel is good too, warm, soft, smells floral but not oppressively so. I forgot what clean is like, it's been so long. Clean is like taking one or two big steps away from crazy.

There's a full-length mirror in the bathroom, fogged. A swipe across it with my palm reveals my face and damned if it doesn't scare me. My skin is grey, except for where angry redness rims my bloodshot eyes and dark circles loom like storm clouds. Cheekbones and chin jut out at sharp angles, threatening to pierce the thin skin underneath, in counterpoint to my sucked-in cheeks. Been a while since I've shaved too.

On impulse, I wipe the rest of the mirror with my towel and see the rest of my body. I look like a corpse, a goddamn walking corpse. My ribs are all picked out in great detail, the skin on them is not taut, but clinging, hanging on for dear life. Even freshly cleaned, the colour is grey, not pink.

I look like I just walked out the gates of a concentration camp, or something. Veins, tendons, and what little muscle I've got, they're all visible, like ropes or wires under my skin. What I find particularly disturbing is the fact that my veins look grey like the rest of me. Just what sort of crap is circulating around in there?

I use Harold's deodorant, hope he won't mind. Just one more thing I haven't been able to afford. I wonder if they'll consider burning it, along with the towel and washcloth after I leave? Probably should.

What the hell, I've already polluted his deodorant, so I grab his razor and give my spotty beard a shave. Luckily it's never managed to grow in thick, or I'd be in a lot of pain. Hopefully Harold intended on changing to a new blade tomorrow, or this one is going to pull his face off in chunks.

Scrape my face, wipe the remaining shaving cream off, and then try and rinse the stubble down the drain. There I go, swirling and down the drain. Yeah, hope not.

For a moment, I contemplate using a toothbrush, but I don't know which one to use, and the idea of someone having to stick anything in *their* mouth after I've used it in *mine* is off-putting. I know I wouldn't do it.

Razor, shaving cream, deodorant – put them all away, best as I can remember where they go. And then pause.

Staring right at me, right on my eye level in the cabinet, are all the pill bottles in the house. Nothing really entertaining, by the looks of things and remembering just whose house I'm standing in. Pills for headache, sinus congestion, allergies, menstrual cramps, and a bunch of other stuff – the stuff that *normal* people have.

I look at the cabinet for a few seconds, weighing options. Yeah, sure, as if I'm not going to come to the same conclusion, no matter how long I wait. Each and every one of the bottles is flirting with me, doing a seductive little song and dance – no, not literally. I don't hallucinate. Okay, not much. Not right at the moment.

Anyway, it would be rude to ignore the pills, after they've put so much work into their presentation. Good work, everybody, nice rehearsal. Stay focused, curtain goes up soon.

Every bottle gets opened in turn, and each one gets a pill scammed out of it, and tossed down my throat, and onto the next bottle.

There is, of course, no way of knowing what the combination will do to me, whether I'll get high, or need a trip to the hospital, but I don't really care. There's many different kinds of risk takers; mountain climbers, stock market investors, cowboys, and then there's people like me who will happily take a random handful of mystery pills without a second thought.

It's like gambling, but in this version, it's actually an advantage if you don't have a full deck.

Well, I haven't started puking, so the mixture isn't going to kill me right away.

Comes time to get dressed. All the rest of my clothes are in the basement somewhere, and there's nothing but a pile of dirty clothes in front of me. Really wish I could put on something clean to match the rest of me, but I guess I have no choice.

So I get dressed.

Immediately, I realize just how filthy I must have been. My shirt feels greasy; the fabric of my pants has an odd texture to it, more like cardboard than cloth. I feel like I'm already dirty again. Two steps forward, one step back.

Oh well, there's nothing I can do about it, except smile and pretend I'm clean all over. A shower, a shave, a proper meal in my belly soon, and the regular indulging of my self-destructive urges. Maybe the pills will kick in soon.

Stepping out of the bathroom, I'm hit by the smell of supper. My God, what was the last thing I ate? Or when, for that matter?

Claire is in the kitchen, standing by the counter, chopping vegetables. I stay out of her domain, leaning on the door jam. I may be clean, but my clothes aren't. Plus, this way I won't get drafted into doing any actual work.

The kitchen is wide and well-lit, clean, bright, decorated with the obligatory picture of Jesus opposite from the clock. I can see our mother in her, as she stands there – taller than our mother, thanks to Dad's genes, but the stance is unmistakably Mom's.

"So, I met Serapion," I say.

She doesn't look up from the cutting board. "Oh, who is that?" I'm watching my sister for anything that would indicate she's feigning ignorance. Perhaps she's become a better actor over the years, but I don't think so. I think she genuinely doesn't know who he is.

Okay, so maybe it wasn't the most plausible idea, but it was about the most reasonable one I had. Scratch her off the list. So where the hell did he come from and why is he so interested in me?

"He's just this guy I met. He reminded me of you for some reason."

"In a good way, or a bad way?"

"An odd way. He's a pretty odd guy." As soon as the words are out of my mouth, I regret them. My sister is rightly insulted by being compared to anyone I might meet who manages to deserve mention as 'odd' compared to the rest of the freaks, geeks and weirdos I would run across in my usual haunts. Then again, much of what I do offends her on some level, so she should be used to it. Wasn't spoiling for a fight this time, though.

We stand in awkward silence for a while, until her curiosity gets the better of her.

"So what is this person like?"

"He's, uh, kind of religious." Claire smiles – maybe I'm finally going to climb on board the god-bus.

"… He also claims he's a bona fide guardian angel."

Claire's face falls. There's genuine anger there. Jesus, why the hell did I have to say that? There's always tension between us, and it's either about religion or family, and as a result, stepping on each other's toes is pretty easy to do – we've just got nothing else to talk about.

"Supper will be ready soon, Alex. Why don't you go and wait in the living room and I'll call you when we're ready." The words are inoffensive, but the icy tone behind them carries the real message – *get out of my face, now*.

Well, running from fights has saved my life so far, and I'm not about to stop yet. Out of the kitchen I go, without another word. I wander around the living room. Sitting would be my preference, but I think my pants would irrevocably stain the upholstery. Standing it is, then.

My sister and her family have the quintessential suburban life – a split-level house, with a pool in the backyard. Very active in their church and community, well liked and respected I would bet. I can imagine an army of statisticians using them as the absolute perfect example of the middle class.

The mantel over the fake fireplace is crowded to overflowing with framed photos. Most are of my sister and her family, but there's some old pictures too – her and me as kids with our parents, one or two of our grandparents. They look good, happy - like they've been short listed as subjects for a Norman Rockwell painting.

The old photos, black and white, faded to grey and yellow. What is it about pictures from years past? Something about the film or the cameras, or maybe just the people, but I look at a picture from then and a recent one, and there's just something missing. The old shots have more detail in the background, or more going on behind people's eyes. Do they just pick up time? Fifty years of stories recounted as they're passed around?

The pictures of me look incredibly dated – the haircut is stupid, the clothes are lame. Man, sometimes I think it's a wonder I ever got laid in high school. I did, by the way, a lot. Ain't bragging but it seems no girl can resist the bad-boy image.

I look even goofier as a child, gangly, teeth too big for my mouth, haircut courtesy of my dad. At least he didn't put a bowl on my head and cut around it, though his efforts weren't a major improvement. I made up for it by being the combination class clown and know-it-all, which I'm sure comes as no surprise to anybody.

I look okay in my graduation photo, or as good as one can while wearing a shiny rented gown. Claire is right behind me in line. Yeah, big surprise – my graduation was delayed by a year because I failed a bunch of courses, while she sailed right through.

After university, Claire came out the other side even more religious and me even less. Away from my parents, away from the church, and the peer pressure, the whole idea of God just sounded ridiculous. My sister just got scared and clung even harder to the concept. Never really understood it myself, that she didn't seem to ever rebel against the way she was raised. Isn't that the natural thing

63

for people to do? No, instead I think the more uncertain she became about the world, the harder she clung to what she knew.

What's more, I don't really know for sure. I've only got my own suppositions about it all. Our family was not the kind to talk about feelings, or express opinions. I think that started with how my father survived living with my grandfather, and trickled down from there. Still, being raised in the same environment as Claire, I suppose I have an idea where she's coming from.

I recognize some of the people in these pics. Others I just know the names, and occasionally how I'm related to them.

Good thing it's my sister who has the pictures. She's got a better head for these things than me and isn't about to pawn the family photo album for crack. It's not that I don't care, but there are priorities.

Yeah.

There's the photo of my father and grandfather, his arm around my dad. Dad sold insurance, my grandfather was an old-school tent preacher, simultaneously disappointed and pleased that his son decided not to follow in the same rootless but holy life. Grandpa was a miserable son of a bitch, I remember. He was pretty old by the time I was born, but still spent much of his life on the road. Just couldn't settle down. Cost him his marriage too – somewhere along the line, his wife left him, never to be seen again.

He would abandon everything to go off on his preaching tour, usually with no warning.

Old grandpa spent enough time in our lives to teach us one thing, though: fear. Fear of God, fear of damnation, of not measuring up to some cosmic list of religious standards, fear of death, judgement, payback. On one hand, we were told that Heaven was assured for us, because we were Saved.

On the other hand, well, what are you supposed to take away from being told that there is someone who watches you constantly, has a very strict set of rules that they demand you follow, has a torture chamber warmed up and ready to go in case you fuck up, but oh yeah, professes to love you? If that person were your neighbour, you'd buy a shotgun to protect yourself, and hope the authorities would drag him off to jail or the psych ward.

At least Dad chose a more stable upbringing for his kids. A less fervent religious life too, I bet. Every once in a while, to scare us into behaving, he'd tell us of the austerity of his childhood, better suited to a monk than a kid. His fear manifested by his devotion to work. He wouldn't miss a day at the office no matter what – he could have had his spine severed in a car crash and would've used his chin to pull himself down the street if necessary.

In the end, he died at the office. Heart attack, predictably, inevitably. According to his coworkers, he kept working, grimacing and with one hand clutched at his chest, even when the ambulance showed up. If he hadn't finally collapsed at his desk, he probably would have brought his work with him for the trip to the hospital.

The photo of my mom is quintessential – hair pulled back, plain clothes, never wanting to draw attention to herself in any way. She could have faded into a crowd standing in a phone booth. And that was just the way she wanted it to be. Laundry was always put away, the kitchen was always stocked. Things just happened around the house with no one noticing. It would have been an embarrassment to her if anyone thanked her for it.

Mom limped on for a while longer without Dad, but there was no spark anymore. She really bought into the idea that her husband was in charge of her and of the family. When he died, it left a kingdom without a king. Her kids, her home and her church weren't enough to fill the void.

God had taken away the captain of her ship and she had to trust it was part of His plan, no matter how much it hurt.

She lasted almost two years without my father, but eventually faded away like ripples in a lake. One day, she was just gone.

For Claire, she frets. Not only does she fear Hell, she sees it around every corner. It doesn't wait for her, though – she's Saved, after all. She prays for me, terrified that I'll die without redemption. Depending on the day of the week, she either thinks she drove me away and is therefore responsible for my impending, eternal damnation, or that it was my choice to leave the church and she should be doing more to save my soul. She's torn between the joy of being Saved, of seeing her whole family again in Heaven, but knowing there will be one person definitely missing if she doesn't save me too. And how could she be truly happy with that hanging over her head?

And for Alex? I avoid the fear of failure by making sure I never succeed at anything. Far better to fail at my own hand than to have someone else judge my efforts unworthy.

I don't blame Dad for who I am. Frankly, all things considered, he made some pretty radical changes from the way he was raised. We lived in a house, not in the back seat of our grandfather's car. We could actually play with our toys on Sunday, where instead he spent the day in quiet prayer, interrupted only by meals, church and more church.

Fear of God, a "gift of the spirit" they call it. I have first-hand knowledge of it, intimate and complete. I've watched it work its special brand of magic on three generations of my family, with an untold number that came before them. The one thing I never understood, and certainly no one has ever been able to give me anything but the most facile of explanations for: why do so many people think "God-fearing" is a good thing? A sensible thing, maybe – fear the vengeful, lightning-bolt throwing, psychopath sky-daddy. But a good thing? Something to emulate?

Back to the living room. There's another very white-looking Jesus staring down at me from the wall. I suspect there's one in every damn room of the house. They have paintings on the wall too. I don't know anything about art, so I'm not even going to pretend to evaluate them. Landscapes, mostly, and they appeal to me, for what it's worth. Nice furniture, comfy looking.

The landscapes are offset by little plaques scattered here and there, sporting either a scriptural sound-bite, or a trite religious poem that's supposed to be inspiring.

What did I learn from all the religiosity around me? From Sunday school and church services and relatives' homes filled with religious knickknacks? Nothing much, other than I would prefer to sleep in on Sundays, and the people who make devotional plaques and posters are lousy poets.

A small table between two chairs holds the family bible. It's big, old, worn – damn near monolithic. No idea how old it is, and it ain't like they bother putting a copyright in it. That was the bible that held the place of honour in my parents' living room, the most important guest, the son that never disappointed them.

Assuming Claire hasn't changed her habits, there's a bible in every room of the house, except for the bathroom.

I know the kids are standing by the door, sneaking a peek at the weirdo in the living room. Kids always think they're being so damn stealthy, and the only explanation they have for getting caught is that Mom has eyes in the back of her head – certainly that's what I thought.

I ignore them and keep looking at stuff. Let them think I don't know they're there, while I keep an eye on them, watching their reflections in the photo frame glass. They're shy, despite their curiosity, hanging onto each other and to the door jam.

Going by my own childhood, I have a fair idea what their upbringing is like. For damn sure they've never seen anyone who looks like me. Yeah, like Sunday morning they're going to find my kind sitting in the church pew next to them.

I'm probably the first taboo thing they've ever seen in the house. But what do I do with this golden opportunity? Convert them? Scandalize them?

Nah, I don't have the energy for all that.

Instead, I spin around and yell "boo!" They shriek and run, and I can hear the giggles all the way down the hall.

Kids are okay, I guess. Not babies, I mean – people stand there, holding them and cooing away. I don't understand the attraction. It's when they're older that they get interesting, when they can start talking. Kids say some weird things, totally inventive, creative things, and I can respect that. It's later, when grownups start teaching them what to think that the problems start.

What else is in the room? Valentine's Day cards on the end table – construction paper ones from the kids, store-bought ones for the grownups. I guess that means I missed my birthday. Congratulations, Alex, you made it to 30 without dying. A few brass gewgaws lying beside them. The thought occurs to me that some of this stuff might be worth a few bucks in the pawnshop. Maybe get enough to buy some smokes, or get high?

Man, I am a lowlife. If I asked for money, Claire would give me some, no doubt. Yes, I would be forced to listen to a brief sermon in exchange, but it's better than feeling like a worm because you stole stuff from your sister.

My finger traces the outline of a small brass ashtray, the little whorls engraved deep into it. Neither of them smoke, so I don't know why they'd bother having one set out. Maybe it's for me? That idea gets shot down quickly. I just can't see them allowing someone to light up in here – purely decorative. They probably set out a chair and ashtray on the porch for my use already.

On some level I feel guilty, but what can I do? Junkies are, by definition, not good at controlling their impulses, or being controlled by guilt. Hopeless, that's me.

I know what I am. I'm not a tough guy with a heart of gold. I'm not a misunderstood rebel. I'm an asshole and a junkie – plain and simple. So why do I feel qualms about stealing? The short answer is: I don't. At least, not normally. Stealing from the only person who gives half a thin shit about me ... the outcome will be the same, but I'll feel worse about it.

My finger stops, having made it to the center of the spiral. Biting my lip and a quick glance around, and the ashtray gets dropped into my pocket.

"Hey, supper is ready," says Harold, popping his head around the corner, and startling the hell out of me. I don't think he saw anything, but just barely. Following Harold out of the room, I catch a glimpse of my mother's photo. I'd swear she's giving me a disapproving glance. Yeah, Mom, I know – you raised me better than that. You also didn't expect I'd become a junkie though.

Jesus, what could I have done differently? I think I've asked myself that question a hundred times, searching for that one moment, where I could've decided A instead of B, or left instead of right. I never do come up with an answer though. I guess life doesn't work like that.

The table looks nice. Claire hasn't gone overboard, like it was Thanksgiving or something, but she's laid things out well enough. There's salad, there's bread, and a roast chicken.

My stomach lets out a threatening growl. *Easy, big fella.*

I notice a bottle of wine on the sideboard, unopened, and that the table is set with water glasses but nothing for the wine. I'm sure that was a conscious decision, not serving wine with dinner. Probably a good choice on their part; it's guaranteed that I'd be downing most of it. It takes a fair amount of willpower for me to stop looking at the bottle.

Before I sit down, I take a peek under the table to look for the dog. I don't know what it's got against me, but no sense in taking any chances.

Peek, sit, help pass around the food as it's doled out on the plates. I've got my knife and fork, but just before I can dig in, Claire clears her throat, meaningfully.

"Alex, would you say Grace?" asks Claire, and the words spill out of me automatically, words I haven't thought about and certainly haven't said since the last time I had supper before moving out of my parents' house for college, what, almost a decade ago.

Although my mouth is on autopilot, my brain is still working. There's a point where I suddenly realize what I'm saying, and at that moment, the trance is broken, my words falter and I have no idea what comes next.

So, I stammer.

Everybody just stares at their food, although Claire gets increasingly anxious, the longer my pause carries. Harold clears his throat and mumbles "Amen," even though the little magical food-blessing spell isn't finished. I'm only too happy to echo him and reach for a serving spoon.

Claire doesn't though – doesn't speak, doesn't move, just stares at me blankly. I can't read what's going on behind her eyes. Is she mad? Hurt? Does she want to denounce me as an infidel?

Another heartbeat or two and she lowers her head, finishes the prayer silently and picks up a fork.

There's no conversation for a few minutes. Fine by me, that would just get in the way of shovelling food down my throat.

"So," says my sister, finally breaking the silence. "Alex, you're looking … not well." Didn't I hear much the same from my mother, or whatever that was, recently?

Harold shoots her a look that says *"what the hell?"* but doesn't say anything. He might be thinking the same, but it just isn't in him to blurt things like that. My sister is much better at meddling in other people's business.

I shrug, stop eating for a second. "Yeah. Things have been rough lately."

"Are you in some sort of trouble?"

I shrug again. "It's not so simple as that. Nobody is out to get me, if that's what you're asking."

She sighs. "Then what is happening, Alex? I've been worried sick since your phone call."

How do I explain what's been happening to me? Where do I start?

"Well, uh, first off, I've been having these dreams. For a while now, that is." Yeah, it sounds lame to me too, but every once in a while, I go with the truth. "Anyway, that's probably the most definite thing – I haven't been sleeping well in months."

Nobody says anything. Claire just takes it in, Harold eats and the kids can't figure out whether to eat or listen to what promises to be a juicy grown-up conversation.

"Other than that, I've been feeling edgy and nervous. Been trying to work on my script, but nothing much happening on that front."

I want to tell her that I'm spending my days awake instead of nights, but how do you explain to someone, especially one like Claire, that that is actually a bad thing? The day shift is an inextricable part of normal as far as she's concerned, so I don't mention it at all – best not to make the situation any more confusing than it already is. There's more than just a few things about the whole concept that she wouldn't understand. Trying to educate her as to the different varieties of lowlife, yeah, that'd be interesting.

And then, to get her to understand why it's important and why it says to me there's big problems ahead. Damn, Claire, couldn't you just take it on faith? You do it with so much else in your life. As long as the guy clutching at the pulpit shouts it at you, you'll believe it. Me, though, that's another story.

She cares for my soul, for all the good that's doing me. If she really cared for me, though, she'd be more willing to help me out in the here and now. I know she thinks that, and it tears into her.

"And, I think I've started seeing things. Hallucinating." Shit, Alex, did you have to blurt it out like that?

"Is it drugs?" asks Claire.

"No, I haven't been taking. I mean, no, this hasn't been happening when I've been stoned. I know what that's like and this is different. Haven't you ever just found yourself experiencing weird things?" Nobody says anything, but the look that passes between Claire and Harold is highly revealing.

Conversation stalls again at the table. Forks and knives scrape over plates, sounding like a subway train going around a corner in the quiet.

"There are treatment programs you can get into," Clair says, breaking the silence. "Our church has a group that meets in the basement. Maybe they could help."

"I don't need help. Not that kind of help, at least."

"Why do you push me away, Alex? I don't understand what you want."

"I'm not sure what I want either," I say, a little more harshly than I intended. How do you put your finger on what's wrong, when *everything* is wrong? "Things are … off, right now and I'm trying to make sense of it. There's stuff happening that I don't understand, and it has me worried, that's all."

Claire doesn't say anything, just looks at me and chews on her lip. It has her worried too.

"I don't get you, Alex. You call me for the first time in months, and tell me you're in trouble, and when I try to get you the help you need, you don't want it. What am I supposed to do?"

"I don't know either," I say. "I've seen a lot of people going into programs, 12-Step, that sort of thing, and despite all the talk, it doesn't seem to actually do all that much."

"Well," she says. "Maybe you might stay with us for a while and pray for guidance and healing." She's ignoring the look that Henry is shooting her way, the one that says *"we need to talk about that first."*

The pills are kicking in finally. Took their goddamn time too. I'm feeling the little flutters of being stoned, a tingling at the end of all of my senses. I wonder if they would have had any effect if I were less wrecked? I don't speak, just sit and rub my hand on the table, enjoying the sensation of being even the tiniest bit stoned.

Her napkin is clenched in her hand – something she's done since she was a kid, whenever she got frustrated or anxious, which is often. I don't want to get all pop-psych, but it always seemed to me like she was hanging on for dear life, afraid of being sucked down by the emotions.

She always tries to hide it, keep it subtle, but I don't think she's aware that her whole body radiates it.

"I've seen incredible things, Alex, miracles. The power of prayer can change your whole life, if you'll just let Jesus into your heart."

"Already did that," I sigh. "Who do you think was sitting next to you in church when we were kids?"

At any moment, I'm expecting Clair to take my hand and ask me to join her in prayer, kneeling on the hard dining room floor. It'd be the standard for this family. Ill? Pray. Unhappy? Pray. Generally dissatisfied with the life you've got and underneath it all seething with bitterness? Pray and feel unworthy and unloved by your god because the feelings don't go away.

"God is trying to help you, Alex, if you just let it happen. He sent you to me so I can take care of you. Don't you feel Him in your heart?" At the thought of it, I get a pang, a twinge in my chest, but it's not Jesus letting me know He's there, it's just … something. And a memory, too elusive to bring to mind.

"Don't you ever feel weird at times?" I ask. "Unsettled, but you can't put your finger on why?"

"No," says Claire, but only after she and Harold share a glance that contradicts her. What the hell is that all about?

"Kids," says Harold. "Don't you have homework to do?" They just stare at him, uncomprehending – they just don't get the hint. He sighs. "Go watch cartoons," he says finally and the both of them take off like a shot out of the room.

"Underneath it all, Claire, nobody is really happy."

"That's not true. I'm happy, Harold is happy." Harold nods his assent, his mouth full of food.

"You think you are, but you're not," I say. "You're comfortable. You've got a roof over your head, and food in the fridge, but under it all, it doesn't make you happy."

She tries to protest, but I stall her with a gesture from my fork. "I've seen it all before, Claire. Remember Dad's funeral? Everybody was saying to Mom that he was in a better place, or it was all part of God's plan. But they weren't saying it because they believed it, but because they hoped it made her feel better. We're only happy when life is good. God has nothing to do with our happiness. It's what we were promised by the church, but we never receive it."

"They were telling her the truth."

"They were telling Mom what they needed to, to make her feel better. If people really believed what they were saying, there'd be far fewer tears at a funeral. Hell, they could forgo it altogether and just go to church to pray and thank God."

There's silence in the room, not even the sounds of eating. I can hear the TV in the other room, playing some classic cartoons I remember watching as a kid.

"Is that why you didn't go to Mom's funeral?" she asks. A quick change of subject – one of her tactics when she feels uncomfortable.

"I missed it because I missed it. You couldn't reach me, and that's all. No ulterior motive."

"If I could have, would you have come?"

I let out a sigh. "I don't like family reunions at the best of times. They're even worse with a casket at one end of the room."

Everybody is silent, and there's a definite chill in the room. No one eats. Harold pushes his food around the plate with his fork.

There's an old song that says that you always hurt the ones you love. Well, there's a good reason for that – the people you hate aren't much motivated to let you past their defences. It isn't that you want to hurt those you love, but the opportunities to do so just show up more often. And, I always seem to take advantage of those moments.

"Alex, I think it was time you were heading home. I need to put the children to bed, and Harold gets up early for work."

"Come on, Alex," he says. "Your clothes should be dry by now. You pack up your gear and I'll warm up the car."

Clean, dry clothes. What a great idea. Head off to fill my duffel, but the dog meets me at the top of the stairs. Still isn't growling, but there's no question that it's on the verge of attack. No false moves, Alex, though I'm not really sure what those would be.

Keeping as far away as possible, I edge my way around the corner and down the stairs, facing the dog the whole time. No way am I going to give it the opportunity to bite my ass.

Down in the basement, I grab my duffel. And indeed, it appears someone threw my clothes in the dryer. Claire, probably. So I throw my newly clean, still warm clothes into the bag and head back upstairs to get my boots and coat on. The dog is gone. Claire and Harold are talking quietly, heads close together when I reach the top of the stairs. She glances my way and they split apart, suddenly guilty, like secret lovers.

I get the most perfunctory of hugs from my sister and, "I'll be praying for you."

"Yeah, be thinking about you," I reply. We're both saying the same thing really.

Harold and I don't talk at all on the drive back downtown.

Well, that could have gone a whole lot better. When will I learn to just shut up? I want the help, I asked for the help, but in the end I push away the thing I need and the only person in the world willing to give it to me.

We reach the street corner, still in silence. My peers have given up the stairs for the night, and a couple of hookers wander over to the stopped car. Harold looks distinctly uncomfortable. They shrug and walk away when we don't roll down the windows.

Even after the women drift off to other cars, he still hasn't lost that look on his face.

"Listen," he says. "Alex, can I give you some money? Help you out a little?" He pulls $20 out of his pocket. Obviously he had taken it from his wallet in preparation, before we even got in the car. I wonder if it was his idea or my sister's?

Either way, I take it.

He looks, I don't know, disappointed. I guess he was expecting a little "oh no, I couldn't" from me, but this isn't about courtesy, it's straight survival. Does the drowning man say "after you, please"?

"Take care of yourself," he says, as I climb out of the car. I mumble something back, but my mind is already elsewhere. I don't wave, or even look to see him drive off. A plan has occurred to me, and it might not be a good plan, but it's all I've got right now.

First, a stop into the convenience store. I need cigarettes, and I want chewing gum. No, I'm not a chewing gum addict on top of everything else. What I really want to do is not go to sleep, not right now at least, and to achieve that I need to score some speed. The voice of experience says gum is a good idea – I hate, really hate, the dry mouth I get when I'm on speed. It's stuff like that they teach you at Junkie School.

Besides, pushers aren't known for being good at making change. Best I break the $20 first.

Pull open the door and walk in. It's hot and humid in here, like a greenhouse. The lights are brighter than ever too. Grab a pack of gum at random – don't care what brand I get – and stand in front of the cash.

The guy behind the counter looks worse than ever. In addition to looking like a fishbelly, it's pretty obvious he hasn't been sleeping. I hear there's a lot of that going around. The only colour to his face is the dark circles under his eyes.

Push the gum across the counter. "That," I say. "And a pack of smokes. Whatever's cheapest." He reaches back without looking and tosses them down in front of me, plucks the $20 from my hand and likewise tosses down my change. Doesn't say a word, and that's fine by me. His face is blank, expressionless. It's like there's nobody home behind his eyes, or he's a robot. Whatever.

Stepping out of the store, I'm once again rendered blind by the shift from intense brightness to dark. Again, I stand and wait for my eyes to adjust. I light a cigarette and drag the smoke back into my lungs – don't need to see, to do that, for sure. Oh my God, I forgot how good a cigarette could be. I have no idea how someone ever figured out that sucking back tobacco smoke could be such a trip, but I'm glad they did.

The traffic is quiet, with the piles of plowed snow absorbing and muting the most of it, taking out the general rumble. I hear a dog pass by, its claws clicking on the pavement. Then another dog passes by, and a third. Click, click, click. Their claws sound just like beads being rattled on a table top.

My vision adjusts, finally, and I get to actually look around me. No dogs. Weird.

Anyway, back to the plan. Who can I score from? The drug pusher situation shifts rapidly, so knowing who was selling as little as a month ago is no indicator of who might be now. It's just a tough profession – like every job in this neighbourhood.

For those lucky enough to qualify for welfare, the cheques come at the end of every month, what we call Welfare Wednesday. That's when the dealers come out in force. This late in the month, demand is as high as ever, but finances are dangerously low. There has to be *someone* though.

I seem to do better when I have a plan. Or at least if I'm moving purposely to some goal, no matter how ill-advised or unattainable. Walking a couple of blocks in the cold isn't as daunting as it might otherwise be. I'm going to get high, I won't go to sleep, and I'll be all right. Or, if there's no speed available, I'll get high to the point that when I fall unconscious I won't be capable of dreaming, and that will be all right too.

And it occurs to me that I know somewhere to go – Niko's. There has got to be someone dealing out of there, one of the rodeo clowns I saw earlier. Buoyed by the meal in my belly, and the smoke in my lungs, off I trot. Okay, so maybe not quite a trot, but I'm at least walking in the right direction.

So I keep walking.

Now, in so many ways, being an almost homeless, worthless, substance-abusing lowlife is not good for you. For instance, one's perception is warped; right now I keep feeling I'm being watched. There's no one on the street but me, no cars on the move, no nothing. I'm fed, clean. Even got a cigarette, for Christ's sake. I should be dancing down the street and belting out "Singing in the Rain." But, at the same time, there's ripples running up my spine, making the hair stand on end, making it almost impossible for me to just put one foot in front of the other and not break into a run. It's got to be those stupid pills I scarfed. Plus side – body buzz. Down side – creeping paranoia.

I stop. I want to spin around to see what is sneaking up on me, but I know there's nothing there.

Are you going crazy, Alex? No, I say. Not if I can help it.

Walk, Alex, move one foot, then the other. Stupid pills.

Under no circumstances will you give in to fear, or the encroaching madness. You will not look behind you. Grudgingly, one foot takes a step forward. The other, after some trepidation, follows suit. And another step, and then I'm walking again. Yeah, the plan.

Then I hear it – the clicking again, the dog claws, coming from behind me, before drifting off to my left and away.

It's a relief to be able to pin my paranoia on something. I'm not going crazy.

The question remains as to why there's all these damn dogs wandering around tonight. Maybe someone left the back door open at the pound or something. Anyway, mystery solved. Onward, brave drug-seeker!

The spring in my step returns, and off I stride. Alex 1, craziness, 0.

The feeling of being watched returns, however, which is really aggravating. It'd be one thing if I was just being crazy and paranoid – and I've already proven that I'm not. Damn dogs.

So I turn around, half expecting to find a dog sniffing at my pant leg or something, but there's nothing.

Hell.

Back to walking. Focus, Alex, you've got a plan. Score some meth, stay awake, avoid the dreams. Stick with the plan.

Scoring in the winter is tough, especially at night. Nobody wants to stand around in the cold, so you either have to find a dealer sitting in his car, or know where they hang out. The latter is an attractive option, because the only place to hang out is a diner or something like that, which means I can buy a coffee and smoke a cigarette. It's amazing the possibilities that occur to you when you've got money in your pocket, and you have a destination in mind.

On the whole, I don't like dealers. If I could buy what they're selling somewhere else, I absolutely would. It takes a special kind of lowlife to prey on the weakness of other lowlifes. You see a crack-head with a bike, guaranteed it's stolen and he's about to trade it for a hit. Some of those bikes are worth a couple thousand dollars, but they don't care if they're being cheated, they just want their hit. As long as they get their dope.

Some of the truly desperate might break into a car – smash a window and grab whatever they can reach, but addicts generally make lousy thieves. Prolific, and prone to taking stupid risks with zero planning. They get caught, perhaps not the first time, but inevitably.

Luckily I'm a coward. I'm too afraid of being caught to do that sort of shit, no matter how impulsive I might feel.

Where I live is mostly safe, I guess. Apartments are harder to break into than houses, though that's not absolute. Mine, at least, hasn't been broken into. Funny, that my shit-hole apartment feels like safety to me.

Niko's now too. I'm going to get some dope, and drink coffee all night until they close up shop. I'm even relatively clean, which means I definitely won't get kicked out if all I buy is coffee.

Once I get there, I'll look for the dealers. If they're not there, though, what then? Can't exactly ask around. No big deal, I've got time. Sit, have a coffee, smoke, observe. If someone in there has stuff for sale, I'll figure it out soon enough.

As I walk, I hear the clicking starting up again. You'd think the mutts would find somewhere warm to sleep, instead of wandering around like, well, like me, frankly. I'm more fucked up than any dog will ever be.

The sound of the first dog is joined by another – one on the left, one on the right. I guess they're not friends. They keep pace with me though, not moving ahead of me, not falling back.

I want to tell them, don't follow me, I have no clue where I'm going either.

A third dog joins in.

What. The. Hell.

Knowing it is absolutely the wrong thing to do, I start walking faster. Yeah, go ahead and find me a dog that doesn't enjoy a good chase. They like it better than sex or food.

From the sounds of it, the dogs have moved further away from each other. The two on the outside peel away from the middle, like wingers in hockey.

Or like hunters, cutting off escape routes.

Oh fuck.

Don't bother with going to Niko's, Alex, just make it home alive.

I can't help myself, I look over my shoulder. Not big dogs, no, but big enough that I couldn't just casually kick them in the chops and be done with them.

There are three of them, and yeah, they're keeping pace with each other and widely spaced. And, just in case I wasn't sure before, they're all staring at me. I am most definitely the object of the exercise. Another thing I can confirm – dogs do indeed smile.

One of the dogs lets out a bark, just a short one. When I hear other dogs baying, from farther away, I figure out he's calling his friends. Things are about to get very crowded, very soon.

Trying hard, very hard to resist the urge to run. They are not attacking me … yet. I am not surrounded … yet. This is not the time to start panicking.

The baying gets closer, and my will gives out and I break into a run. The dogs behind me go wild with barking, letting everybody know the chase is on. Fuck it, now is *definitely* the time to start panicking

And I run, and I run, and I run, in blind animal panic. I can't hear the dogs over the sound of my feet slapping on the pavement and the ragged rush of my breath. *Keep running, Alex.*

There's no time to think about what route I'm taking, or whether I'm heading down a dead end. Turn a corner, jump over a low wall, run some more.

I could duck into Niko's – it's close by. But I'm running in the wrong direction, and I can't exactly just turn around.

Run across the road, dodging the cars as they zip past me and honk their horns. Somehow make it to the other side without being hit. I chance a look back over my shoulder, and see the dogs. They've got more sense than I do, not to run headlong into traffic.

Doesn't stop them for long though – I can hear the barking getting louder behind me again. Keep going.

Skid around a corner, and nearly slam into a phone booth. Ain't the greatest protection, but it'll have to do. But before I can get inside and hold the door shut against them, one of the fuckers has caught a corner of my coat. He's growling and throwing his head around, and I yank it free and keep running again.

The mall the thought occurs, *I can hide out in the mall.*

It should still be early enough for me to get in. I hope it is, because I can't think of another hidey-hole. And I'm dead otherwise.

Around another corner, and down the street. Run, damn it, run!

The sidewalk is clear of snow, so I'm making good time on it, while the dogs are stuck scrabbling on the pavement. Yeah, hurray. Maybe I should run backwards to give them a sporting chance.

The mall comes into view ahead of me, a shining beacon of hope and consumer goods. I keep running, even though my lungs are burning and my legs feel like rubber.

The furry bastards are right on my heels, barking and snapping, still eager to dig a tooth into me. All it'll take is one little patch of ice under my boot, and I'll find myself at the bottom of a pile of very motivated, very angry dogs.

There's a bunch of people outside the mall doors. It's never the same faces, but it's always the same crowd – waiting for a taxi, or grabbing a quick cigarette because there's no smoking allowed inside, or bored teenagers. Right at the moment, though, I'm not looking for a friend, or someone I can bum a cigarette off of, I just need sanctuary.

Nobody pays any attention to me as I run at them, which isn't a surprise – I'm just one more person late for a bus, late for a meeting, late for a date. All I know is, I don't want them to get in my way and slow me down.

So I do what any self-respecting crazy junkie street person does – I scream and wave my arms.

Of course it works. Nobody wants to find out if crazy is contagious, and they scatter away from me in a hurry, like pigeons taking flight. Just as I reach the doors, there's someone coming out and I deke past him and into the mall, and safety.

The dogs are a split-second behind me, but that's all it takes for me to yank the doors closed. I'm on one side of the thick glass, and they're left to howl and bark on the outside. After what they put me through, I want to mock them mercilessly, but I can't. My lungs hurt, legs are wobbly. Time to find a place to sit before my heart bursts.

But first I'm just going to lean here, until my legs can carry me. Close my eyes for a moment while the world spins a bit.

I can hear the dogs barking their damn heads off outside, and a few people shouting. Yeah, go ahead, bark all you want. I'm not coming out until the lot of you are good and gone. If they don't wander off on their own, the pound will be by eventually to round them all up. Or the cops will shoot them. Whatever.

It boggles my mind, the thought that there is a pack of feral dogs roaming the streets. Sure, the city has seen better days, but it isn't that far gone. Or, maybe it is now. I can imagine the documentary, with a sober-voiced narrator explaining that every day here is a struggle for survival, with images of me running for my life with a pack of dogs hungry for a taste of my ass.

A momentary pang of guilt crosses my mind. Hopefully nobody gets bitten too badly, when the pack goes off in search of new prey. But, as fast as I think it, the feeling is gone. People can look after themselves for all I care. It isn't like they'd stop to help me out if I were lying bleeding in the street, so pardon me if I don't feel the Good Samaritan urge. Besides, they all looked like they were running away faster than I was.

If they were smart, they'd duck inside like I did.

People in the mall are staring at me, not even trying to be discreet. And why would they? I don't look dangerous, at least I don't think I do, but I'm sure I look ill or dying or both. Gasping, sweating, clutching the wall to hold myself up.

On the plus side, everybody seems happy as hell to vacate the bench when I lurch over to it. Thanks, citizens, for giving me a place to plunk my ass down.

The plastic bench is hard under me and cold and uncomfortable as hell, but I don't really care. They make them like this intentionally, I think – keep people from sticking around too long. *Quit sitting there! Get up and buy stuff already!*

The mall is like every other mall in the world – an endless hall with stores left and right as far as the eye can see. Much like a casino, there are as few windows as possible and probably for the same reason: to keep the patrons from realizing just how much time they've spent. Likewise, there are as many twists and turns as possible between each exit, so just trying to leave becomes a drawn-out affair. A few months of street-life and I know this place like the back of my hand.

Anyway, I only want to stay here as long as it takes for my heart to quit doing its little ferret dance in my chest. It's been a long day and I'd like to go home.

And then, oh god, a wave of nausea washes over me. It's my good luck that I'm sitting on the end right next to a garbage can, because the urge to puke hits me so fast that I hurt my neck in my urgency to double over. Wouldn't have cared overly much if I had puked on the floor instead, but that comes with the risk of covering myself.

There goes dinner, rocketing into the trash as fast as my stomach can pitch it. My throat hurts from being roughly violated by my meal, and my mouth burns from the bile. I can taste it, I can smell it.

It does not make me feel better, the vomiting. There is no relief. The nausea is in command, my stomach trying to fulfill its tyrannical requirements, heaving, heaving, painfully. My eyes are watering as I stare down into the garbage can. Sight, touch, taste, smell, hearing – yep, every sense gets offended in turn.

Get yourself under control, Alex, you do not want security tossing you out those doors until the dogs are long gone.

Slowly, slowly, things calm. The nausea retreats, growling like some creature lurking in a cave, ready to pounce again if I look away. There is definite mental effort involved in pushing it down.

While I'm wiping my mouth with my sleeve, I catch sight of the security guard out of the corner of my eye. Trouble, and heading my way. He does not look pleasant. He does not look reasonable. He does not give me the impression that he would like to politely urge me to seek accommodation elsewhere. In fact, he looks like the type who knows where the security camera blind spots are, so he can slap my type around for a bit.

Time to move.

I don't feel good, not even close to it, but every person on the street knows when it makes sense to cut and run, even the craziest ones.

Grab my duffel and haul ass.

It would probably be the most prudent to head back outside, but I'd rather give the dogs more time to wander off, and find someone else to chew on.

Plus, I still feel like crap.

Up on my feet, and off I go. Still not steady, but that'll come in time. Down the hall, turn a corner, down another hall and duck into the men's room. The door cuts off the continuous babbling noise from outside, and the quiet is damn good. Nothing in here but the sound of a tap dripping.

Things are running my way, at least a little – there's a stall free. Step around the puddle of indeterminate origin. Inside the stall, close the door, lock it. The duffel sits at the bottom of the door, blocking the opening just in case the security guard is still looking for me.

Nothing to see here, just Joe Consumer taking a dump after shopping for luggage.

Probably I'll be able to stay in here for a long time if I wanted to. Who's going to bang on the door and ask "hey, are you the detestable lowlife who just puked in the garbage can?" Depending on when the last patrol went through here, it'll be a while. They won't catch on until they've come through a few times, and see the same duffel sitting there.

The men's room door opens and shuts – someone just came in. Although I don't pick up any footsteps, I hear the water running in the sink. The water shuts off, but I don't hear the hand dryer. Maybe it's broken, maybe he just prefers to wipe his hands off on his pants – hey, the world is a weird place, I wouldn't be surprised.

Minutes pass and I still haven't heard the door again. What's this guy doing? Just standing there, admiring himself in the mirror? Waiting for someone? That's a possibility. Maybe a drug dealer – the thought of which reminds me that I never managed to make it to Niko's. Could be a golden opportunity to score, providing I don't spook him into thinking I'm a nark. Can't exactly call out "pardon me, but are you dealing drugs," while hiding in a stall – a mental images crossed my mind of a dozen cops stuffed in the stall like clowns in a tiny car. I stifle a giggle.

It's tempting to open the door and look out – finding a dealer in here would be goddamn fantastic – but there's another possibility. It could be the guard again, tracking me down. I'm not blowing my cover just for that goon. I can chance a peek out from under the partition wall, but I don't see anything, no legs. Maybe he's left already? Quietly? No, no matter how softly the door opened or closed, I'd still hear the crowds in the hall.

Sit tight, Alex. If you can't be patient, you at least can be fearful. You do not want to be kicked out just yet.

Slowly, ever so slowly, I become aware of a quiet, distant hissing sound. It isn't the hiss like from a leaking tire, or like a snake, more like a long, audible exhalation, an impossibly long one.

And as I listen, I realize I hear more than one hiss. There's a few, three at least, and coming from different corners of the room.

Air vents? Heaters maybe?

The sound gets louder, in tiny degrees.

Looking out the little crack between the door and frame, I can't see anything. Where the hell is that sound coming from? A movement catches my eye, but I can't figure out what I saw. Shift left, shift right, trying to see out that tiny crack without going permanently cross-eyed.

Might already be too late for that – I'm starting to see colours. Sit back, blink, rub my eyes and look again.

Still see colours, but they've moved.

Yeah, a little tint, drifting slowly, oranges and greens, mostly. Look at my hand, at the stall walls and the stained ceiling tiles, and they all look normal. Peek out through the crack again and watch the colours swirl. They're stronger now, more vibrant. No question about it – something out there is moving.

It's amorphous, liquid motion. Bubbling, seething, nothing graceful or gentle about it. More colours now, in pure, sharp, eye-splitting hues.

The hissing too, louder and more distinct. It sound almost like voices heard from a distance, or almost like animals growling low.

The fog is rising like a tide, filling up the room. Jousting, fighting, jostling, the colours push against one another. There are sparks flashing out among the colours now.

The walls of the toilet stall rattle, like they're being buffeted by wind, or like a big truck just rumbled past. I've got my hands braced against the walls, and my feet planted against the stall door, pushing at it as hard as I can, and still it feels as if it'll collapse at any second.

The noises are louder now, hurting my ears and I'm forced to clap my hands tight to them, to shut it out.

The frenzy keeps building, threatening to crest over the top of the stall and come crashing down on me. One second it's waves of colour and the next it is like fog or steam. The sparks still shoot through it. And then, disembodied fanged mouths snap and chase each other around.

All I can do now is grit my teeth and hope like hell I survive this – whatever the hell it is.

It all whips past, faster and faster, blurring, a cyclone of colour. The noises too, blending and speeding up, like a buzz saw, the intensity increasing. Press my hands more tightly over my ears and clench my eyes shut tight against the lights.

And then, pop, like a soap bubble, gone. Vanished.

Me, alone in the men's room, with nothing but the sound of a dripping tap.

I'm shaking, head to toe, and right out to my fingertips, trembling. It's like being in a car accident, when your body has all this adrenaline coursing through it, but there's nothing for you to do but sit in the car. Slowly get to my feet, and pick up my duffel. Wait a moment, listening, before I unlock the stall door and peek out into the washroom. Nothing.

I stagger out of the men's room and lean against the corridor wall. I'm tired, so goddamn tired. A glance around, and I see the storm trooper coming my way. He's definitely pissed now, and I'm in for some deep trouble if he gets his hands on me.

I start walking a straight line – no need to make him think I'm about to wander into any of the stores. That would definitely get him riled. Can't have a bum ruin the shopping experience for Mr. and Mrs. Consumer.

Everybody just take it nice and easy, and nobody, namely me, needs to get hurt … more than I already have been, that is.

And just like that, I'm out the door and into the cold air again. Security dude just hangs out at the threshold and stares at me, chest puffed out, hands on his hips, daring me to turn around and try his patience. Yeah, whatever. I'm sure that approach just wows the teenagers, but I've got better places to be. Niko's, for one.

Go there, then go home. So damn tired from running that it might just be possible to sleep, and not worry about the dreams. That'd be fantastic, a full night's sleep.

As I walk, the thought occurs that maybe I should just go home, forget about the drugs. And I probably would, if I were anybody else. But I'm not, and the allure of getting high is just too strong.

That's the decision then. Drugward ho!

While I was inside the mall, busy vomiting and hallucinating, it started snowing out. Big, fluffy flakes are falling, the kind one normally only sees in Christmas movies.

I owe myself those drugs now. It's been a fucked up day and a little oblivion would suit me fine. No more thoughts of family, or dogs, or fog with fangs.

Is this how normal people feel after a rough day at the office? What the hell is normal anyway? I wouldn't know, I've never felt normal a day in my life. Alex Mackie, the eternal outcast. Is it any surprise I ended up on the street? Normal people develop lasting bonds, and develop friendships, associates, acquaintances, networks, people who notice when your life is going down the crapper.

I'm not whining about my life. Isn't anybody's fault but my own. Just, sometimes I wonder what it would be like to be one of those people. Sometimes it sounds appealing, but often not. To have a steady paycheque, a full belly, of course that's appealing. It's all the things that go along with those perks that I struggle with.

Manage to walk another block or so before it starts up again, the creeping paranoia, like I'm being watched.

Resist it, Alex.

I keep walking.

Eventually, though, it gets too strong to ignore, and I stop on the sidewalk and just stand there for a bit, hoping that it'll pass but it doesn't.

So I look over my shoulder. There's a dog behind me, a scruffy little thing like they'd have in a movie as a mascot to some woeful, big-eyed kid. It made me jump when I first saw it, which makes me laugh. The damn thing isn't big enough to be harmful – maybe a bite on the ankle, but that's all it would get before I'd kick it down the street.

It barks at me, one of those yappy, high-pitched barks. Again I laugh, until I hear more barking from further away. Son of a bitch, they're after me again.

Run for my apartment. It's not too far away now, and if I can make it before the dogs close in on me, I'll be safe.

There's a hot spot on my neck from where the duffel bag strap is rubbing, taking the slow way to saw my head off as I run. Damn thing is heavy and it's slowing me down.

Shuck the strap off my shoulder and toss it back at the dogs. I can always get more clothes. I know a laundry bag isn't going to take the fight out of them but maybe they'll have their fun tearing it apart and leave me alone. The sounds of barking fall back as I run, changing to growling and snarling. Looks like they're interested in the bag after all. But almost before I can finish the thought, I hear the barking start up again. The chase is back in session.

Goddamn run, Alex, just run. Don't think, don't speculate, just run. Once more, my world is filled with nothing but the sound of my boots slapping against the pavement and the ragged sound of my breath and the howling of dogs behind me.

My legs are getting rubbery, and it's getting harder to run. They're going to catch me after all. C'mon, Alex, keep going, keep going, goddamnit.

The apartment building looms in front of me suddenly, and I don't think I've ever seen anything more beautiful in my life. Squat, dirty, neglected, but goddamn beautiful.

Up the few steps to the door of the building, hoping desperately that I don't wipe out on the ice. Fumble with the stupid door that hasn't worked well since before I moved in.

It opens suddenly, pitching me onto my face in the lobby and giving me an instant taste of blood in my mouth. Shut the door, Alex, shut the goddamn door. I manage to slam it closed, just as the dogs come into view. They're so hungry for me that they barrel up the steps and slam hard into the door, making it rattle in its frame.

When I finally get to my feet and take a look, there's got to be a dozen or more barking, snarling mouths out there, teeth flashing in the light streaming out the lobby window.

"Nice try, guys," I say, sounding braver than I feel. "Maybe we can try again tomorrow night?" Fuck, I hope not. Not tomorrow, not ever again. The score is now 2-0 for me, and I'd like to retire now with my undefeated record.

I think I pissed my pants in the excitement. Better than being torn to shreds, for sure. Today's hero would have been tomorrow's dog poop. Hell - I threw my duffel bag, I don't have any other pants to wear. Great – one pair of pants to my name, and they smell like piss. Hope I can find the damn bag tomorrow.

With the sound of dogs still barking at the door, I turn to face the lobby. There's a bunch of bodies, sleeping the night away. One or two are awake, looking my way and wondering what the hell all the noise is about.

"Dogs," I say, like that's much of an explanation. Like any moron couldn't figure out that dogs are barking. Whatever.

To the stairs, then, and to my apartment. I didn't manage to score, but I don't think that matters. There's the distinct impression that I will not be getting to sleep tonight no matter what.

Halfway up the stairs, the shakes set in. Holy crap, I don't think I've ever come that close to dying. My heart is pounding in my chest, hard and fast, like a goddamn jackhammer. I'm afraid I'm going to have a heart attack or something. The stairs suddenly feel like an excellent place to sit as my legs give way, yeah, very comfortable, like they were made for sitting. Yeah. A bag of broken glass would feel like a cushion right now, I'm so goddamn tired.

My head is spinning, I've got the shakes all over, and I can barely breath. Where the hell is Serapion? Where's my supposed guardian angel?

My heart tries to remember what normal is. I'm sucking in air like a jet engine.

My chest hurts, my legs hurt, and now my head hurts too. The wall is cool, and feels good against my forehead. Cooling, calming. Steady up, Alex. Calm enough to just sit and look around me. A distraction would be good right now.

Look up, lose myself in space, peer up the stairwell, all the way and try to see all the way to the top. Five floors of what used to be a posh apartment building.

Even the stairwell reflects the former glory of the building. The stairs are made of marble slabs, worn smooth by countless feet, a shallow, wide groove worn down the middle. The railing is ornate, weighted down with a thousand layers of paint. And the walls, well, they're covered in graffiti. Can't win 'em all.

Heartbeat, just about under control. Breathing slowing. Resting my head against the cool of the wall eases the headache. Slowly, slowly coming back to normal. Normal for me.

There's a sound from the bottom of the stairwell. Clicking. It's important, but in my state, I can't figure out why, or what it might be.

Oh fuck, dogs.

Up, Alex, up. Go, go up the stairs. Tired muscles don't even bother to complain, as the heart goes into overdrive again. Pound up the stairs, quickly now. The dogs are running now, abandoning their cunning approach, howling and scrabbling up the hard, smooth stairs. That's the only thing that's saving me right now – if they get anything suitable to run on, I'm dead.

Their baying fills the stairwell, echoing, piling noise upon noise. I'm screaming, but it doesn't make a dent in the din.

All I can think is, who was the moron who opened up the goddamn door to the lobby?

Nearly wipe out on the landing, rounding a corner. Only my hand on the rail keeps me on the move. One more floor to go, unless I've miscounted, in which case I'm dog food.

Yank open the stairwell door, and race down the hall. Stupid door slowly swings closed, with one of those fucking stupid arm things preventing it from slamming shut. Dogs are already spilling into the hallway as I run.

Keys, keys, get your goddamn keys, Alex. I fumble them out of my pocket as I run. There's a couple on the ring, but only one fits anything I own, the only possible one I could care about right now.

And the key drives home into the lock and the door opens, and I lunge inside. But before I can get in all the way, I feel fire in my calf. Screaming, I yank my leg free of the dog's mouth, not caring about the pain or whatever damage has been done. Close the door, Alex.

The first dog has his head in the apartment. He's got my blood all over his muzzle, and a piece of my pant leg hooked on a tooth, and he's in a real hurry for more of me. He looks like a bear trap with glaring, feral eyes. Big dog, big fucking dog.

I'm getting a real good look at him because the door is clamping his neck against the jam and I'm shoving hard against the door with one foot, and kicking like crazy with the other. The kicks just piss the dog off more, something I didn't think was possible. Dog spit is flying everywhere as it barks.

Then the other dogs start in, throwing themselves against the door and trying to force through the narrow opening. More mouths poke through, all struggling to get a taste of me.

The door thunders with the impacts of the dogs, again and again. They're big, they're motivated, and there's way more of them than there are of me. Every time I kick, a spray of my blood flies across the noses of the rest, driving them to a higher state of madness and urgency.

I'm trapped – with the dog's head wedged, I can't close the door, but if I open it to kick him out, I'll be giving the rest the opportunity they crave. And the longer I fight, the weaker I get. Hot tears run down my cheeks.

So, in desperation, I stick my boot right in its face, push it up his nose and keep pushing, forcing him back. The other dogs try to get around him, or get at my leg, but he's in the way. I can see his eyes, rolling with canine fury, as he twists and turns. And then he twists just right, gets his mouth around it and sinks his teeth into my boot. He pulls and pulls, not willing to let me get away.

And suddenly, the boot pops off my foot, and the dog rolls backwards with it. A quick kick, and the door slams shut, with me right behind it, throwing my body against the door, hoping, praying, *really* praying for the first time in a dozen or more years, please God, don't let the lock fail.

I barely hear a whimper amidst all the barking and howling and the slamming of the dogs against the door, but it takes me a few seconds before I realize the noise is coming from me. I'm dying here on the floor, even if the dogs don't get me. My leg is throbbing, there's blood all over the door, the frame and floor, my heart is beating too fast to count, and I can't breathe. Spasms wrack my arms and legs.

Please, God, don't let the lock fail.

The room is spinning. Feeling bad, and all that noise in the hallway makes it impossible to concentrate. Swirling noise. Can't stand up, can't move

Can't nothing. I pass out.

I wish I knew how long it is before I come to. Long enough for my heart to lose its jackrabbit pace and for my lungs to catch up – supplying oxygen again. That much I can figure out.

There's no more noise from the hallway. Either the dogs have called it a night, or the cunning bastards are lying in wait for me. There's no way I'll be opening the door to find out, either way. It seems God answered my prayer, and it would be ungrateful of me to go and unlock the door now.

No, instead, I painfully pull myself to my feet, and spend long, unpleasant moments of light-headedness, vision tunnelling down to a pinprick, a high-pitched whine in my ears, and I'm in danger of falling to the floor. I don't think I can reliably sit down though, so I'm stuck standing. Man, I'm having trouble remembering the last time I felt as bad as this.

When my vision clears, and much to my surprise I'm still standing, I limp off to the bathroom, making a clump, slide, clump, slide sound as I walk. Hurray for small apartments, where it's never a long trip to cross the floor. My leg is an artist's study of red – brilliant, slick scarlet butts up against more subdued crimson smears, fading to mottled, dried burgundy. I've painted a trail on the floor too. Never thought of myself as a visual artist, and now is not the time to start.

Blood, sweat and tears of an artist.

Fuck off.

At least the bathroom light works, filling the room with its meagre glow. Fuck, I look terrible. Was it only a couple of hours ago that I stepped out of my sister's shower and stared at myself in the mirror? Yeah, well, any progress I made towards appearing healthy, happy, sane, whatever, has been flushed down the toilet. The circles under my eyes aren't just dark, but puffy now and purple, like angry bruises. The skin hangs even further, the tone more grey.

Right, let's see the damage.

With a hiss of effort and a wobbly moment, I manage to sit down on the edge of the tub. It's uncomfortable under me – my ass doesn't provide much padding for my hip bones. Roll up what's left of my pant leg, and pull off my sock. What a bloody mess, literally. My father would've called it a dog's breakfast, but that's just too close for comfort. Blood everywhere, smeared all over.

Start running the water. The tub is filthy, but I'm not planning on getting in, I just want to rinse my foot. On goes the cold water. It pulls a little yelp out of me. As it sprays across my leg, I'm grateful for just how cold it is. My calf is instantly numb, the throbbing stops, and I can take a look at it, clearheaded again.

It's almost disappointing to see how little damage there is – a couple of puncture marks, really, a bit of gouging, that's all that's left after the blood is washed off. Little threads of pink trail off from the holes. Seems that it still moves properly, so I guess nothing essential got hit. That's my kind of luck, I get fucked up, but not so badly that I can't do more to myself tomorrow.

There's one towel in the room, in the whole apartment actually, in colours not found in nature, with 'Viva Las Vegas' emblazoned across it. Right now I couldn't imagine anything more beautiful in the world, as I wrap it around my calf and hobble out of the bathroom.

At the door to the apartment, I hesitate, one hand on the doorknob. No, Alex, it isn't worth knowing.

It takes a little time to limp to the couch, simultaneously using the wall to hold myself up, while removing my coat and dropping it on the floor. Put my foot up, smoke my cigarettes, and spend whatever still remains of the night wondering what the hell that was all about.

So just what *was* that all about? I can understand a bunch of feral dogs going after an easy meal, that's just dogs. But, these bastards were driven to attack me, hunt me. They wanted *my* blood. They chased me, lost me, found me again and kept after me. That's not a random attack. They wanted *me*.

What's it all about? I told Claire that I'm seeing things but this wasn't a hallucination. There's some very real holes in my leg and real blood on the floor. Not a single thing about last night was a hallucination.

Okay, there was the weird shit I saw in the men's room. I don't know what to call that, maybe it was something from the pills I took and the running and the puking? Everything else was real though.

What would drive dogs to do that? I can't imagine them being that focused on catching a cat or a rabbit, let alone a human, in the middle of a city full of humans.

Wonder if the newspaper is going to have my exploits on the front page again. I can see the headline: "Area Lowlife Leads City's First Annual Running From the Dogs Festival."

There's rustling in the hallway, so I limp over to the door to listen. Voices. Neighbours going to work, the few of them who have straight jobs. Since there's no sound of people being eaten alive, I chance to open the door.

No dogs. Just my boot, smelling of dog slobber, sitting in the middle of the hall. Wave 'hi' to the neighbours. They nod back, cautiously. Can't blame them, probably unsettling to have a walking corpse greet you.

"Bit noisy last night," I venture.

"Yeah, dogs," says one, an older guy, chubby, balding. "This place is going to hell, I swear. I called the cops, but they weren't too interested."

"Yeah. What happened to them? The dogs, I mean."

"Dunno. They went nuts for a while, and then they just got quiet and went away."

"Weird."

"Yeah, weird." They turn and wander off down the hall. That was the longest conversation I've had with anybody in the building since my former roommate Beaudry moved out, other than "hey, can I buy some of that dope?" If they noticed the towel around my foot, they didn't bother to ask. I like neighbours who don't delve into other people's business.

Retrieve my boot, and I'm about to close the door when I notice that my keys are still dangling from the lock. Good thing dogs aren't hip to working doorknobs.

Back inside, lock the door, limp to the couch. Gingerly, I unwrap the towel from my calf. There's a few spots where it clings to dried blood, but it comes free with a little tugging and a bit of pain.

I was lucky, damn lucky, and I know it. The dog that tagged me, if he had kept a grip on me ... I have a mental flash of what it must look like from under a pack of dogs, the world consisting of nothing but hungry mouths and chomping fangs and my bloody hands trying to push them all away. Close Call – that should be the title of my autobiography, assuming I live long enough to write it. A shudder runs up my spine. Then another. And suddenly, I'm sobbing. There are tears running down my cheeks, dripping off and soaking my shirt.

The sobbing hurts my throat. I feel it constrict like a noose every time I try to breath in. Snaps tight, hurts, then relax and the air comes in, again and again.

I exhale with a wail, pain trying to escape, but it's inexhaustible, going on and on as the sobs rack my body. Throat is tight, so is my chest, my gut. Hands balled into fists, all the muscles in my body are complaining, crying, howling at the insults heaped upon it. Why me, God? Why me? Six billion people on the damn planet, and I'm the one getting shit on. Why?

I understand what it is to be god-forsaken, when nobody, not even an eternally loving deity gives a damn whether you live or die. The pain is abandonment, by everything.

Then, release. A big sigh, the sobs quiet, the heaving stops, the muscles ease. There is no reason why it should be me and not someone else. If there was, then that would also mean there is a God, and that all the shit that has happened to me was part of some master plan. I'd be a latter-day Job. And I'm not.

This day has not started well. The only consolation is that I didn't sleep, didn't dream. Yeah. Never mind that I've got a bunch of holes in my leg, probably going to get rabies now, my boot smells like a dog's tonsils, I lost my duffel bag with all my clothes, and the one pair of pants I have are covered in blood and smell of piss. Yeah, and they weren't washed to begin with.

But I'm alive. Yeah. So it's not a total write-off.

Shuffling off to the bathroom, I strip off my pants, wash them as best I can in the sink and throw them over the radiator to dry. They smell, of course, like a wet dog.

In the medicine cabinet, there's a pack of bandages. Nothing else, except for a toothbrush with dust on it. Definitely no painkillers, of course. Those got cleaned out a long, long time ago, and not for their recommended use. Too bad, my leg is throbbing again from all the walking around. I don't know a damn thing about first aid, but the bandages seem to be the logical thing to use.

Start slapping them all over my calf. Stupid cheap things don't cling very well, so I make up with quantity for any lack in quality. And then, since they don't seem to be doing much of a job, I wrap the towel around my leg again anyway. Ah well, another layer can't hurt.

Hey, hang on, for once I actually have money. I could go and buy something for the pain. Yeah, there's the plan: wait for pants to dry, head down to the corner, get some aspirin. I would go to the free clinic to get patched up, but what I really want is something for the pain, and they make sure everybody knows not to bother attempting to get pain meds from them. They put big signs on the front window telling the junkies to fuck off, but in the nicest, most professional way.

I look in the cigarette pack, but it's empty now. Smoked them all while I was thinking. Crumple it, chuck it at the overflowing garbage can in the corner, and watch it fall short. Didn't even hit the rim.

Yeah, well, I'm not a basketball player.

Look around for another pack, pat my pockets and find a little cardboard scrap. The job offer on Beasley Street. Geez, what the hell was that all about? The whole thing comes back to me in a rush, the phone call on a dead phone, seeing my mother, looking up at a building that isn't there anymore.

Feral dogs, hallucinations, just what the hell is happening?

I am goddamn losing it.

A thought occurs: While I'm sitting and wondering what happened to the building on Beasley St., I realize I don't know what happened to my parents' actual house. Dad died, Mom died, and then I guess it was sold, but what happened to the money? Is there an inheritance waiting for me that Claire didn't tell me about? God knows I could use the money.

I'm going to have to call her, first chance I get.

For the next couple of hours, I observe a little routine. Sit on the couch in my underwear, until I really crave a cigarette. Try and distract myself by wondering how much time has passed. Stand up, shakily. Shuffle to the bathroom, check on my pants, swear expansively because they're still wet. Shuffle back to the couch, sit, pretend my leg doesn't hurt and I don't want a cigarette. Repeat. Discover the pack of gum I bought along with the cigarettes. Ain't tobacco, but maybe it'll do in the meantime. Chew a piece until its flavour is gone, stick it under the coffee table. Again, repeat.

It takes a while, but eventually my pants make it past whatever standard of dry I'm using. Still smell terrible, still feel greasy, but hopefully less so. Yeah. Pissy smell is gone, though.

Sit on the toilet to put them on, because falling over right now would suck. Take time to stand up. Waver a bit, like a toddler, but eventually succeed. Guess this counts as starting the day on a high note. They're still a little damp, but hopefully I won't get too cold wearing them outside.

Shuffle out of the bathroom, grab my coat off the floor, shrug it on. Poise precariously on my good foot, as I slowly wedge the other into a boot. It's slow going with the towel wrapped around my calf, while I'm clutching anything I can to keep from falling over.

Same process again, but this time standing on the bad leg. The throbbing has started again, and my balance is even more suspect. But, triumphant again, I get my second boot on. Well, this day is just going swimmingly.

Listen at the door again. Open the door a crack and peek outside, ready to slam it in a heartbeat if I glimpse anything even close to the colour of dog hair.

But, nothing. Only a carpet that deserves to be burnt and buried, and a dingy, ill-lit hallway.

Close and lock the door behind me, shuffle off to the stairs, giving the elevator doors a slap as I pass by. Right, junkie on a mission. Cue theme music and off I go.

Working my way down to the lobby makes me feel like an old man. I can't just walk. Instead, it's step down with the left foot, catch up with the right foot. Limping downhill. Seems to take forever. Probably does. Luckily there's no one sleeping in the stairwell right now, because it would be a bitch to climb over them.

My slow descent means I get the full effect of the stench of stale urine, cigarette smoke and – only God knows where it's coming from – motor oil. I can't go any faster, so I breath through my mouth.

The lobby is empty too, which I didn't expect – I guess the dogs made it very clear that everybody should find somewhere else to sleep last night.

Step outside, onto the postage stamp of concrete at the top of the little flight of stairs leading to my building. It's cold out, maybe more so than last night.

The sky is grey, still. Overcast. There's the occasional break in the clouds, letting a little sunlight through, just enough to remind everybody that there really is a sun up there.

I take a deep breath of the cold morning air, and fire it out again with a painful coughing fit. I'm used to smoker's cough, but this is far worse. Maybe I hurt my lungs running around last night? Can you do that, sucking back cold air? Probably, maybe get frostbite on my lungs or something.

The snowfall during the night has left a lot on the ground – nobody has had a chance to shovel it yet. Makes walking treacherous. Better to take it easy, because I can guarantee I'm going to hurt myself if I slip and fall, and getting back to my feet is going to be a pain in the ass. It's slow going. I manage to catch up to one of the other bums. He's walking ahead of me, pushing a shopping cart full of his crap that acts like a snow plough. It's still slow, but at least there's less snow.

As usual, my esteemed colleagues are taking up the steps on the corner. I've got more important things to do before I say hi, so I duck into the store.

From the outside, the store is like any other mom and pop convenience store the world over. One day it'll be bought out by a big chain and it'll get a snazzy new sign, but nothing of significance will change. The windows sport sun-faded movie posters, and hand-drawn advertisements that should have come down months ago – although, it'd be fun to set off fireworks in February.

Indoors, though, that's where the difference hides. First, there's only two kinds of clientele that come here – bums and office workers. For us, it's our grocer, entertainment centre, news outlet and pharmacy. We can get anything we could ever need here, though usually "anything" means cigarettes and junk food – probably not that different from the office workers in that regard.

The second difference is the lighting. It's still amazingly bright in here, and I still can't figure out why. Hurts the eyes just to be in here.

They don't keep stuff like aspirin out where people like me can get them, so I need to ask the guy behind the counter. I just want to pay for my shit, stuff as many little pills down my throat as I can, and make the pain in my leg go away for a while. I don't want to make conversation, I don't want to explain myself, and I sure as hell don't want some dude behind the counter trying to figure out if it's a good idea or not to sell anything to me.

The same damn guy as last night is behind the counter. Does he just never go home? Certainly it doesn't look like he's slept. Dark circles under his eyes, with colours like old bruises – purples, shading out to green at the edges. They're a stark contrast to the rest of his face with its unnatural paleness, and a texture that reminds me of clay. There's no expression either. Totally bland. There's nobody home behind those eyes. Creepy as hell.

No preamble then. I walk up to the counter, look him in those dead eyes, and say "aspirin, and a pack of smokes." No question, no request.

He stares at me flatly for a few seconds, before turning from me and taking down the little bottle off the shelf behind him, tosses it down between us and stares at me again. Not a word. Reaches back again, grabs a pack of cigarettes at random and tosses them down too.

Drag out my money from my pocket and drop it beside everything else on the counter. My money goes, my change comes back. Probably enough there for coffee at Niko's. Pain in the ass to limp all the way there, but better than sitting around in the cold.

I figure it's safer to take my pills now, here in the store, than out on the corner. I've already seen how it works out with cigarettes, and I have no interest in finding out if it holds true for pain pills too.

So I find myself a little spot over by the magazine rack where I can have some privacy. Nobody, *nobody* wants to see what the derelict is doing over by the porno mags, so I'm safe. Takes me forever to figure out how to open the little cap, and then there's a seal below that too, one that I think is tough enough to handle a frickin' rhino. Tougher than my thumbnail, at least. Pulling at it with my teeth finally rips it off. If there's something below that, I think I'll just drop dead. It'll be easier.

But there isn't. Out goes the little pack of stuff that's supposed to keep things dry, and I shake a bunch of pills into my mouth. How many, I don't know – why should I bother counting? Careful, Alex, you might ruin your health. Yeah, there's a laugh.

Swallowing them, though, is another story. I haven't had any water or anything since yesterday at my sister's I guess. My mouth is already pasty, and the pills greedily suck up any moisture they can find, sticking to my tongue and gums. Every single pill grinds its way down my throat, pulling, cutting, sticking. The taste makes me want to puke too.

I briefly contemplate spitting the damn things out, but the throbbing in my leg is pretty ominous, so I struggle to swallow. Trying to work up some spit doesn't do a damn thing, and I'm left with no option but to stand there, pretending to look at the magazine covers, and swallow again and again. Each time, I can feel a pill rasp a little further down the pipe.

Don't want to be in the store, don't want to be anywhere right now. Just want to be done with everything. Being dead seems like an attractive choice at the moment.

My patience pays off eventually, and there's a handful of pills in my gut, hopefully working on easing the pain. Limp out the door, mindful that I don't slip in the slush, and over to the steps. Nobody really says anything to me, a few nods in my direction is about all. Good. Don't want to talk, just want to sit.

I feel horrible in so many ways – my leg is still throbbing, my throat feels like I swallowed sandpaper, and there's some nausea too. Haven't slept, haven't eaten, haven't had any booze or drugs or nothing. Wish I could sleep it off, but I don't want to do that either.

Should be going back to my apartment, let the pills kick in and rest a bit.

Instead, I sit on the corner with the rest of the lowlifes.

It hits me very quickly, just how much everyone around me smells. I've had my immunity stripped from me by last night's shower, and despite the smell of my clothes, the stench around me assaults my nostrils. Piss, and cigarettes and unwashed bodies, and who knows what else, mixed together and left to ferment – sometimes for years.

I never really noticed it before, but man, we stink.

It makes sense, though. The corner, it draws us in like flies to shit. We just can't escape it. If it weren't made out of concrete, some of us would be putting down roots.

And maybe, some of them are. I'm not the only one who looks this bad. I think nobody is sleeping, or eating lately, and whatever they're managing to score isn't filling that hollow space inside of them, going by appearance. Whatever is affecting me is hitting them as well.

Street Corner of the Living Dead, coming soon to a theatre near you.

One could take the faces on view here, and use them to string together a narrative of the hard life. Weathered skin, bad teeth, and scraggly beards provide the setting, the climate we live in. Only some of us sport burnt lips from overheated crack pipes, but all of us have tobacco-yellowed fingers, and smell of booze – those are just the tangible signs of what passes for motivation here. And then, the smell of unwashed bodies, some of us with the white-man dreadlocks that only come from extreme filth, that writes of how far we've fallen from societal norms.

And crazy as shit-house rats. You can listen around you and hear several channels of crazy, like it's a radio station in an asylum. Just have to tune in.

"Gotta keep control," says the guy sitting one step below me. "Control, right, control. Control rods, keeps everything safe. Control rods, like Rodney Dangerfield, respect, he never got any respect ..."

I could listen all day if I wanted to, probably end up crazy too. More crazy. I could have a sign that said "will rant for food."

I note that Dingle hasn't shown up yet, which isn't a big deal, considering that nobody here owns a watch. He'll be by eventually – nobody dares miss panhandling the morning rush.

There's another thing he's about to miss if he doesn't hurry up. It's a symptom of this sort of life that it doesn't take much to make us happy. Okay, not long-term happy. Not slap your knee and sing out that this is the day when you'll dry out and fly straight, but the kind of happy that reminds you that there's that little nugget of hope and humanity deep inside you, that maybe if you could just hold onto it long enough, you'd be all right.

Case in point: there's a mother and child we see every morning, as she walks him to school, and then again in reverse at the end of the day. It's part of an unspoken code that you don't ask moms with kids for money. I don't know why, and I don't think anyone could explain it adequately, but it's just something that isn't done. If it had to be explained to you, you wouldn't understand it anyway.

Anyway, the mom is nice enough, never stops to chat, but at least she acknowledges our existence and maybe smiles a little. That feels pretty good. Like I said, it doesn't take much.

It's the kid, though, who we all wait to see. He doesn't just smile, he beams, like there's a light source within him. Again, we don't ask them for money – he's the one who initiates conversation. Asks us how we are and really wants to know. Wishes us a nice day and really means it.

Mom rushes him along a bit usually – he's got to get to school, and probably sitting around talking to winos and junkies isn't the kind of education she had in mind for him.

We've come to crave it, the twice-daily visit from the child of joy. Even me, who hasn't been on the corner for that long, I feel it too.

So, it's troubling, startling, to see him this morning, shy, withdrawn, staring straight ahead as he walks past our corner. His mother whispers something in his ear, an encouragement perhaps, and he gives us a side-long glance, his gaze seeming to linger a bit on me. A shy little wave, and then snapping his face to the front like a soldier to continue on his way to the front lines.

Our moods turn as grey as the overcast sky. What was up with that?

Doesn't take long before I'm feeling the cold. It always wins in the end anyway, but it's more of a question of when I'll feel it, not if. I'd have a cigarette to take my mind off of it, but I know pulling out a fresh pack here would be a bad idea.

Pull my legs in close, and wrap my arms around, trying to build up some warmth. Wish I had a longer coat, then I could cover my shins, make a little tent.

But, I don't. My coat isn't bad, as they go, and there's some out here who manage to survive with less. A Christmas present from my mother, and at least a decade old, worn, but functional. Wish the same could be said about me.

Wrap my arms a little tighter, and rest my head on my knees. The pressure on my eye sockets feels good.

I find myself standing on the steps of my apartment building, and it is day - brightest, hottest day, with the sunlight pouring down on me. The brightness of it washes the colour out of everything. The snow is long-gone and I can see heat shimmers in the distance.

But around me, everything is shadow, hazy and indistinct despite the white light all around. Not everything is like that ... the buildings, cars, that sort of stuff is throwing your regular crisp shadow.

It's the people around me, they are shadow. They don't cast shadows, they're made of it, looking like smudges that walked away from a watercolour painting. They drift, wander, cluster all around me, contemplating me.

From where I'm standing on the steps, I can see more of them coming, from every direction.

And they all want me.

With a snort and a jump, I realize I was asleep where I sat. Not long, I think, just a minute or so. There's commotion. Everyone around is wondering what the hell is going on, and being loud about it, and for once none of it has anything to do with me. After a few pointless attempts to ask what's up, I spot what they're looking at.

Just down the street, right around where my little hobo haunt sits, there's lights flashing, couple of cop cars, ambulance, I think a fire truck. Wonder what that's all about?

It isn't unusual to see emergency vehicles around here, but seeing that many together means something interesting is happening. A few of us are drifting off to see what's up. The rest of us follow, since we've got nothing better to do, and when the inevitable and endless dissection of current events ensues, there's just no substitute to having seen it first hand – all the better to see all the details and then make your own definite pronouncements on the events. We make our own entertainment, in a way.

The sidewalks still haven't been ploughed and probably won't be for a while yet, but thankfully foot traffic has beaten a path.

Still, I'm in the back of the pack, however. My leg puts me with two old guys and the Skipper, who pointedly keeps plenty of room between him and me. My leg still hurts, but it's lost the needling aspect. Now it's dull, like being repeatedly tapped with a hammer. About damn time the pills kicked in. Still doesn't mean I'm moving fast. We'd be the ones eaten by wolves in the wild, I guess. A sudden flicker of last night crosses my mind, of being hunted, and sour bile rises in the back of my throat. Yeah, best not to think about wolves.

Anyway, I'm moving slowly, so by the time I catch up, most of what I see is a wall of people. The cops are trying to move everybody back, but not with much success – one person takes a step away, and somewhere else another two move forward. It's like pushing a wall of jello. One cop is rolling out a strip of yellow tape to mark the perimeter but it doesn't get much respect – it is, after all, just tape.

We're not much for obeying cops because there isn't much they can do to us. Arresting your normal citizen, or even detaining him for a few hours, will create all sorts of havoc in his life – "yeah, sorry honey, can't make it to dinner with the Wilsons, I'm in the slammer" – but for us, so what? We get to stay somewhere warm, three hot meals per day, and a jail cell is a lot safer and cleaner than sleeping at the shelter. Plus we get something interesting to talk about when we get released the next morning – what's not to like? We know it, the cops know it, so neither side is particularly worked up.

The normal people, though, they've got routines to protect. They clear out first, jobs to go to, or coffee break is over, or off to some place warm, leaving space for me to limp my way closer to the action.

The first thing I get to see is blood, and lots of it. The snow of my little corner is gaudily decked out in bright scarlet, from one end to the other. It gleams fresh, wet, even brighter than I would have expected against the white snow. There's still a crowd in the way, so I only get to see glimpses between people as they lean left and right trying to get a better look. Not much in the mood to try and push my way to the front.

The cops eventually give up with pushing us away from the scene, as long as we don't try to make it past the tape. That's fine, nobody here is that brave. We don't need to be on top of the action, just witnesses to it. The cops have their job, we have ours.

I can see the paramedics, but it doesn't look like they're sticking around. Rather than unloading gear, looks like they're schlepping it back to their ambulance. That speaks volumes about the condition of whoever did all the bleeding. He needs a morgue, not a medic.

We have respect for the paramedics, because unlike cops or other representatives of officialdom, they actually do something useful instead of busting our balls with a bunch of stupid questions. We all move out of the way so they can roll through with the stretcher. Ain't a thing they can do for a dead guy, and there's plenty of other people in the city waiting for them.

One of the pair is a woman, and I can't take my eyes off her. Never mind that my leg still throbs, and my lungs ache, and I haven't eaten, and I'm going crazy, and there's a dead guy over there in the alley – all of that is staying put. I can get back to it after I've checked her out. Yes, I'm a pig, and I'm comfortable with that knowledge. It isn't like I meet a lot of women these days, and frankly, I haven't been laid in months. Just about any woman would do it for me right now.

This one, though, I'd have noticed her no matter what condition I was in. She's got a cute butt, and a nice face with just enough of the exotic in it to really peak my interest. Her hair is black, as are her eyes, and skin with a hint of darkness to it.

The one problem with her is a typical one for winter – heavy clothing. She's got a bomber jacket that obscures any of the interesting details between the neck and waist. And then I'm lost in a little reverie, imagining unzipping her jacket, undoing her shirt button by button, peeling it back to reveal lovely, curvy skin, listening to her intake of breath as I run my fingers …

"There's the body," someone says, yanking me from pleasant fantasy world. Damn.

I can't see what he's referring to, but a general murmur filters through the crowd. But I keep craning and weaving back and forth, trying to get a look.

Finally, I do see, but it isn't the body. No, instead I see a familiar duffel bag, one I picked up years ago in an army surplus store, ripped to pieces. That's mine - my bag, my clothes, and someone else's blood. Again there's the taste of bile in the back of my throat, and my vision starts to swim. Aw fuck. I grab onto the sleeve of whoever is standing next to me, but he shrugs off my grip and I fall.

Falling, falling. The trip to the sidewalk seems to take forever. Sounds mash together. The first indication I have that I'm all the way down is the feeling of cold, wet snow on my cheek, next comes the pain from having rapped my skull on the sidewalk. Damn, just what I need – more pain. Clears my head though, and suddenly vision and sound return.

At first all I see are boots and snow. Nobody is interested in helping me, but at least nobody is stepping on me either. I'm just about to start the laborious process of standing up, when something catches my eye through the forest of legs.

There's a yellow plastic sheet spread out in the alley, conspicuous by how clean it looks compared to the omnipresent grime and blood around it. No doubt, it's covering the body. What else could it be?

And then a cop, curious, morbid, who knows? He picks up a corner of the sheet and peeks underneath, giving me a perfect view.

Dingle.

Poor dumb stupid bastard Dingle. Goddamn too stupid to find somewhere safe to hide when there was a pack of feral dogs on the loose Dingle.

His corpse stares directly at me, eyes wide, mouth agape in an expression that doesn't speak of surprise or terror, but instead asks "why me?" The face is unmarked, far as I can tell, although there are splatters of blood on the cheeks and forehead. His glasses are missing.

Why you, buddy? Because I ran like a rabbit, and you just ran out of luck.

I can't see the rest of him, but considering how much blood has been splashed on the snow, that's probably a good thing.

For most of these guys, all they can hope for is a death marked by a lack of anything interesting. Fall asleep on a thin mattress at the men's shelter, and just don't wake up the next morning, that's a good death. Dingle, though, alone, cold, and ripped into bloody chunks by a pack of feral dogs. And for what? Because he had the bad luck to be the first to find my duffel bag.

Suddenly, Dingle is gone. Replaced by the Yeller, leaning in so close to me that I can feel the heat off his face. "Gimme!" he yells, spittle flying. I try to scuttle back away from him, but he's got his hands dug into the collar of my coat. I try again anyway.

There's no way I can fight him, not now. Hell, probably not during my best days – I'm not built to be a fighter. And right now, I'm so far gone I'm actually hallucinating. The Yeller seems a lot bigger than before, bigger than a man has a right to be, and someone has been playing with the knobs on the television, because his colour is off too. His face is fire-engine red and glossy like it was polished or something

In an instant, I'm vertical again – the Yeller yanking me to my feet with little effort, and shaking me like a dog with a hunk of rope.

"Gimme," he yells again.

"Hang on" I yell. "You can have my cigarettes." But he keeps yelling and shaking me.

I'm getting an up close look at his face, which I never wanted in the first place. He's got the obligatory beard and greasy hair sported by all of us 'urban outdoorsmen'. His skin is pock-marked from acne or chickenpox or something. A scar runs across the tip of his bulbous nose. The colour, though, it's incredible. It's so red that I actually flinch away, expecting heat from it. He is hot, but not like the stove element he resembles. There's a smell of something burning too.

From behind the Yeller, I see an arm snake around into a choke-hold on his neck, as a cop drags him back. It doesn't do anything – he just ignores it and keeps shaking me around. There's a full-grown man on his back, and he's lifting another, me, bodily off the ground, and none of it seems to be causing him any strain.

"Gonna rip you apart," he yells, and suddenly the world spins again, with me ending once more in the snow. Another cop is wrapped around the Yeller's knees, dragging him to the ground and me along with him. He's still got the bruise from Serapion, but now it reminds me of an ember in a campfire – dull in colour at the edges, but with the promise of fire on the inside. I didn't know skin could look like that.

A third cop joins in, prying off the hands currently choking the living shit out of me.

I should thank the Yeller for a new experience – I'm actually glad to have the cops around. The hands pop off my collar, and I scurry away from the tangle of people.

Serapion detaches himself from the crowd, and strolls over to me. He squats down on his haunches, looming over where I'm sitting on the icy sidewalk. Seems every time I see him, I'm sitting on the pavement, looking up at him.

"You're nothing but trouble, you know that?" he says.

"Serapion, where the hell were you?"

"Over there," he says, indicating the crowd with a tilt of his head. "It didn't seem that serious."

"You suck as a guardian angel."

He shrugs. "Your words wound me."

"I wish. Why didn't you help me?"

He shrugs again. "I was on hand if things went sour, and I had confidence that he wouldn't be able to beat all those big, tough policemen."

We both look over to where the Yeller is. There's four cops on top of him, struggling, and a couple of firefighters standing by, looking brave and wisely not jumping in.

"Okay, I need somewhere to sit before I totally fall apart. Help me up."

"Nope. Get up on your own; it'll be good for you to exercise." Serapion isn't joking. He stands up and steps away from me. I couldn't grab his coat even if I wanted to. Climbing to my feet is an involved process. I don't want to slip on the ice, there's one leg that needs favouring, and I think I hurt my ass on the sidewalk. Slowly, like an old man, I stand up.

"Thanks for nothing," I say. My guardian angel inspects his fingernails, as if any dirt would dare hide there.

Again slowly, limp back to the corner. I want to be sitting before the adrenaline gives out, because I don't know if I'll be able to stand after that. As it is, I've got a serious case of the shakes going on.

Serapion and I have the stairs to ourselves, at least until the last of the emergency vehicles have left. Even after that, I bet we'll probably still be left alone. Although my peers are inoculated against personal tragedy, they also have a heightened sense of fear and superstition. There is no chance anybody is going near the stairs until some favourable omen comes by. At least I get to claim the best piece of cardboard.

Plus, I can have a cigarette without inciting a riot in the process.

The ambulance drives by, working its way through the morning rush hour traffic. I can just catch a glimpse of the cutie I saw in the alley. Nice.

The alley. There's still a crowd – all the bums, plus the transient flow of people passing by.

Today has been full of entertainment for them. First, Dingle's death, and now they get to watch as the Yeller thrashes around in the snow, cuffs latched on to both his wrists and his ankles, and *still* the cops are having a hard time with him. I can see that weird redness to his face all the way over here.

The bums hoot and holler, shouting encouragement to the Yeller – one of our own striking back against society, as it were. Or maybe just enjoying the excitement of the fight and they don't care who wins.

Behind them all, I see the yellow plastic sheet still covering Dingle. Sure he died horribly. The exact same thing is happening to the rest of us, just at a more sedate pace. It isn't death we're afraid of, just the rapid change that accompanies it. And the pain, and the fear and the uncertainty of what happens next.

Damn, Alex, that's just cold. A man dies, a *friend* dies, and all I can do is wax philosophical about it. But isn't that what people do? Try and make sense of it all? Among the crowd I grew up with, it all would've been placed in the happy protective custody of God's master plan. *"It was his time,"* they'd say, or *"God called him home."*

"Hey, Serapion," I say. "If you're an angel, you can answer this for me: does God have a master plan?"

103

"Not one that would make anybody happy or comfortable if they were familiar with it. If it does, that's just coincidental." He's looking off at the alley, at the Yeller and at Dingle, and I guess in some way I understand.

God, I'm tired.

There's a guy across the street, making a bee-line for where Serapion and I are sitting. I'm hoping he's an outreach worker – they give out toiletries, dry socks and hot coffee, and I can use all of that. Instead, by the looks of him, I'm getting a street preacher, with nothing but free bibles and a canned sermon. He's easy to spot – uptight, paid far too much attention to his hair, and he's smiling at nothing.

Yay. All of this and a guy claiming to be an angel sitting next to me. It promises to be an all-out, tag-team wrestling match for God, with me in the opposing corner.

Serapion says he's here to protect me, but I doubt that extends to defending me from proselytizers.

Typically they work the street in groups of two or three – one takes the lead and does all the talking, while his buddies hand out pamphlets, and add the occasional "amen." There are bigger groups - some of them are really into putting on a show, with loudspeakers, and signs, occasionally musicians. Anyway, they take great pains to make sure they don't collide with a rival group, which I guess could be professional courtesy, but could also be a strategy to avoid contamination or holy war. Sure would be entertaining to see.

Today, though, there seems to be a labour shortage in the god squad, with a single preacher making his way over to us. I'm pretty sure I've seen him before but he's always been a second stringer. Looks like there's been a battlefield promotion.

He looks keen, eager to prove himself, and makes it over to us, dodging traffic to cross the street. That a car didn't hit him is direct evidence that prayer doesn't work.

I am really not up for this. Right now, I want a chance to calm down. A drink would be fantastic. A sermon on the wages of sin would be decidedly unpleasant.

Despite the sour expression on my face, he comes over to us. "Hi there," he says, beaming with the joy that only small children, lunatics and the extremely religious possess. "How are you today?"

"Crappy. Well, actually, shitty make that."

Pastor Bob (that's what it says on his name tag) ignores my crudity and looks sympathetic. He's not a very good actor, though, more like an amateur game show host, making him look like a grinning jackass instead.

"Have you found Jesus?"

"Nope," I say. "But I saw his picture on the side of a milk carton. I hear it's very important to find them in the first 48 hours after they go missing."

The preacher's eyes get the tiniest gleam in them. He's out to earn his spurs, I think. Bag a few for the Lord, as it were. For a moment, he looks for a place to sit, but thinks better of it. Although the bums have swept the snow off the steps, it isn't warm or comfortable. Fine by me, I'd rather have him in front of me where it's easy to keep an eye on him. I know his type, seen them a thousand times before, and I don't trust them.

"So," he says. "Let me ask you something: have you ever told a lie?"

"Sure," I say. "Not a surprise, really."

"And what do you think that makes you?"

"Uh, human?" I say. *C'mon, Captain Obvious, hit me with a tough one.*

He chuckles, but it sounds forced, just another part of the script. "Well yes, but it also makes you a liar. Now, have you ever stolen anything?"

"Not today, but the day ain't over yet."

"So you're a thief then," he says. "Have you ever felt lust?"

I blink a few times at the stupidity of the question. I'm a man – just about every thought I've had since puberty has been inappropriate in one way or the other. The preacher takes my silence for assent.

"Well," he says. "All that makes you a sinner, and that means a guaranteed trip to Hell, and eternal damnation."

"At least I'll be warm, which is more than I can say for right now." I hold up a finger to interrupt the beginning of his protest. "Frankly, you're going to have to do better than that," I say. "I'm hungry, I'm really fucking hurting, I'm cold turkey – not by my choice, I might add. I'm already strolling through Hell, thank you very much."

"Then pray with me, brother. You've already acknowledged that you are a sinner, now all you have to do is accept Jesus into your heart and the Lord will come into your life and make you a new person. The Bible says 'Whosoever calls upon the name of the Lord shall be saved.'"

I snort. "Bob... can I call you Bob? I've done more praying in my life than you might ever suspect, and all I got out of it was a near terminal case of guilt and sore knees from a hard floor. Unless God is going to fix me up with a pizza and a six pack right now, I'm not interested.

"See that fire truck over there? It's hosing away the remains of my dead friend. I can guaran-fucking-tee you that he was screaming for God to help him, probably right up to the moment that the dogs ripped his throat out. You want to tell somebody about the power of prayer, go talk to him."

Bob stares at the trucks for a long time. I think it's having an impact on him, but it's hard to tell. He lets out a deep breath in a whoosh, before turning back to me, but before he can open his mouth, I throw that finger in his face again. "Don't," I say. "Not another word. I'm done talking with you."

I sit and stare right through him, like he wasn't standing directly in front of me. Eventually, he shrugs, sidesteps, and stands in front of Serapion.

"Hi there," he says. "How are you today?" Just like our little conversation had never happened.

"Can we skip the preamble and get right to the heart of your argument?" asks Serapion.

Bob is taken aback for a moment. You can see him mentally hitting fast-forward on his monologue before he finds the right spot.

The whole time I've been talking with Pastor Bob, Serapion was silent. It wasn't what I expected, but I'm grateful – didn't really feel the need for both of them to be telling me my business. It'd be like having a lecture from two parents. I was hoping that maybe Bob would recruit Serapion and they'd both go away. But, a guardian angel having it out with a god-walloper? That could be major entertainment.

Bob fires his opening salvo: "Jesus loves you, and wants to save you from the fires of Hell, if only you welcome Him into your heart."

"That's damn decent of him, although you're getting ahead of yourself. First, you can prove to me that *any* god exists, and maybe then we can get to the specifics of your very generous offer."

He smiles. "There is only one god, the God of the Bible, whose son came down from Heaven to save us all from eternal damnation."

"And? Again, where's your proof?"

"There must be a God – it just makes logical sense."

"Really? How's that?"

"Every effect must have a cause, correct?" asks Bob, warming to his topic. "And everything that is built has a builder, yes? We see a painting; we know there must have been a painter. We see a watch;

we know there was a watchmaker. Cause and effect. If we keep going back along that chain of cause and effect, eventually you would find the thing that started it all, the first cause, the first builder. For there to be a Creation, there has to be a Creator, and that is God."

Serapion smiles. I don't like his smile very much. "So every river has a riverer, and every thunder has a thunderer – maybe some things don't have a creator as such. And for that matter, what created God? Seems to me you're drawing a fairly arbitrary line in the sand, saying that God gets to be an effect without a cause. Maybe I'd prefer to worship whatever created your god."

"There is nothing that created God. He always was."

"I'm unimpressed. Really, I didn't have high hopes for you anyway, but your arguments are terrible. I'm unconvinced."

Bob waves his hands in the air like he's trying to disperse a fart. "Think about what you're risking, by denying God. Are you willing to bet that you're correct? If you're right and there is no God, you've lost nothing, but if I'm right then you are dooming yourself to eternal damnation and punishment."

"Well, if we're talking about what it's prudent to believe in, have I got an offer for you." Serapion leans in closer to him, providing an air of confidentiality. "You see, I'm actually an angel."

Bob starts to move away, a scowl on his face. "No, wait, hear me out," Serapion says. "If you believe I'm an angel and I'm not, you've lost nothing, but if I really am an angel, then you've just made friends with one of God's very close servants. It's in your best interests to believe."

"I can't just choose to believe you're an angel – belief doesn't work like that."

"Where's your faith, Bob?" Serapion asks, loudly. A few people passing by look up from their thoughts at the sound.

He starts to retreat, just a step back, but his weight is on his heels now.

"So tell me something, Bob – you don't mind if I call you Bob too, do you? Why are you all alone? I thought your type always went in teams."

Bob looks around nervously, like he's hoping the reinforcements will finally arrive to rescue him from the very intimidating man. Of course, he's still alone. Serapion leans close again, a predatory gleam in his eye. And then, when he's very close to Bob, he jerks forward suddenly. Just a tiny amount, less than an inch, but it's enough. Bob's nerve breaks, and he turns on his heel, and strides off purposefully, like he remembered an important appointment.

I want to laugh and jeer at his retreat, but I can't work up the energy.

"Serapion, why do you think he's all alone? Or were you just messing with him?"

"Being religious is sort of like being trapped between two very different propositions. On one hand, there's all the assumptions one makes based on reasonable expectations like the sun will rise tomorrow, or that gravity will keep working – the stuff that a sane human needs to get through the day. On the other hand, the devotee has a whole raft of ideas for which he has not a shred of proof, no evidence whatsoever.

"And," he continues. "That's just the way they like it. As long as their god is vast and unknowable, there's nothing to impede them from imagining their invisible best friend any way they want to. You can tell them God made the universe in six days and they're okay with that, but tell them that the paint on a bench is still wet, and they have to find out for themselves."

"So, what you're saying is, you have absolutely no idea why Bob is alone today."

"I know exactly why," he says. "Right now, he, and all his friends are finding the rational and religious sides of their brains are having a major showdown."

"But why?"

Serapion lets out a long sigh. "Because things are happening that will make it very difficult for true believers to continue to maintain their willing suspension of disbelief."

"And that would be?" I ask.

But Serapion clams up, a wall of stony silence.

"Okay, so where are his friends?"

"Calling in sick, in droves. Sitting in their homes doing whatever self-destructive habit they've got that they hide from the world. Secret drinking, mostly."

"Why?'

"Because if the true believers were given actual proof of the existence of God, they'd reject it," he says. "Soon they won't be able to."

I mull on that for a minute.

"For a second there, it looked like you gave Bob something to think about."

"You kidding? God himself couldn't do that."

I give him a sidelong look, eyebrow raised.

Serapion shakes his head. "Problem is that guy has faith, which is the sworn enemy of reason. He didn't reason his way into where he is today, and ain't no way it'll work to get him out either. He and I have one thing in common, belief in the existence of God. The difference is, I don't need faith. I've got direct evidence of God's existence. And, in fact, I'd rather be there right now, basking in the Presence and singing the million names of God."

"God has a million names?"

"Give or take."

"That's a lot of names," I say. Serapion shrugs in reply. "I still don't believe you're an angel." He gives me a sidelong glance, then shrugs again.

I don't want to be here anymore. I don't want to be anywhere, really, but here on the corner most of all. Cold, tired, hungry, beat up. I would wander around a bit, see what's up in the neighbourhood, but it's better just to get away from people for a while.

I'd go to the mall, but that's obviously a bad choice for a little while. It'd be just my luck to run into the same security guard. He'd kick the crap out of me.

Niko's is an option, but it's getting near the lunch rush. If I'm going to spend my money there, it'll be when I can spend hours and hours there.

That leaves the apartment.

But, I don't want to go there, because Serapion is sitting next to me. Old stony face. What can I say or do to ditch him? I sneak a look to see if he's paying attention, and realize he's gone. Didn't make a sound. I'm alone again, and problem solved.

Time to go home. The side walk is easier to deal with now, thanks to the morning's traffic. The beaten path is much wider now, trodden down. Damn near optimal, in fact, for winter walking – it isn't a fresh snow drift, but not so trampled that it has started to get icy. Perfect for a cripple like me.

And while I limp home, recent events rise up in my mind.

Why the hell is all this happening? This is beyond just going insane. Crazy was seeing a cat that wasn't there, or hearing my name on the radio, or seeing … whatever that was in the mall toilet.

The dogs, though, and Dingle, that wasn't hallucination.

Dingle. Jesus, man, I'm so sorry that had to happen to you. Not that I would've traded places, if given the choice, but that's no way for someone to die.

So what's happening? Maybe it's nothing. Maybe it's all just coincidence that this is all at the same time. Yeah, whatever that means. Assuming it means anything.

Damn shame about Dingle. Just, damn.

Shuffle on home, through the lobby, slowly up the stairs, and back to my pest-hole of an apartment. Kick off my boots, drop my coat where I stand. Sit down on the familiar old couch, then lie back so I can put my foot up. God, I'm tired.

~~~~~ Chapter 7 ~~~~~

I can't tell if I'm dreaming or not, or if it's a memory, or if this is happening right now. It's surreal, but I feel it with such intensity. There's just no clear line between what might be a dream and where reality starts. Remember what I said about knowing when I'm dreaming? Yeah, well scratch that.

There's no memory of how I got here, but I'm lying on my back, on the floor. I can move, but slowly and with great effort. My arms and legs are heavy, and the air feels viscous. It makes it a struggle to raise my arm, but likewise to let it drop. Best just to lie here and do nothing.

It is hot, and incredibly humid, and smells of something like ozone.

But it's the sounds that command my attention the most, like a thousand voices, all singing, but some terrified voices, angry, demanding, cursing. The singing is tense, restrained, eager, hungry even, if one can describe a singing voice like that. The song is beautiful and terrifying at the same time.

The sound holds me in place and I'm helpless against it. But it saps me of the urge to move anyway, and I relax.

And when I stop trying to move, suddenly it gets quieter. The singers haven't stopped, but it feels like they've moved farther away now.

Standing next to me and over me is Beaudry, and I want to ask him what the hell is happening, and whether I'm dreaming, but speaking is too difficult to manage.

Beaudry is dressed like some sort of stage wizard – long robes, fancy headgear, dramatic lighting and sound effects. I get an answer to my question; I must be dreaming. Granted that he was a weirdo, but costumes weren't his style.

How refreshing – I'm dreaming but I'm not terrified. Fan-fucking-tastic.

"Hey, Alex," he says, leaning closer to my face. "I won't lie to you, this is going to hurt, and it's going to hurt a lot."

The singing doesn't let me get worked up at the thought of impending pain. Everything is going to be fine. So, happily I shrug as best I can and I'm not worried when he holds up a ball of some sort, glassine, iridescent, crackling with sparks. It fascinates me – colours swirl and emerge and coalesce and disperse. I can see faces, shapes, even ideas portrayed all at dizzying speeds. I could look at it all day, except that Beaudry takes a deep breath, steadies himself, and then plunges his hand and the ball right into my chest.

And before I have a chance to marvel about all the wonderful, improbable things that can happen inside a dream, the pain hits me. Every muscle in me is on fire, clenching so hard that I fear they're about to rip. I want to scream, but I can't make my body do anything as it shudders and jolts.

It goes on and on, this agony, to the point that now I'm struggling for breath too, but my chest is locked in a fierce combat with itself, my muscles fighting against one another. The pain keeps going and going, and at the point where I can't believe it can continue, that a human can feel such incredible pain and still remain conscious or sane, I find out that yes, the pain can continue, and no, the brain doesn't shut off. I'm forced to be a mute, trembling witness to it all.

And kneeling beside me, his face floating over mine, is Beaudry. He's not looking at my face, but at my chest, which is still impaled by his hand. There's furious concentration written in his expression, he's working at a puzzle, it seems.

 Chapter 8 ~~~~~

I'm awake and lying on the couch, and realize it was indeed a dream. I'm awake, I'm not in pain, Beaudry is not in my apartment, and hasn't been for months. Judging by the light filtering in through the grimy window, it's still day. Since there's nobody banging on the wall, I'll assume I wasn't screaming out loud in my sleep this time.

"It wasn't a dream, Alex," says Serapion, sitting crouched like a vulture on the arm of the couch above my head, with his overcoat draping like wings.

"Whuh," I say. I'm not a morning person, and neither are my powers of repartee – not that it is morning. I'd like to leap to my feet in surprise, but that ain't happening.

"Do you really think you were having a dream? You were remembering. That was the beginning."

"Beginning of what?" I ask, sitting up and finally getting my mouth to work.

"All of this," he says, gesturing at the apartment, but indicating everything beyond the walls. "It was at that precise moment that your life was absolutely, irrevocably fucked."

"What do you mean? How do you know what I was dreaming?" The pitch of my voice is climbing, threatening to crack as my fear creeps upwards. "And how'd you get in here? For that matter, how the flying hell do you know where I live?"

He sighs, pinching the bridge of his nose again. "We've talked about this before. I'm your guardian angel. That's the answer to your last four questions, and probably to the next half-dozen."

"I don't understand any of this," I say. There's something wrong here, fundamentally, elementally wrong. I can feel it. In a blink, I'm up and off the couch and bouncing around the apartment, with no idea what I'm doing. Open a cupboard, peek inside, slam it shut. I go through the whole filthy kitchen doing that. There's no food in the place, there's no booze. Coffee, God, I'd kill for a cup of coffee right now. I don't care how much my foot hurts, I need to move. There's that animal part of the brain that's solely focused on finding an escape route right away, and it doesn't care if it means chewing off the leg caught in the trap.

But there's no coffee, and not enough money to buy any. I do have cigarettes though, yeah. Fish one out of the pack, try and light it, but I'm having a hard time making the lighter work with my shaking hands. Takes a few attempts, with both hands clenched tight on the lighter, and eventually get the cigarette lit. Suck back a lungful of smoke, calm down.

Peek into the pack to count how many smokes I've got left. I owe Dingle money still but I'm sure I can trade him for it instead. Then I remember. Dingle is dead. Suddenly my cigarette doesn't taste so good anymore. Slowly, back to the lumpy green couch, to sit heavily upon it and stare at nothing.

"You done?"

A long sigh, and then "Yeah, think so."

We're silent for a while, him standing now, motionless, and me rocking gently back and forth. The ancient springs of the couch groan quietly in time with my motion.

"Okay, let me know when you want to take another crack at your questions."

"Sure, sure," I say.

The uncompanionable silence continues, initially because I'm clamping my mouth shut against the words that threaten to shoot out of my mouth like a fire hose. But after I've reined it in, I don't want to be the first to speak. He seems mountainous in his patience, though, and eventually it gets to me – I break first.

My hands slap my thighs, and I turn to face him. "How did you get in here?"

"Through the door, moron, same as anyone else."

"Through a locked door?" A quick glance confirms that the door is indeed still attached to its hinges, that he didn't kick it down.

"Yeah, locked. Whatever."

The thought gets filed away that later I will need to check the door to see if Serapion has tampered with it, or if it's just as rundown as the rest of the building, and needed only the most gentle of coaxing to swing open. Maybe the pounding from the dogs has done it in.

"Okay, why are you here?"

"Because I'm your guardian angel."

"You keep saying that like you believe it," I say. "And like I should believe it too. If you're really a guardian angel, couldn't you just float invisibly over my head? You wouldn't have to use the door either."

"I don't really care. I only told you in the first place so you wouldn't panic every damn time you saw me hanging around you."

"Well then, why *are* you hanging around me?" I ask. "I've got all the friends I could possibly need."

"Yeah," he says. "About your friends. Let's just say this is about a memory you have of one particular friend, that you have convinced yourself is a dream."

I'm trying to act cool, which is made doubly tough by the fact that my body still wants to bolt off the couch and start pacing the room again. Adrenaline is a bitch. "How would you know what I was dreaming?"

"Wasn't a dream."

"Yeah, yeah. Fine. Tell me what I remembered, then."

"You're testing me." There's real amusement in his voice, for once.

"Sure, call it a test of faith," I smirk. "You tell me what I was dreaming, and I'll believe you're really an angel."

"You sure about that, Alex? Maybe you'd be much happier in your ignorance."

"I'll take my chances."

Serapion shrugs. "Well, you were warned." He cracks his knuckles – first one hand, then the other. Looks like my day is about to start with a beating. I'm just about to sprint for a hiding space, when he laces his fingers together and starts talking instead of punching.

"Beaudry was dressed in purple robes, with red trim. You lay there, naked, happy as a clam, while he plunged his hand into your ribcage, and you both had a wild ride while he rearranged your plumbing."

He folds his arms on his chest and smiles. It is not a smile of happiness. I'm still sitting, mouth open now, like a big fish. About the most I can do is blink.

"Oh, also," he adds. "You have a very shrill scream, like a nine-year-old girl or something."

And once again, I'm on my feet and pacing, lost in spinning implications. Hands clapped over my ears, shutting out anything more that Serapion might say. I stop, mostly because my leg is seriously throbbing again. Back to the couch, throw myself down and put my foot up on the coffee table. As always, the couch springs complain like an old man.

"I don't believe any of this."

"Doesn't matter if you do or not. Belief or the lack doesn't change what is. You can say you don't believe in gravity, but it ain't going to make you float away. I hope you see my point – believe in it, don't believe in it. Doesn't matter either way. It is."

"Then why?" I ask. "Why are you telling me this if it truly doesn't matter?"

"Well, first because despite my warning, you still wanted me to tell you, and second, it makes my job easier if you're not being a complete idiot. There's only so far you'll be able to fight against your natural tendencies in that regard, but I'm hoping a little information will go a long way.

"You remember when we were blessed with the company of Pastor Bob, and how I said that the rational and religious sides of the true believers were about to suffer from a major collision?"

"Sure, and you were prevaricating then, just like you are now. Fill me in, already."

He ignores me and continues. "You are a very small, but extremely important cog in the grand works of what is going on," he says.

"Very flattering, which makes me want to ask you what you're trying to sell to me."

"Got nothing to sell," he says. "It's just an accurate interpretation of current events."

"I'm getting tired of obscure hints. Can you just tell me what the hell is going on?"

Serapion sighs, but I'm not buying into it. I sit there, arms folded over my chest.

"Alex, you hold within you, the key to the survival or destruction of life as you know it."

Is there no end to the run around? "For the love of God, speak plainly."

"This is for the love of God. Certainly it isn't because of any affection I might have towards you, which plainly I don't have. And Alex, once again, I am not being metaphorical.

"The key," he says, leaning very close to me. "Is. Right. Here." He taps my chest, exactly where Beaudry thrust his hand.

It hits my stomach in a rush, like an elevator suddenly plunging downwards. There's a phantom sensation on my chest, where Serapion tapped me, where Beaudry thrust his hand into my chest. I realize. It *did* happen, it *was* a memory. Oh my God, I believe it, I believe it.

And if Serapion is right about that, is he telling the truth about being an angel? Or about the destruction of life as I know it?"

~~~~~ Chapter 9 ~~~~~

"You ready to hear more?"

I still feel sick to my stomach, but there's nothing else I can do. I nod.

"Some of this will no doubt be hard for you to understand, but it is important for you to listen carefully. Your co-operation will go a long way toward making my job easier."

"And what is your job?"

"Preserving your life. I have been assigned as your bodyguard, while the current situation exists."

"Which is what?" I ask.

"Ask yourself: why would someone need a bodyguard?"

I shrug. Someday he'll get to the point. "I don't know, because they're famous or rich? Said something that pissed people off and now they're angry enough to kill? Hey, that one is half-way plausible for me."

"You forgot one," he says. "A person could have something in his charge which is very valuable – gems, or state secrets, for instance."

"So what? That doesn't apply to me."

"Don't be so sure. Picture yourself as Beaudry for a moment. You've got something very valuable on your hands, but there's others closing in on you and they want it for themselves. What do you do?"

"Give it to them and hope they don't beat me up?"

"Right," he sighs. "Forgot who I was talking to. Okay, again, you're not you right now, you're someone with a spine. The other thing someone might do is hide it somewhere in the hopes that it can be retrieved later."

"And that somewhere is supposed to be inside me?" I ask.

"Hallelujah, ladies and gentlemen – he *can* be taught."

"Yeah, except I don't believe it," I say. "So you're telling me my weird old roommate had this thing …"

"The key."

"Yeah, right. So he had this key and the best place he could find to hide it was inside my chest. Have I got it so far?"

He nods.

"Problem is, that makes for more unanswered questions, not less. How did Beaudry happen to have this key? How could he possibly manage to pop it inside my chest without cutting me open or leaving a scar? Hell, and just what *is* this key?"

"I'm getting to all that. Reality is like an egg," he says, and before I can open my mouth with some sort of wise-ass remark, he stabs a finger in the air at me. "Beings like you will never know what's beyond the shell. The egg, that's your entire universe. Same situation for beings in the other eggs."

"Others?"

"Yeah, like a pot full of eggs. A whole bunch of universes, filled with people just like you with no inkling of what else is out there. Now, say we fill the pot with water and set it to boil. What happens?"

"Breakfast in five minutes?"

"Movement, ass-hat. The eggs, the universes, are in motion. They can come in contact with one another and move away, and no one can predict when or for how long it will happen.

"If you know what's beyond your shell, you've got the potential to cross that barrier and enter into another universe, see? But once that contact is lost, so is your opportunity.

"Now, here's where you come in. Every once in a very rare while, an item comes along which could drastically alter the course of the war."

"The war?" I sputter. "What war?"

"Shut up, I'm getting to that. In this particular case, this item is a key, one that would allow the wielder to open or shut doors, allowing a degree of control over the process.

"And," says Serapion, leaning in close again. "That key is presently sitting in the middle of your ribcage."

I think I'm going to puke.

~~~~~ Chapter 10 ~~~~~

It's like being seasick, this feeling, even though I'm standing still and on dry land. I'm used to a wide variety of nausea: too much alcohol, or shitty food that a goat wouldn't touch, or bad trips, or being ill when there's no one in the world to take care of you. Plenty of ways to be sick to your stomach.

This one is different, and feels more like I'm sitting in a chair that suddenly starts tipping backwards, except the fall doesn't end.

"Now, about the war. It is ancient, although considering the setting, time is a suspect concept. Regardless, as far as you're concerned, God has been fighting it a long time."

"God versus Satan?"

Serapion makes a face. "Oh please. God appointed Satan to his role. There's no battle there."

"But doesn't the Bible say ..."

"It says a lot of things, Alex, but I didn't think you believed it. No this is a war between God and his rivals."

"His *what*?"

"Rivals, other gods, other deities, trying to exert their control over as many universes as they can. The problem is the shifting nature of these multiple realities. It's hard to hold a definitive advantage when you never know what's going to happen with the territory. The key can change all that."

I continue to feel distinctly unwell.

"How does Beaudry fit into all this?"

"Beaudry was a wizard."

"A *what*?"

He shrugs. "Well, you can call it what you want. I figure wizard will make sense to you. There are rare individuals who are aware of the shell separating the various realities, and are able to use that awareness to control the nature of reality to a degree. Pretty wizardly, wouldn't you say? Comes at a price, though – since humans are essentially fragile, there's a lot of madmen in their ranks."

"So all those loonies I hang out with on the corner are wizards? I can't buy that."

"You don't have to – they're just crazy."

"I have to piss," I say, and head off to my dingy bathroom. Lock the door behind me, piss, flip the lid down, sit on the toilet and think. Doesn't matter really that Serapion is out there unattended. What's he going to steal? And even if I told him to get out, he'd probably sneak back in, or just laugh in my face.

I can't remember who introduced me to Beaudry – friend of a friend, I guess. He needed a roommate, I needed a place to throw my duffel bag and typewriter.

So, I met Beaudry. Wild hair, bushy beard, clothes like something out of an old movie from the 1930's or 40's. Never did figure out how old he was.

He said, you got money? I said yeah. He said fine, you get the couch. I asked him what he did for a living, and he said he did oil paintings on black velvet, usually matadors, but the occasional portrait of Elvis too. After a 10-second pause, we both started laughing. I didn't get around to asking him again, and he never got around to telling me.

As roommates go, he was okay. He didn't touch my stuff, didn't ask me about my comings and goings. I can appreciate that, and did the same for him. It was a nice change to have a regular place to live, instead of couch-surfing.

Only problem with him was he'd get weird sometimes, furtive, angry, jittery. Back then I thought he was on speed or something. Now I guess it was some cosmic wizard problem.

Beaudry was a wizard.

I must be going crazy, because I almost believe it. I'd say it makes sense, but nothing makes sense these days. But, I've thrown out all the other possibilities. Doesn't that mean whatever remains is the truth? And if that's true, if all of it is, then I've got more problems on my hands than a few bad dreams.

I lived here, what, like two or three months before Beaudry decided to stick his hand in my chest and fuck up my life.

Fucker.

It was probably just a short time after that, that I last saw him. Not his proudest moment, I'm sure – running down the street, butt naked, screaming his fool head off and slapping at imaginary bugs.

I assumed he was having a bad trip. I suppose I know better now.

Probably should go back out and see Serapion. Been sitting on the toilet for a long time, and I'll be way more comfortable on my couch. That is, assuming he hasn't gone and looted the place in the meantime.

Get up, flush, open the door and shuffle out.

"You didn't wash your hands," he says.

I ignore it. "Hey, what ever happened to Beaudry?"

"Not sure," says Serapion. "Nobody can find him which you have to understand, is pretty damn unusual, considering how many people are looking for him. Died probably, and in an unpleasant fashion."

"Oh," I say. What are you supposed to say to that kind of news?

"But," he continues. "Whatever caught up with him, they didn't get the key, obviously. Bet they were pissed." He laughs.

Yeah, great. Ha ha. Pissed and coming after me. The sound of dogs barking echoes through my head as I wander around the apartment. End up in my writing room, like I always do. Sit in the chair – I can see Serapion from here. He stands, unmoving, not talking. Certainly he doesn't sit on my worn, old couch.

After I was pretty sure Beaudry wasn't coming back, I started pawning and trading off his stuff, mostly so I could get high. Lots of weird stuff in there, trinkets, books in foreign languages, things that I gave away or chucked, since I couldn't get any money for them.

Pretty quickly his bedroom was empty. That's when I moved my typewriter in and set up my little shrine. Could have set up a bed in there, but I was happy with the couch, and by the time I realized I could have just used Beaudry's bed, I'd already traded it for a couple of joints. Never had a blanket or a sheet, so I slept in my clothes – or my underwear during the summer. Beadry never said anything about it, and didn't offer me a sheet. Didn't bother him, I guess. A great roommate, like I said.

The couch looks like it's been here forever, never moved from its spot except for the occasional search in hopes of finding spare change. It was here before I was, and I'm sure it'll be here long after I move out.

I call out to him. "Serapion, why are you telling me all this, if it doesn't matter? Why not just let me go around, blissfully unaware of all this stuff?"

"Because it makes my job easier. I need to protect you and if you're wandering around, getting into trouble, it's nothing but work, work, work. You would be safest if you would stay in your apartment as much as possible, but it is unrealistic of me to assume you will just because I said so. Thus, some incentive is needed – some insight into what is going on.

"You are at the eye of the storm, made up of circling factions, powerful ones. The sheer magnitude of their proximity makes things happen in this reality. Their visitations are marked by side effects, like hallucinations, or bad dreams or voices … or street lights showering glass all over the place." The more he says, the more numb I feel, like my body is no longer my own, like I'm seeing it at a distance. How can he know these things?

"The short version of that is: stay put."

"Hey, bring me some food and cigarettes, or maybe some dope. I could happily stay here all day."

"Yeah, ain't going to happen," he says. "Maybe if I had an expense account."

Do I believe him?

The thought occurs to me that I think I might believe Serapion is really an angel. It scares the crap out of me, both him being an angel and me believing it. Always figured that going crazy would be more of a subtle process. Nope, apparently it happens right in front of you.

"So what do we do to get this key out of me?" I ask. "Can we get a doctor or something?"

Serapion shakes his head. "This isn't something covered in medical school – theological school either, for that matter. In fact, the key has been inside you for, what, four or five months now? By this point, it has become very comfortable right where it is, probably made itself a happy home. Trying to remove it now would be …
traumatic."

I don't have any idea what his version of traumatic is, but I'm not in any hurry to find out. Bad I figure, all around.

"In fact, the key and your ongoing health, are intimately connected," he says. "We don't know what removing the key would do, but we can guarantee that if you die, so does the key."

That sounds bad at first, but the thought occurs to me – "So, it's in everyone's best interest to keep me alive then."

"For some," he says. "Mostly those who want to use the key themselves. Others want to make sure that it doesn't fall into the hands of a rival, and would just as soon see it destroyed."

"And you?"

"I would have thought you'd know. Weren't you always taught that God wants to save you?"

My chin has the beginning of sand-papery whiskers growing. Stroking my chin in thought isn't as effective, now that I've shaved off my beard.

All I know is that I need time to think about this, to process it.

Does this mean God is real? And I mean *really* real, not just willing sense of disbelief like when you're watching a movie. God wants to save me, apparently. It's a good thing Claire isn't here right now, or she'd be insufferably smug.

Serapion has been talking while I've been thinking. "All of this makes you a very valuable commodity. Some want the key, some want to prevent them from getting it, some would prefer to destroy it. In any case, it means there's a lot of very powerful factions unpleasantly interested in you."

"So everything that has been happening to me ..."

"... is a direct result of the key," he finishes. "Not just you, though - your downward spiral plus that of everybody associated with you, your nightmares, and even being able to see me."

I don't get it. Serapion can tell from the dumb look on my face.

"Maybe you haven't noticed," he says. "But I'm not a local. It means this realm, your reality, and mine are drawing closer together and faster than we thought."

"Nope," I say, shaking my head. "Still don't get it."

He's rubbing the bridge of his nose again. "Think of yourself as a radio, a cheap, crappy radio."

He ignores my protest. "The further you get from a transmitter, the less you'll receive, right? Stronger signals the closer you get? Well, let's just say the radio station is currently barrelling down at you like it has a rocket strapped to its ass."

"You're mixing your metaphors."

"And if you don't catch my drift soon, I'll be reduced to finger puppets, and drawing diagrams on your walls. I think I know why

Beaudry stuck you with the key. It wasn't expedience. He just really needed someone truly stupid."

"Where did the key come from? Who made it? Maybe there's a way to get them to take it back."

"We have no idea. And trust me, if it's a mystery to us, then certainly your little brain isn't going to figure it out."

"Who is 'us'?"

"Me, my commander, and all the way up the org chart to the Big Cheese himself. Only extremely powerful entities, wizards, children, or the clinically insane, should have been able to see me."

"Maybe I'm a wizard," I venture.

Serapion snorts. "Yeah, and maybe you're a vanilla milkshake too. Have you ever held a job? Yeah, once or twice. Happy family life? For many years, yeah. Ever troubled by hallucinations before Beaudry stuck his hand inside your chest? No? Not a wizard. However, the other option is a definite possibility."

"Which one?"

"That you're going insane," he says. "As a container, you are definitely not rated to be carrying artefacts of incredible power. There's bound to be a host of unpleasant side effects."

Great, I think. *Consult a physician if you experience dry mouth, blurry vision or creeping madness.*

"So, here's what we do," he continues. "We wait." He holds up a hand to forestall my inevitable objection. "The key has a very definite 'best before' date. After that, the crisis has passed and the gods can go back to ignoring you and the rest of mankind like usual."

"And the key is gone?"

"Well, can't guarantee that. Can't guarantee it won't drive you irretrievably insane or kill you either, but you don't have much of a choice, do you?"

No, I guess not.

"Anyway," he says. "I have to go. You've got a lot to think about and I've got work to do."

Can't imagine what job he might have otherwise. Mob enforcer? Yeah, something like that would suit – he has the people skills.

"What kind of work? Day manager at the Angel Store?"

"Just work. Stuff. Things that need doing. You might be surprised at how much it takes to keep you alive these days."

He turns and leaves, with me still sitting on the couch. The door closes soundlessly behind him – makes me want to check to see if he's just hiding in the front hall, going to jump out at me and yell "boo" in 10 minutes or so.

Chapter 11

"Is the battleship gone?"

Before I even turn around, my mind is running through the possibilities: someone else has broken into my apartment, someone has just walked in because Serapion broke the damn door and now anybody can just waltz in, or, I'm hallucinating.

When I look up, though, all I see is that damned cat. It's actually a relief to see it, to be able to say to myself "yes, a cat *has* been sneaking into my apartment."

We stare at each other, staring, staring, before the cat looks away and delicately sits, washing itself. Lick the paw a few times, wipe the head, repeat.

Don't bother getting in a staring contest with a cat, because even if they lose, which they rarely do, they don't care.

A moment longer, and then I remember, someone spoke. There's obviously no-one in my living room, since I could see them from where I sit. Ditto for the kitchen, and most of the writing room. Which leaves the bathroom. Well, for the sake of completeness, and my sanity, I should check.

I'm barely on my feet, when the voice speaks again: "Alex, down here."

I will not look down, I will not open my mouth, I think to myself. *Buy into the hallucinations, take a step closer to complete madness.*

"You can speak," I say. *Fuck! Alex, you moron!*

The cat is already bored of the conversation.

"You never have anything worth eating," it says, as it strolls into the kitchen, and leaps up on the counter. I follow. We're on a more equitable level now, height-wise. It's a good looking cat, really – green eyes, well-cared for fur, well nourished. I guess if you're a talking cat, you're smart enough to take good care of yourself. Or if you're going to hallucinate one, might as well make it pretty.

"How'd you get in here?" I ask. "I'd notice the cold if a window was open."

"I've always been here. At least, longer than you." The voice is soft, with a little throaty rumble to it. It's not male, nor female – it's just cat.

123

"Don't think so – I would've remembered seeing a talking cat before, stands out from the other cats, you know."

The cat looks impossibly bored now, and resumes cleaning itself.

"Listen, this has been very entertaining, but I have to go. Keep your head down, Alex, and you just might make it through this." It leaps down from the counter and pads out of the kitchen and around the corner into the living room. Of course, when I take a look, there's nothing there.

A talking hallucinatory cat that knows my name – might have been a boring day without that.

I don't put a lot of trust in psychotherapy, psychiatry, all that head-shrinking stuff. People don't just fit in pigeon holes and they don't change just because they talk to someone willing to listen.

But, what the hell is happening in my head. Is the cat hallucination my subconscious trying to tell me something? *Yeah, don't trust Serapion.* Well no frickin' kidding, like I don't know that already.

Or maybe there's nothing deep to it at all. My brain is just misfiring and this is what comes out – bad dreams and talking cats. And what about Serapion? Either I'm a junkie on a downward spiral, going crazy, or according to him, I'm at the center of a battle across the universe.

Isn't that just my luck? No matter what direction I go, it comes out crap. Not too hard to figure out which is more likely: I'm a nothing, a nobody, and I'm not the pivotal figure in the play. Ergo, I'm crazy. Sort of comforting in a way, admitting that.

What's next, though? Have I just opened the gate that normally keeps the rampant craziness at bay?

No way of knowing, really. When it's all over I'll be able to look back, maybe, and say "yeah, shouldn't have done that."

Step back into the kitchen. There's a few stale crackers in the cupboard, so I grab them and head to the writing room. It shouldn't be called that, as such, since there's not a lot of writing that actually happens, but "tinkering room" just sounds wrong.

Accurate, mind you. I spend the rest of the day there, late afternoon until the night, sitting, reworking a little dialogue here and there, smoke a cigarette, eat a few crackers. Occasionally back to the kitchen for a drink of water, but for the most part, I stay put and rest my leg.

Chapter 12

I'm tired, but I'm awake, but I'm tired, but I'm awake. My body wants sleep, lusts after it. Probably would dream about sleep, if only I would lie down and let the dreams come. At the same time, though, I'm feeling tightly wound and awake. That's fine by me, totally happy to stave off dreaming for a little while longer. Sleep doesn't promise peace.

Hasn't for a while. My leg hurts on and off. When I find a comfortable position, it doesn't last. That's keeping me awake too – if it isn't a pervasive dull ache, it's a sharp, jolting stab.

Shuffle back to the couch and sit down. God, I feel old.

How much of what Serapion said is true? He could just be bullshitting me for his own amusement, or maybe he really does believe it all. Hanging out with fringe artists and the like, I've met plenty of people like that – crazy enough to believe some bat-shit weird stuff, but still able to hold down a job, keep themselves fed.

So, now I know why I'm having the dreams, assuming that Serapion was telling me the truth. Should be comforting to have that much, right? Knowing is half the battle and all that? Well, it probably would, if the reason was something other than my wizard roommate used my chest as a safety deposit box for a super high power skeleton key, which is slowly driving me insane, and attracting interested divine and demonic parties from all around.

That's not to mention the very real-looking cat, albeit a talking one. Okay, that's 100 percent hallucination, but one that seems to be dispensing reasonable advice.

I don't think I left anything out there, other than I'm scared shitless.

Staying in my apartment isn't good, because it doesn't distract me. I could sit on the corner. My peer group has abandoned it until morning, so I wouldn't have to speak to them. That'd suit me fine.

I don't like walking. Exercise in general has never appealed to me, and I wish I could just stay in my apartment, but sitting isn't relaxing, neither is lying down, and certainly I'm not sleeping.

So, I get out and walk.

The hookers are, of course, out for their evening stroll. They each give me an appraising glance, but quickly figure out I'm not buying and look away, scanning for more suitable customers.

Ain't that they're picky – I bet half of them would screw a pit-bull in a mudslide if it paid enough. Doesn't take a financial genius to figure out that I'm broke.

Once again, I'm sitting at the corner. Inescapable, like gravity. Sit alone, and watch the nightlife, which is almost exclusively hookers and their customers. Nobody else has a reason to be here this early in the morning.

Cops, I guess, but not very often, and it'd take someone being shot right in front of them to drag them from their warm car.

The only time I ever saw a woman dressed like a hooker out of popular culture – fishnet stockings, and 5-inch stripper heels – she was an undercover cop. As soon as I spotted her I knew something was up. In the winter, the girls wear coats, not mini-skirts.

The moment I saw her potential customer get busted stays with me, in a moment of artistic purity, his face filled with the anticipation of getting his rocks off, and the excitement and risk and "ain't I a bad boy." Then, confusion as a man steps out of a parked car, takes him by the arm and starts talking to him. Finally, his face losing its colour, and all the wonderful tingly emotions he was just feeling drain out of him, to be replaced with fear, doubt, and the dread at having to tell his wife what happened.

It was like a miniature play. I wanted to capture that range, that gritty human condition in my own writing. I tried, but I don't think I managed it. I could see what I wanted, see the whole scene in glorious detail, but making it translate into cold words on a page – more of a challenge than I was capable of. My script, my life.

So now I sit and watch the night traffic – car stops, woman walks over, gets in the car. Ten minutes later, she's back, strolling the sidewalk again. It's cold though, and after five minutes, I can feel the chill slowly creeping up through my boney hips. Time to move, before my ass freezes in place.

Standing up hurts my leg, so I shake some more pills down my throat. Running low, unfortunately, and I won't be able to get more. Nothing else I can do about it. When the pills are gone, hopefully my leg won't be hurting so much. Or maybe I'll panhandle enough money to get some more.

Until then, walking is free, and not as cold as sitting, and it keeps me from sleeping. So, I walk, sort of. My present limping shuffle resembles walking, and it gets me around.

The air has a dampness to it that I really hate, because it seems impossible to shake the chill it brings. Get cold, stay cold. I wouldn't mind winter otherwise, but this way, it starts worming into my coat.

One thing I *do* like about the cold is the clarity it brings, to thought, to vision. Now if only it could bring a little clarity to my life.

Walking out towards the bridge is a little more pleasant – the further I get from the tall buildings, the more the wind dies down. The bridge has some historical significance I guess, but I don't know much about it, other than it is named after some dude, presumably a local politician, definitely dead.

Underneath it flows a river, the original impetus for building a city here, an artery of trade and commerce, pre-railroad. In modern times, it transports, well, nothing really. During the summer you'll see the occasional boater, a couple of grumpy ducks and some decidedly unhappy fish. The bridge is low enough that some people go fishing off the side of it, but I don't really understand why. I don't get fishing as a hobby in general, but it isn't like you'd eat anything coming out of this river, and any fish you toss back in probably thinks "aw fuck" as soon as it re-enters the water.

Right now, though, it has a whole lot of ice. It's split in places, cracks as deep and wide as my hand, thanks to some up and down weather in January, and then a February of cold and wet, rather than the deep, to-the-core cold that it needs to freeze solid.

Except for desperate idiots like me, and the occasional car cruising by, the streets are deserted. When I see the two guys coming from the other direction, it makes me wonder just what they're up to. People like me don't normally walk with purpose, since we don't have anywhere important to go, and these two have a destination in mind. Other than the fact that one is taller than the other, they're pretty much nondescript. Nothing about them says, well, anything. They don't look like cops, or street people or anything in between. I'm not fond of mysteries.

They aren't talking, just walking straight ahead and paying no attention to me, until they're just about past me, when the shorter of the two turns to me.

"Hey bud, got a light?" he asks.

"Yeah, hold on a sec," I say, as I go through my pockets.
"Maybe I could bum one of those smokes off of you?"

And while I'm concentrating on finding my lighter, they attack. I'm grabbed by both guys, one yanks on my coat, the other my legs, and before I can even let out a yelp, I'm halfway over the rail and looking out into empty space.

Sheer animal instinct saves me. I manage to hook a foot against the rail, and tangle my hand in the coat of one of my attackers. I'm yelling and screaming too, total gibberish, but as loud as I can.

Going, going – it's just a matter of time, and a countdown of only a few seconds at that, before I'll be over the rail. But, I hold on, even though I know I will fail and die. Stupid old rat-like will to survive. Really I should let go, take my death like a man, but I'm far too cowardly to go out with anything approaching nobility.

Yes, I am fully aware of the irony of fighting for your life because you're a coward. Irony is a driving force in my life recently – and for what few moments remain.

But before they manage to chuck their burden off the bridge and into the river, there's a voice behind them. "Excuse me, but I believe you have something I want."

The taller of the two lets go of my legs and faces Serapion, jamming his hand inside his coat as he turns. The little guy keeps pushing at me, of course. I try to bite him but only get a mouthful of sleeve. I don't stop biting though; I'll hang onto whatever I can.

And the big guy pulls out... a whistle. Fighting for my life, I still double-take – yeah, he has a beat up old dog whistle, glinting under the street lights. I was expecting a gun or knife or something. Serapion takes it as a serious threat, though, throwing his arms wide and yelling.

All over, I feel my skin prickling, like recovering from having your foot fall asleep, but over my whole body. The air smells weird too.

Suddenly, the world is made entirely of white light and ear splitting noise. I start to slip off the edge, until I remember what the hell is happening to me and grab my attacker's coat again.

Just what *did* happen? I can't see anything but I can feel, and I'm not being pushed over the edge. Did Serapion knock him unconscious? Or kill him?

"Serapion? Are you there? What's happening?"

I know I'm talking, but I can't hear myself speak. Whatever happened has deafened me. If Serapion is answering me, I can't tell.

Doesn't matter though. I think he's dead, slumped over the rail and slipping fast, with me still clinging to him. There's nothing I can do to stop the fall. Inching, sliding, the body is coming over the rail with me.

I'm falling.

It's a small comfort that I can't see a bloody thing at the moment, flash-blinded by whatever the hell that was, because I can't see what's coming. Let me die, please, let me die.

I don't want to look down, I don't want to look down, even if I can't see. Please, just let it end. Here's hoping the fall kills me, because if it doesn't, then I'm going through the ice and the cold water can do the job.

In my mind, I have enough time to howl, and rant, and curse God and gravity and that stupid moron who is supposed to be my guardian angel, who fucking stands there yelling instead of just saving my ass.

Then, impact and an explosion of sparks across my flash-blinded vision. I thought it would've been louder, but it's a dull thud, and then complete silence.

I'm lying on my back, spread, with arms and legs flung wide. For a moment, I can't feel a thing and there's a sudden panic that I'm a cripple now.

Small mercy, the pain hits a second or so later – just about every inch of my body feels like it's on fire, making me grit my teeth and writhe

I don't know where I am. I mean, I know, the bridge, the fall, the ice. But, there's a disorientation. Can't see, or hear, can't really figure out which way is up. Everything hurts and makes it tough to figure out if I'm lying on my back or my belly, or what.

One by one, the systems come on line. I realize I'm rolling side to side in my pain, and that I keep bumping into something on my left. Then I can tell, it's the guy who fell off the bridge with me.

He's not moving – I think he must be hurt worse than me, or maybe he's unconscious. When my hearing comes back, I can tell he's not groaning, and eventually pick up that he's not breathing either.

Geez, he's dead. I'm lying next to a dead guy, and for sure I don't want to be. I need to move.

Arms, check. Legs, check. The smell of burnt coat, hair and flesh hangs in the air. I can feel everything, so I guess I didn't break my back. Yeah, holy cow, I can feel everything, and all of it hurts.

"Don't stand up," says a voice from above me. When my vision finally clears, I see Serapion's silhouette is leaning over the rail, looking down at the two bodies sprawled on the ice. One of the bodies gives him the finger. Way I'm feeling, I wasn't going to stand up any time soon anyway.

"The ice is patchy in sections. If you get up or try to walk to shore, you're liable to go in."

Great, the impact didn't kill me, so now I'm in a race between drowning and freezing to death.

Lying on my back, I could get a great view of the stars if they weren't washed out by the street lights shining down from the bridge, or blocked out by the bridge itself. Wish I knew something about astronomy. I could pick out the Big Dipper, which means I could find Polaris too, I think. That pretty much exhausts my knowledge.

Not much to see down here either.

"Serapion, what the hell happened up there? I was fighting that guy and then there was this incredible light."

"Yeah," he says. "I called down lightning. It was the expedient thing to do."

Serapion called goddamn lightning down from the sky. And I'm lying next to a dead man who was very vigorously trying to kill me as little as two minutes ago.

It's damned impossible, starting with lightning from a clear, cloudless sky, followed by the fact that neither Serapion nor I were fried by it, and lastly, who calls down lightning like they're ordering pizza?

An angel, that's who.

He really is an angel, sent to protect me. Damn.

"Serapion, aren't you going to rescue me?"

"Can't."

"Can't? You just blasted two people into barbecue ribs, but you can't get me off the ice? What are you? Allergic?"

"You're not technically in danger at the moment, and my rules of engagement are very clear."

"What do you mean not in danger?" I say. "I'm standing on a frickin' ice floe."

"No you're not, you're lying down. And you're in as much peril as you were when you were standing up here."

"Well, what if I decided to just walk to shore?"

"Wouldn't recommend it, that's pretty treacherous ice."

"But if it cracked, you'd be forced to save me."

"No, I'd be forced to let you die."

"What the hell? Get me off this ice!"

"No, really I can't," Serapion says. "If you decide to walk, it's your own choice. I cannot interfere with your free will. You stand up, your choice. You try to walk to shore, your choice. You die while doing so, not my problem."

"So go for help."

"No can do. You're a sitting duck there, and I'm not going to risk anything nasty showing up for you while I'm gone." Serapion looks around. "Besides, someone will come soon. Meantime, sit tight."

So, I stay where I am. Goddamn guardian angel, should damn well fly down here and rescue me. Or, he shouldn't have let me fall in the first place. Like in that old movie It's a Wonderful Life. At least *that* angel didn't let a guy fall off a bridge.

It doesn't take long before the cold of the ice worms its way into my clothes. I was already cold. Now I'm, what, ultra-cold? My teeth are chattering.

"Spread out the dead guy's coat and lie on that. It isn't much, but it should help."

I would prefer to pretend there isn't a corpse lying next to me, or barring that, I wish it wasn't within arm's reach.

But, freezing is freezing, and I lose my distaste soon enough. Carefully, so that I don't shift around too much on the ice, and likewise, avoiding any contact with the dead guy, I manage to pull his coat out a bit so I have something to lie on.

Several times, the ice lets out an ominous crack, and I stop dead. *Don't use that term, Alex.* I have nothing against dead people, but there's not much to build a relationship on.

Serapion is still leaning over the rail, looking down at me.

"See anyone?"

He scans right and left. "Nope."

"Man, I could use a cigarette right now." It is dawning on me that it's been too long since I've had a smoke. I'd have the shakes really bad right now, if I weren't shivering so much.

"Give me a second," says Serapion. He disappears from view, but he's back in less than half a minute and tosses down a pack of smokes. They hit me dead center on my chest.

"Where'd you get these? They look pretty beat up."

He snorts. "I looted a dead body. Didn't think he'd mind."

An image flashes in my imagination of what the other stiff must look like, up on the bridge where the light is. Man gets killed by lightning, can't be too pretty.

I would swear the cigarettes in my hand smells of death.

Whatever you do, don't think of the corpse next to you.

For a moment, my craving for a cigarette pops its head up and complains, but it gets shouted down by my stomach, which currently wants to puke all over the ice. I just may have discovered an entirely new method of breaking nicotine addiction, but much like the way I overcome writers block, there's not much to recommend it.

My current surroundings don't provide much to take my mind off my troubles, so I look back up at Serapion. Backlit by the streetlights, all I can really make out a black silhouette. I can't see a goddamn thing.

"Why can't you rescue me, again?"

"Like I told you, free will. You're not in immediate danger, and whatever you do to rescue yourself is outside of my ability to control, or interfere with. You drown on your own time, Alex."

"You told me that before, but it still doesn't mean anything to me. Why?"

I hear him sigh. "Because that's the limitation of being an angel. We can't affect whether you choose good or evil, salvation or damnation, cheeseburgers versus tofu. Just the way things are."

"What about the dead guy down here? Seems to me you interfered with his free will in a big way."

"The hell I did. First of all, if he didn't want to be blasted by lightning, there was nothing stopping him from standing somewhere else. Besides, now he can file a complaint direct with the head office. Second, he was not what I would call exactly human."

"What the hell does that mean? Either something is human or it isn't. What, you think they're androids or something?" I don't know what his game is, but I still don't feel comfortable. Bad enough that I'm lying beside a corpse; even worse if that corpse is … something else.

"Don't bother trying to figure it out," he says. "You aren't up to the job, intellectually. It's a very human insistence on thinking of things being what they appear. A man is a man, a building is a building. As long as you can hang onto your sanity, that's a comfortable reality for you to work with."

Serapion doesn't say anything after that for a while. I shut up too.

"That's partly why you are in the mess you're in," he says. "Not your present situation, mind you, but in a larger sense. I'm here to protect you, but I can't protect you from yourself. I'm not your mom. If you want to drink yourself into a stupor, or shoot up, or walk into traffic, so be it, fill your boots."

"Hey," I say. "You *did* stop me from walking into traffic – saved my life."

I can almost hear Serapion rolling his eyes. "Dumb-ass, you weren't walking, you were standing. The bus jumped the curb and I was obligated to act; same as when you were about to get punched out. Right now, though, unless that ice under you decides to crack, I'm not budging."

My hips and shoulders are really starting to ache from the cold, as is my back, as is my butt. The bit of coat I'm lying on doesn't provide much insulation. Can't walk around to stay warm. Hell, can't even sit up to change my position. Rubbing my hands on my legs doesn't help at all – just makes my hands cold.

"Hey," I call. "What if I get frostbite? Lose a couple of toes? I might get gangrene. Would you have to intervene then?"

Serapion thinks it over. "Yeah, I guess so," he says. "But, you don't have frostbite yet."

I want to ask him how he'd know, but the answer won't be satisfying.

Crap. Looks like it'll be a long time until morning.

Finally I give in and light up a cigarette. Boredom, cold, dark, cravings, they all conspire against my resolve.

The cigarette tastes good, though. Being hit by lightning doesn't seem to have harmed it, at least not in the important ways. The nicotine hits me with a punch and a rush, as I suck the smoke back into my lungs.

Once again, I try and fail to blow smoke rings, puffing streams of smoke up above me, to be faintly illuminated by the meagre streetlight. Then again, with nothing to do but practice, I keep trying.

"Hey," I call up. "What was with the whistle the one guy had?"

"It was a dog whistle."

"Yeah. I saw. What was the big deal about that? You allergic to high-pitched noises, as well as ice?"

I hear Serapion hawk and spit, hear it land on the ice somewhere close to me. Asshole. "What responds to a dog whistle, moron?"

Oh. Right. Dogs.

"If he had blown that whistle, you just might have ended up like your buddy Dingle."

Considering that it was supposed to have been me dead in the alley and not Dingle, it'd be poetic justice for the dogs to get me now. I'm safe from them down here though, no way they'd come on the ice. Safe, yeah. One could almost forget what sort of situation one was in, except for the corpse, the freezing cold, and the fear of going through the ice and drowning. Yeah, don't want to think about all of that too much, lest I get shit-scared and do something stupid.

"Is that what you meant earlier about something nasty coming by? Dogs?"

"Dogs are a possibility, but not the only one. There are things on the prowl that you most definitely do not want to see."

I lie there, occasionally rolling onto my other side, contemplating that idea. And I wait.

"Hey Serapion," I say. "What happens to us after we die?"

"What are you, a five year old?" he grunts. "Fine, you go to heaven and you get to play with kittens and ride ponies all day long, and at night you sleep in a big princess bed."

"Hey now, I was just asking a question."

"And it was a dumb question. You don't have the faculties to understand the answer if I gave it to you. In fact, you don't have enough on the ball to comprehend just how dumb you are."

I chew on my lip for a bit. "Well, can I ask a question?"

"Of course you can. You can do whatever you want to. Free will, remember? Whether or not I answer your question is still to be revealed."

Well, here goes nothing. "So something I've been wondering: Is there free will in heaven? I mean, you're a good guy, you get into heaven. They're about to start in on the fifth or sixth rendition of the million names of God, and instead, you decide to go do something really sinful. Can you actually do that in heaven?"

I can hear him shift his weight from foot to foot. "It's complicated."

"So you can't sin in heaven?"

"You could, you just…won't want to."

"So," I say, feeling the smallest sliver of smug. "There's no free will in heaven. Whether or not I *could* choose to sin, I won't, which to me seems to be the same as saying I can't."

"It's complicated," is all Serapion says in response.

There's another long silence, interrupted only by the sounds of me shifting around, trying to find a different part of my body to take on the cold for a while, and the occasional far off sounds of the city. When the hell is someone going to pass by? Is Serapion even *trying* to get help? My nose is running now, making me snort constantly to deal with it. Every time I do, I taste blood. I'm trying to spit it as far as possible, but that's not easy when you're lying on your side. Hope I'm not drooling all over myself.

His voice cuts the silence.

"You people have really screwed things up when it comes to religion. It's like you're all obsessed with over-complicating everything about it. Rules, laws, dogma, apologetics, discourses, interpretations … and then holy wars when your text inevitably disagrees with your neighbour's text."

"Hey now," I say. "That's sort of a cheap shot considering you told me you're part of a holy war too."

"Nothing holy about it," he says. "You're confusing your little wars where rulers use their made-up religions to justify what they're doing. It's nothing more than a tarted-up version of the regular ones. In the end, they're still fighting for territory, or resources, or influence."

"And your wars?" I ask.

"Perhaps nothing different, in that sense. The scale is much greater though, in terms of time, and of space and the power we can exert on the fabric of the universe. Also, we don't harbour illusions about why we're fighting – we've no need for a propaganda campaign to win over the troops."

I could gauge the passing of time by the movement of the stars, if I could actually see them creep out from behind the bulk of the bridge. Okay, no, I couldn't – no idea how long it takes for stars to move across the night sky but at least it gives me something to do. If one of my street compatriots was down here instead of me, it probably wouldn't be such a bad stretch. Typically, I don't think there's much happening behind their eyes. No internal monologue, no getting bored. Easy for them.

Me, though, I've got a demented monkey for a brain. Always jumping, running, digging into things. It's a pain in the ass, because it means I never get anything done. Three-quarters of the way through and I'll get bored and move on to the next thing. Right now, there's no next thing for me to jump to.

I'm on my seventh or eighth cigarette, and getting mighty twitchy with the nicotine jitters competing against my body shivering, when I see the light up on the bridge. Flashing lights, cops I guess.

Some dude pokes his head over the bridge rail and yells down "Anybody there?"

It takes me two attempts to yell back, I'm so cold.

The silhouette waves. "Okay, hang in there and we'll get you out in a jiffy."

A jiffy, I think, *great, sounds like I'm being rescued by my dad.*

There's more voices up there now, and I can hear them moving around. My eyes ache suddenly, as they open up a bunch of floodlights, filling the space below the bridge with light. It's like a cavern up there, with icicle stalactites and a century's worth of bird shit clinging to the girders.

Once my eyes adjust, I get to see everybody peering down at me. Cops are there, as I guessed. Fire department, maybe some paramedics. I don't particularly like getting attention from the authorities, and this is a lot of people. The whole bridge is lit up with vehicle lights, blinking and flashing red and blue.

"How's your buddy down there?" calls the same voice. I can see him now. Yes, it's a cop, and yes, if my father was still alive, they'd be of an age, somewhere in their 60's.

"He ain't my buddy, and just between you and me, I think he's dead."

The voice doesn't say anything more and I'm left with my thoughts – thoughts like, where the hell is Serapion? Is he up there? And what do I tell the cops? *No, I don't know who the dead guys are, but they tried to kill me, until an angel smote them Old Testament-style with a big ass lightning bolt. Oh, and they're not quite human.*

Yeah, right. Never been in a psych ward before – bet they have some absolutely awesome drugs. Well, it'll probably be another half hour or more before they can get me up there, so it would be time well spent to come up with a story.

I think I'm fucked.

"I thought you would just pull me up," I call up.

"No can do. If you're injured, that would just make things worse. You just stay right where you are and we'll come to you."

I hate waiting, and I've been on this ice for hours now. "I'm fine, lower a rope and pull me the hell up."

They ignore me.

Over on the shore now, I can see a few people getting geared up to come out on the ice. Damn, I was hoping they'd use a crane or something like that. How many other times in my life would I get the chance to ride a crane? Nope, looks like they've got harnesses, and ropes. Two of them for me, and two for my unwanted companion.

I'll hand it to them; they make it over to me pretty fast. Guess they don't want to be out on the ice any more than I do. As they cross, I can hear the ice crack under them, even though they're crawling. I would've gone through trying to walk to shore, no doubt in my mind. They don't talk, just get to work instead. I can't see what they're doing with the dead guy, but then again, I don't really care much either. Get my tired and frozen ass off here and take me somewhere warm.

Gear gets laid out next to me, including a big yellow backboard. The board opens up down the middle, making it look like a giant, deformed Pac Man, poised to eat me. Best behaviour, Alex. *Don't laugh and make the nice men think you're crazy. That'll come soon enough.*

When the two halves snap shut under me, it damn near bites off a chunk of my ass. I let out a yelp and "careful, assholes!" but nobody responds.

Quickly, brusquely, I'm strapped in, and I'm sliding my way to shore.

There's a neck brace holding my head immobile so all I can see is what is directly above me - the sky, shot with the beginnings of false dawn. Occasionally I catch a glimpse one of the rescue guys, as they carry me. Nobody looks at me, or talks to me. My head is strapped into immobility so looking around is out of the question.

Off the ice, up the slope of the riverbank, and onto the bridge, and still no one talks to me.

The backboard is laid down on something, not dropped exactly, but placed with less care than I would have thought customary. Care is, I suspect, reserved for the more stable, tax-paying citizens of this fair city. My view of the sky is replaced by the ceiling of the ambulance, as they slide me in the back.

A face looms into view above mine, coming in at an angle. A woman, and an attractive one at that. I've seen her before, and it takes me a few seconds to figure out where. Dingle. Yeah. She was one of the people dealing with what was left of him.

Should have figured she wasn't someone I see on a day-to-day basis. For one thing, she doesn't look like hell. For another, the cops aren't arresting her.

With nothing else to do, I take the opportunity to study her face, scope her out. Again, I like what I see – black hair cut short, and dark, dark eyes. Can't figure out her ethnicity, though – Hispanic, maybe? No, that's not right, but I can't pin it down. She smells good too, the clean smell of soap.

I'm so busy checking her out, that I totally miss what she asked me. Typical. If I were in a bus going over a cliff, I'd probably use the opportunity to peek down the shirt of the woman next to me. We all have priorities.

"Uh, sorry, again please?"

"I asked you what your name was," she says. There's no annoyance in her voice. She's had to do this a thousand times before.

"Alex Mackie. We meet again."

"We do?"

"Yeah," I say. "I was friends with the dead guy in the alley yesterday – the dog attack? I saw you there."

She nods, remembering, and then moving on. "Okay, Alex Mackie, how are you doing?"

"Not bad, considering. My nose itches, though."

There's a hint of a smile. "We aim to please," she says, scratching my nose.

"You're a brave woman."

"I'm wearing gloves."

While we're talking, her hands are probing me for injuries, my head, my neck, chest, belly. "Listen, I'm only going to let you feel me up for another 20 minutes or so before I ask you to stop, okay?"

I can hear her smirk. "I'll try and respect your limits."

There's a little draft of cold air as she peeks underneath the towel wrapped around my calf.

"What happened to your leg, Alex?"

"Dog. I must smell like gravy."

"You and your friend don't get along with dogs, I take it," she says, and I can hear the scissors as they cut open my pant leg.

I try to shrug, but the neck restraint makes it impossible. "Well, some people just prefer cats."

She makes a noncommittal noise and keeps checking me over. I'm not enjoying it. Yes, it's the most contact I've had with a woman since … in a long time. However, it isn't exactly a fantasy of mine to be strapped to a board while it happens. It's a mood-killer. Frankly, I just want to be lying down on my couch, getting warm again, smoking a cigarette or a joint and thinking about absolutely goddamn nothing at all.

"Listen, I'm fine," I call out. "How about you stitch up my leg, give me something for the pain, and a tetanus shot, and I'll be on my way."

"First, we don't do the stitching or the shots – you need to be at the hospital for that," she says. "Second, you're already on the board, and in the ambulance, you'd be better off if you let us take you in, and get your leg looked after. Be nice to the nurse and maybe she'll scrounge up some of that hospital food I hear everyone raving about. I think I saw chipped beef and jello on the menu."

"Wow, you sure do know how to sweeten a deal. Really, I'm fine. I'd rather just go back to my apartment."

"They have coffee."

Damn, my Achilles heel. "I bet it tastes like crap, though."

"Of course, but it's better than the chipped beef and there's plenty of it."

She's got a nametag pinned to her jacket. Alana, it says. Just a first name and a five-digit number. Wonder what I would have to do to get a last name out of her, or a phone number. Step 1 would be: don't be a lowlife who hallucinates. Sure, but get that out of the way and I'm betting on the Alex Mackie charm to win the day. As long as

138

you don't care what a woman thinks of you tomorrow, it ain't so hard to talk them into the sack today.

Seeing the flashing lights of the police cars casting their little multi-coloured blips of light on the ceiling of the ambulance reminds me of where I am, and what is happening. There's a bunch of cops waiting on the bridge for me and they're not going to just escort me home. This morning's adventure is going to be reams of paperwork for them anyway, and I'm sure it's disappointing not to have a warm body to show for it afterwards. Two corpses and no answers.

Options, options, options. Do I decline the trip to the hospital and go directly to jail, or let the pretty paramedic do her work while I flirt with her, take a ride, maybe get fixed up with some drugs, and after that, get arrested?

Well, if I'm going to jail anyway...

"All right, sweetheart, do your thing."

While I was thinking, she kept working. She knew what I was going to answer, even if I hadn't figured it out yet. I always thought it would be great if I could find the secret to the patterns of people – how they respond, what they're going to do. I guess the first step would be to actually give a shit about people. If I cared about them then maybe I'd pay attention to what motivates them.

Her voice is close by me. "Okay, Alex, we'll be on the road in just a minute."

It's a rare experience, being treated nicely by someone, at least for me. Part of that is environment – my friends, if you can call them that, are rightfully primarily concerned with survival. There's very little room left for altruism.

The other part of that is me. Most definitely I don't make it easy on a friend. I lie to them, cheat on them and generally take advantage of the relationship.

Wow, that's pretty unpleasant, when I think about it, but that's not 100 percent me. I'm also the guy who's always got a joke, or ... Or what? Is there anything left in me that makes me a worthwhile human being?

The ambulance makes a little lurch. She's true to her word, and we're on the move. Probably just miss the morning rush hour traffic – prime begging time, if I wasn't strapped to a board and packed into the meat wagon. Then again, considering my luck lately, begging wouldn't have been very profitable anyway. That's why I like begging with Dingle – he's the perfect foil to my technique, the good cop versus my smart-mouthed one.

Then I remember the reality of things. Dingle is dead. Shit, yeah.

"Hey, how come I don't get any sirens?"

"Because you're not dying," she says. "Better luck next time."

Figures. Only time I've been in an ambulance and I don't get sirens. What a rip-off.

Life is just one big disappointment. And then you die. And after that, presuming there's an afterlife, probably more disappointment.

Drive, stop, drive, stop, turn a corner, drive some more. Traffic seems heavy already. I can hear the two of them gossiping away, and the occasional chatter of voices on the radio. I've got nothing to add to the conversation, so I keep my mouth shut.

Very slowly, I'm starting to warm up under the blankets they tossed over me. God, it feels good.

The ambulance pulls to a stop and the back doors open. A little cold air puffs in. "All right," says a voice, not the woman. "Last stop, everyone off the bus."

"Great," I say, to the roof of the ambulance. "Hope you don't mind if I just lie here."

"No problem, door-to-door service," he says, unlatching the stretcher and pulling it out into the open air.

Out of the ambulance, and into the hospital. The stretcher bumps around a little, as we travel. Outdoors, indoors, down a hall, around a corner and I'm still staring at the ceiling, watching the lights go by as we go, before stopping somewhere, in a corridor. People are talking all around me, but I can't see anything but up. I can hear the paramedic talking to someone, and probably about me. I like the sound of her voice – warm honey tones and confidence. Then I'm on the move again, down a hallway and around a corner. We stop, and almost immediately, I feel the brief sensation of flight as the backboard gets moved off the stretcher and onto a gurney. I can hear the rails get pulled up, to lock with a definite clack.

She drifts into view again, and again at a weird angle. If it weren't for the neck brace I wouldn't be able to resist trying to crank around to see her face straight on.

"Okay, Alex, this is where we part company. We're having a busy morning and I have to go. Sorry about the straps and collar, but they have to stay on until a doctor can take a look and clear you for spinal injuries."

"No problem. As first dates go, I think this went pretty well."

She laughs. It's a good sound. "I've already briefed the nurse about you, and she'll be right with you. I told her you weren't a problem case, so don't be a jerk, okay? If you're still here by the time I come through again, I'll say hi."

"Thanks. I'd like to complement you for probably being the sanest person I've had the pleasure of meeting in a while."

"Alex," she says. "That is without a doubt the oddest compliment I've ever been paid. Remember what I said – be nice to the nurses."

And then she disappears from view, and unfortunately I'm left alone again. Considering how much time I spend wishing people would just fuck off and leave me alone, it's pretty hypocritical of me to want someone to talk with right now. The need for human companionship is built into us, I guess. We aren't much more than herd animals, seeking the company of others. Convince a bunch of sheep to stand on their hind legs, clip the wool off of them, and voila, you've got commuters waiting for the morning train to work. Oddballs like me resist the urge to herd as long as we can, but eventually we're drawn in.

Plus, I want the goddamn nurse to come and undo the straps. I want the paramedic back here so I can flirt some more. It felt good. It felt human.

So I wait. After sitting all night on an ice floe at the bottom of a bridge, I am really tired of waiting, but strapped to a board, there ain't much more I can do.

Noises, rubber wheels on floor tiles, curtains being drawn open or closed. Voices float all around – close, far, drifting past. Can't tell if I'm the subject of conversation. Man, what an ego I have. I wonder if the cops are here, waiting for a doctor to check me out, and pronounce me fit for incarceration. A couple times I think I hear my last name, spoken low by male voices – yeah, definitely cops.

I've never been in jail before, which may come as a surprise to the casual onlooker but it's true. And considering that it never made it onto my list of 50 things to do before I die, I have little wish to do so.

Geez, yeah, I actually did do such a list, back when I was in college. Wow, haven't thought about that for a long time. But, then again, ain't like I've got much else to do but wait and think.

There's a few that got checked off: have sex in a public place, Mardi Gras in New Orleans, sex in a moving vehicle … Plenty still on the list, though: go skydiving, visit the seven wonders of the world, have sex atop the seven wonders of the world, drive a race car.

That was mostly back when I was young, ambitious, idealistic, but before I became an artsy fuckup.

And, I always figured that if I was in jail, it would be sitting next to a friend, saying *"that was fucking awesome!"* Not much chance of that these days. First, I don't have any friends left, and second, I don't get to have stuff in my life that deserves to be called awesome.

The thoughts have barely finished flitting across my mind before it hits me just how whiney I'm being. But, I don't deserve just a little bit? My life is fucked, my mind and body are fucked; it's the perfect time to whine.

Yeah.

I wonder if they'll have to give me an x-ray? Probably, no telling what stuff I've broken internally. Could be bleeding to death just lying here, for all I know. Will they be able to see the key? I'd love to see their faces while they try and figure out what it is.

With no warning, something gets dropped on my chest. It's light and soft, compact, like a bundle of something. Like a rolled up blanket maybe? Whatever it is, it startles me enough to let out a "hey, watch it," to whoever threw it, even though it didn't hurt.

No one answers. And then, the package starts to move, taking distinct, light steps up my chest. I can't see it, and I can't bat it away with my hands. Just before I scream for a nurse, though, the cat's face comes into view, less than a hand span away from my nose. Makes my eyes feel funny trying to focus on something so close.

"You need to learn to talk less, and listen a great deal more," it says. "Especially to me."

Little needles of pain start dotting my chest, along with tiny rip, rip, rip noises.

"What the hell are you doing?"

"Getting comfortable for our little chat. Won't be but a moment."

Rip, rip, rip, as its claws knead and grasp at my shirt and chest. The cat takes its time settling down. I can feel the warmth of its body.

"So," it says. "I see you've been ignoring my advice."

"What advice?"

"That you shouldn't be so quick to trust your angel."

"Why shouldn't I trust him?"

"You should stop asking me questions," it says. "You ask me, because while I answer, you get to avoid thinking about the problems I'm putting in front of you."

"You're crazy," I say before remembering that I'm the one talking to a hallucination. Stupid irony. "Serapion saved my life a couple of hours ago. What have you done for me lately?"

All I want, in the whole entire world at this very moment, is to fold my arms across my chest, enjoy a cigarette, and ignore the cat sitting six inches away from my nose. "You know, I'm going to laugh my ass off if a nurse chases you out of here with a broom. That'd put a real dent in your air of superiority."

The cat is unfazed. "No one will be bothering us. It is becoming a very busy day for medical personnel across the city. Your key is responsible for that."

"Ain't my key," I mumble.

"Indeed. The problem is, Alex, you think like a dog."

"I don't understand what that means."

"It means that on some level, you'll trust anybody who gives you food and a pat on the head."

Do I? Is that what I am? That's just stupid. "I'm the least-trusting person I know. C'mon, I've screwed over so many people that there has got to be a line-up of people wanting to take a swing at me."

"Trustworthy and trusting are not the same thing. And besides, you trust them – that has nothing to do with your inevitable betrayal of them. Why do you trust Serapion?"

"Why should I trust you instead? Isn't like you've given me any reason to believe what you have to say."

"Don't be ridiculous," it sniffs. "I'm a cat. You can trust me."

"I'm supposed to trust something that cleans itself with its tongue?"

"And you rarely clean yourself at all. What does that tell you about yourself?"

I don't have a comeback for that, and I think the cat knows it. "There's not a lot I can do about trusting or not trusting him right now," I say, shifting around a bit against the straps to emphasize my point.

"First," says the cat. "You need to think more like a cat. The enemy of my enemy is *not* necessarily my friend."

I roll my eyes. "In concrete terms, for Christ's sake. I've had enough with everybody's aphorisms."

The cat stares at me silently, in the way that only a cat does, that somehow allows a tiny little animal to make you feel stupid and slow. "Don't go back to your apartment, Alex. It will seem like a good idea, but don't do it."

Before I can ask why, there's a definite change in the air. I feel it, and the way the cat snaps its head around, it feels it too. Things have gotten distinctly quiet in the hallway.

143

Without another word, the cat leaps from my chest, and I'm alone again.

In the end, I'm always alone.

"All right, Mr. Mackie, I'm here to give you your enema," says a voice, from outside of my field of vision. It takes me a second before I recognize it.

"Holy crap, where the hell have you been?"

"Busy," says the angel. "What do you say you and me go for a walk?"

"I don't know if that's such a good idea. The docs haven't checked me out yet."

Serapion makes a noise through pursed lips as he comes into view. "I know I phrased it as a question, but I really don't mean it that way."

I give him the best dubious look one can give while strapped into immobility. "Doesn't matter how you phrase it, I'm still not going to leap to my feet."

He vanishes from view, quickly enough that I'm forced to blink against the sudden reappearance of the light on the ceiling.

And then the gurney starts moving.

"Are you really supposed to be doing that?"

"I'm an angel of the Lord. Of course I am."

"What if someone catches us?"

Serapion lets out a snort. "What, you worried you'll get arrested? Dumb-ass, that was already going to happen. You can't be *more* arrested. Now sit tight and enjoy the ride."

The lights overhead flash by, slowly first, and then increasingly, and worryingly quickly. We round a corner far too fast, the wheels on one side thumping back down on the floor when we're back on the straightaway. I can't do anything but clench the sheet under me.

"Jesus, Serapion, slow down."

"No time for that," he says. "Don't worry. I've got you."

"That's what I'm worried about. You're going to flip the damn gurney."

"You worry too much," he says. "Would you rather I leave you where you're eventually going to get arrested?"

Truthfully, that's not looking like such a bad alternative. Get picked up by the cops, or have my teeth knocked out when we wipe out on a corner.

Serapion ignores me, of course. The lights continue to zip by and then we stop.

"Serapion?"

"Shhh." Then a bell dings, and I can hear the elevator doors open. For sure, then, we're not leaving the same way we came in. Gurney in, doors close, elevator goes down. The Girl From Ipanema is playing softly in the background. I hate that song. Serapion is humming along with it.

Down one floor, door opens, and we take off again at rocket pace.

"Undo the straps and get me off this stupid gurney!"

"Later," says the angel. "I'm in a hurry."

"What? Undo the goddamn straps!"

"Hey," says Serapion. "I can't figure out how to get my DVD player to work, let alone figure these things out."

"You watch television?"

"No, dumb-ass. I'm an angel. I don't have a television, a favourite soap opera, or a place to sit and watch it."

All I can see is the damned lights, but I can hear plenty. People talking, a floor polisher, telephones ringing – they all fly past us. If anybody thinks anything odd about us, we're long past before they can do anything about it.

Serapion barks out a laugh, and comes into view, looming over me. "Sounds like they just figured out you're missing."

"How's that?"

He indicates the PA speaker on the ceiling with his thumb – *"paging Dr. Strong. Dr. Strong to the ER, please,"* it squawks.

"Who's that?"

"It's a distress code, moron." He vanishes from sight and the gurney starts moving again. The first set of doors catch me by surprise, as Serapion batters them open with the gurney. The second set of doors, I'm already gritting my teeth, so the impact isn't as jarring.

By contrast, the third set of doors is almost boring.

"Well," he says. "That was fun." We slow down to a reasonable pace. Serapion is taking his time, strolling along.

"Wouldn't it be better for us to wait until a doctor takes a look at me? What if there's something seriously wrong with me?"

"You mean something more serious than an incredibly powerful artefact in your chest that could spell the end of the world? Trust me, if I don't get you out of here, a boo-boo on your leg is truly going to be the least of your worries."

I chew on my lip over that. "Listen, I really think this is a bad idea."

"You thought it was a bad idea to go to the hospital in the first place. Now that you're here, you want to stay. Let me know when you've made up your mind."

"Why the big rush?"

"Will you stop being a pain in the ass if I tell you?"

"Yeah."

"Because things are accelerating a bit faster than expected. Lots of uncertainty at the moment and it's making a lot of people nervous."

"What people?"

"Well," says Serapion. "Not exactly people. Things, then. Anyway, I'm concerned that we're going to have … things … sniffing around very soon. Hard enough to protect you when you're strapped to a plank, it'll be just as hard or worse, if you're in a jail cell. Time is running out, and I've got to get you to safety."

"How much time?"

"I don't know, and that's what makes me anxious to move - especially now, since your large, loud friend is presently hogtied and lying on a cell floor. Just our luck, you'd find yourself in a cell next to him."

Well, if he's locked up, he's not a problem."

"No, but he won't be for long."

I laugh. "Okay, listen. I know you're an angel and all that, so you can be excused for not knowing how the whole jail thing works. They've got him on a handful of charges that I can think of. Even if they decided he's just a crazy wino and it isn't worth going through with everything, they'll still hold him overnight at the very least."

"No," says Serapion, with finality. "He's getting out."

Again I laugh. "Oh sure, he eloquently convinced a judge that he's obviously not a flight risk, paid his bail and he's out – all in, what, an hour or two?"

"Laugh all you want. He's getting out."

I can hear the rail on the gurney unlock and snap down. One by one, Serapion undoes the straps, and I get to reclaim body parts. My head, my arms, my legs. Slowly sit up, wary of dizziness or anything like that. When I'm confident I'm not going to fall over or pass out, I swing my legs over the side of the gurney and slide off, to stand on a concrete floor.

"C'mon," says Serapion. "We really have to move it."

"Give me a break. I feel like shit."

"Things will be much worse if you don't speed it up."

"What things?"

He turns to face me, so fast that I flinch, thinking he's going to hit me.

"Explanations can come later, but right now, we need to get you to your apartment, and pronto. Beaudry spent a lot of time putting some pretty hefty magical protection into that building. You'll be safe there."

I'm about to ask Serapion what he's talking about but I think I already know. Despite the people sleeping in the lobby and pissing in the stairwell, there was never any real trouble – no fights, no fire alarms, and no break-ins. A relative sea of calm.

"Through here," he says, and slams the crash bar on a pair of beat-up metal doors. Just like that, we're outside. An alleyway, strewn with garbage and snow. The door slams shut behind us. It's cold out here, not just because I've been indoors for the last hour or so, but also my pant leg is cut open and my towel gone who knows where, and the frosty air clings to my bare calf.

There's a pair of dumpsters in the alley, and out of reflex, I want to take a peek inside to see if there's anything worth scavenging. I guess painkillers would be out of the question, but there could be plenty of other stuff.

"Alex," says Serapion. "Keep moving."

"Yeah." Damn, I've sunk low. Going through someone's trash has become a viable life option. Limp my way down the alley. The snow isn't too bad here, but that's not going to be the case everywhere. Hopefully Serapion is okay with us walking on well-travelled routes, because I'm not up to climbing over snow banks.

"Things are going to be getting very weird," he says.

"What do you mean by weird? I thought we were already at that point."

Serapion guffaws. "Nope. We're getting towards the end of the game, so all of the players are throwing down whatever cards they've still got in their hands. Everybody wants that key of yours."

"Ain't mine, goddamn it, and I wish I didn't have it." I feel what he's talking about, though. Feeling an unpleasant body buzz, and sounds aren't registering quite right.

The wind, it can't decide which direction it's blowing from – little gusts seem to come from everywhere, swirling about me, buffeting me. Stinging snow blasts me face on, needling my skin, pushing against me, trying to hold me back.

"Fight through it, Alex. We need to keep going."

"What if it gets worse?"

"It won't. Or, it will until something else interferes."

"I don't get it," I shout, to be heard above the shrieking wind.

And just like that, the winds die down.

"Keep moving. There are still battles going on, even if you're not aware of them. Likely this is only temporary. From this point on, everything you experience will probably be fighting for control."

He turns at a corner. "This way," he says. It's a parking lot, empty of cars, which is weird both because it's downtown, and because it's a weekday morning. Should be wall-to-wall with cars, but it is completely empty. Hell, there's an even layer of snow over the whole thing, untouched, with not a single boot print.

Except for one thing – crows, dozens and dozens of them. All over the damn lot, like they've got some sort of convention or something. Not a single one is making any noise or flying about. They just stand there.

"Serapion, are you sure this is a good idea?"

"Of course I am. They're just birds, for crying out loud."

"Birds acting strangely. I'm not big on strange animals lately."

He casts me a dubious glance, and kicks one of the birds like a football. It lets out a squawk, flaps a bit, but otherwise doesn't do anything to right the insult.

Serapion is striding along, kicking birds out of his path. The damned things don't seem worried about his approach, and shrug off being launched by the tip of his boot. I try to follow closely. Maybe they're just acting casual for him, and as soon as his back is turned, they're going to pounce on me and inflict the death of a thousand pecks on me.

"If you want me to go faster, you could take my arm and help me walk, or something." Serapion isn't impressed with the idea. Hell, he looks like he wishes his ears could spit, just to remove my words. "So that's a no, huh?"

"We'll manage without that. Now walk faster or it won't matter what happens to your foot."

We walk in silence, mostly. I'm still making groans and hisses, and muttering occasionally, but we don't talk. The more I walk, the more I wonder if I should've stayed where I was. Maybe this is a bad idea, and I should've stuck around so the doctor could look at my calf. I might be bleeding internally – what does that even feel like?

I can hear dogs barking in the distance, and my heart starts to pound like I'm already running away from them. Do they know we're here? Are they coming closer?

While I've been standing and trying to figure out which way to run, Serapion has kept on walking.

"Serapion," I say. "The dogs."

He stops for a second, and without turning around says "Don't worry about them. We've come to an understanding."

He starts walking again. I follow.

"What do you mean by an understanding? They're dogs."

"Probably smarter than you are, frankly, now come on."

So I come on. Once again, snow is pelting my face - harder now though, and with gusts that threaten to flatten me. I see faces in the swirling snow, and what looks like hands reaching out, before another gust blows them away.

We're almost back to the apartment, which has me scared. When things are in easy reach, that's when they get taken away from you – life has taught me that.

Rounding the corner, I can see the building now. Oh god, it's so close. Damn near want to cry with joy. But I don't, because I feel distinctly unwell. There's some sort of vertigo happening here; my vision is warping or something. The streets look like they're bending, rising up far away from me, and dropping down close by to me, like I'm at the bottom of some immense, shallow bowl.

"Keep going," says Serapion.

"Give me a second – I'm dizzy."

"No, you're not. What you're feeling is actually happening. Now keep going."

Easier said than done though – I feel like I'm at the bottom of a giant hamster ball, with the ground rolling under me, rather than me walking on it. Plus, if that's not bad enough, every time I blink or look around me, I lose that perspective and suddenly I feel like I'm at the top of the ball looking down and there's the sudden terror that I'm going to fall. I'd like to puke, but I don't know what direction to do it in.

I keep going though, slowly, clutching the curving side of a building, and inching my way along skewed sidewalks. What did he mean by that? This is actually happening? He couldn't have really meant it.

Of course he could. He's an angel; weird stuff orbits him.

It's tough going, the walk. Although nothing is moving under me, I feel like I'm walking the deck of a ship in a rough sea. There's no such thing as straight ahead anymore, and it isn't so much left and right, as clockwise and counter-clockwise. Serapion is striding along no problem. I'd ask him again to help me, but I already know what the answer would be.

I want to puke, but there's nothing in my stomach – fight down the urge, because I sure don't need dry heaves along with the rest of my problems.

Problems, yeah. I think another one just found me. Standing in what I think is the middle of the street, feet planted firmly, is the Yeller.

~~~~~ Chapter 13 ~~~~~

He's even bigger now, a damned giant, and his skin looks like polished obsidian. There's cracks in the skin, with brilliant light shining out through them. I can still tell it's the Yeller, though, because he points his finger at me and screams "Gimme!"

Well I'll be goddamned – looks like Serapion was right about him getting out of jail. Now I just have to make sure he doesn't get a hold of me, but running away from a fight is damn near impossible when you can't tell which direction you're running. And hell, I can barely stand.

He lets out a wordless scream, and all the black shreds off of him, just bursts away and flutters to the street like party streamers, little ribbons of black. Underneath it all, is another layer, like polished stone, golden, but not a metallic shine. It gleams – despite the overcast sun, it gleams like it's the hottest summer day.

His face, though, that's the biggest change, because it's not his face. Starting from the top of his shoulders, sweeping up the neck and over the entire head is a coating of fine, tight feathers. His chin, mouth and nose have been replaced with a sharp, hooked beak. The eyes are black and shiny, like oil.

He stands there, regally, staring at us with the haughty indifference of a hawk. And what do I do? Stand and gape. I know who that is, though knowing and believing what I see are two different things. He, the Yeller, is Horus, one of the old Egyptian gods.

When I was in my early teens, I used to take books out of the library, that my family would have considered contraband. Forbidden thinkers and forbidden thoughts. I read a lot of mythology, trying to figure out what made my religion different than the rest, how it could be more *right* than them.

150

The images of epic struggle always stuck with me, for whatever reason. Theseus fighting the Minotaur, or Thor and the Midgard Serpent. Horus fighting Seth.

In his hand, he has a curved sword, unadorned, but beautiful in simplicity. That can't be good.

"Run, Alex," yells Serapion. "Run until you need to throw up, then puke, then keep running." Just how the hell do I do that? I would try to - better believe I'm no hero, but I'm not exactly sure how or where I go right now. There's no such thing as straight ahead right now.

"Just hang on, and when the next wave of reality hits, go!" he yells, back over his shoulder at me, as he sprints at the Yeller, or Horus, or whatever that is. In his hand is a sword. I don't know where it came from, and I can guarantee I didn't see it earlier.

They crash together like a pair of sword-wielding freight trains. The sound is incredible, not just from its volume. It's like a thousand trumpets falling off a cliff onto the rocks below. It just keeps going on and on endlessly as they clash, spring apart and clash again. They're both chanting or singing or something, with voices like an earthquake colliding with a hurricane. Raw, elemental.

Slashing, parrying, wheeling around each other, all on a street turned inside out. I want to run, run and hide and shut my eyes and ears against what's happening around me, but I can't.

I don't know what way is up or down, can't find a straight line to walk, and just in front of me is a sword fight. I can't even tell how far away they are from me. Are they at the top of the bowl and I'm looking up at them, or are they on the bottom?

Either way, with no better alternative, I hide behind a trash can. It's solid and not moving. Holding on to it gives me a frame of reference to cling to.

The battle would almost be beautiful, if they weren't trying to kill each other. Neither seems to have any problem with the warped reality. Their movements are graceful – artistic, even.

It's obvious, though, that Serapion is being outclassed. Horus is driving him back with every strike, clearly putting him on the defensive. He just doesn't have the mojo.

Taking a chance, I pop my head up to take a look in the garbage can for a bottle or something like that. All I can see is a thick covering of snow. I could dig through it, but that'd mean standing up, and right now hiding is the best thing for me.

And then, I'm aware of my pocket. My attention is drawn there, suddenly, and irresistibly so. It's a feeling of disconnection, as I watch my hand dip into my pocket without my bidding, and pull out a brass ashtray. Claire's, yeah.

Perfect.

With a shout, I stand up and before the vertigo hits, I fling the ashtray at Horus, watching it fly straight and true, like some sort of ninja throwing star or something.

I was never an athlete, so it's gratifying to watch it go right at its target.

It hits. Serapion. Right in the back of his head. Right dead center. It ricochets off somewhere.

He wheels around to face the new threat, only to see me, standing there, still gaping like an idiot.

"Stupid moron," he yells. Horus takes advantage of the distraction, knocks him aside and runs at me, sword held aloft for the killing blow. I'm frozen to the spot, not like I could outrun him anyway.

I can see Serapion behind him, calling out, hand outstretched and arm held high.

Then I can't see anything at all, because my world is filled with the lightning bolt he's called down. My eyes are stunned, my ears deafened, and all I can do is squat down and clutch the trash can for dear life.

Helpless as a newborn kitten, that's me. However, it occurs to me that I'm not dead, which means that Serapion's lightning hit its target.

My sight slowly returns, though I've still got an afterimage of Horus being blasted with lightning – from his body language, I'd say it came as a surprise. I hope that's temporary, because as satisfying as the moment was, I'm not interested in looking at it for the rest of my life.

The good news is that reality is back to being, well, real. Normal, that is. The street is flat, the grey sky is overhead, and I'm standing steady. "Glad that's over," I say.

"Won't last long," says Serapion. He's standing over the corpse of Horus, or, what used to be Horus, sprawled out in the wintry street – it's the Yeller again, though now he's naked, burnt in places, and still smoking. "That was a tough one."

"That was a tough *what*?"

"It would take too long to explain. C'mon, we need to get you to your apartment. Now."

It doesn't take any convincing. As fast as I can, I sprint off down the street. I call it a sprint, but really it's a part stagger, part limp, and not at all fast. The apartment is close though, very close. Serapion strides along beside me.

"Keep going," he says, giving me as hard a push as he can without knocking me over. "I'll catch up." He turns away, still wielding his sword, and I don't stop to ask questions.

Stepping inside the building is like flipping a switch or something. It's instantly calm, peaceful, serene. Reality is strong inside here. I guess Serapion was right about Beaudry's magic. I look around, hoping to see some evidence of it – whatever magic looks like.

The lobby is empty. Almost clean too, which is weird to see, almost unnerving. Magic, I suppose.

Oh God I feel like shit. Count it up. In the last few days, I've had a pack of dogs run me ragged, had one of them chew on my leg for a while, had two people try to kill me, sat on an ice floe for hours, and had a maniac wrestle me to the ground. I've barely eaten, haven't had nearly enough cigarettes, haven't been high in a week, haven't slept. Been seeing things, hearing things. Everything hurts, everything is tired.

And now I have to face the goddamn stairs.

I start climbing. They were bad enough when I was walking down them, and walking up is ten times worse.

Every damn step is a misery. Ain't the first time I've wished I lived on the first floor, but this time it isn't laziness or drunkenness that is the problem. My calf is throbbing mercilessly now. Each time I put even a little weight on it, a spear of pain runs up my leg, squeezing a groan and a hiss from me. Step with the good, drag the bad leg, repeat. Rest at each landing, staring up the impossibly high stairwell.

Stupid stairs. Fucking elevator. Goddamn everything. Next time, God, could you send an elevator repairman instead of a guardian angel?

The thought makes me laugh. That could almost sound like a prayer if I rephrased it a little. Am I religious again? All my life, I've wanted some sign that God is really out there, that all the bullshit from my family wasn't just wishful thinking.

And now, I've got it. Now what? Start going to church again? No, can't stand those assholes. Go see Claire and apologize for everything I've ever said to her? Yeah, probably. After that, I've got a lot of thinking to do.

Reach the fourth floor and stumble out into the hallway. Bleak, poorly lit, with a carpet that looks like they drive trucks up and down on it. Limp, limp, limp to my door.

I get to rest my forehead against the door while I fish for my key and slot it into the lock.

Home. Is there any more wonderful word in the whole messed up world?

I open my apartment door, shuffle in, and stop dead in my tracks. Suddenly, my heart is hammering away in my ribcage, and my whole body is shaking, like I'm running all over again. There's something in my apartment and it isn't human, and that means something else wants to kill me.

Trying to scramble backwards out the door, and not having a lot of success doing so as I bang my head against the doorframe. "Dumb-ass," I hear Serapion mutter. He pushes past me into the room, obviously not perturbed by the stranger, or in any hurry to protect me. There's steam rising from his overcoat.

"Jerkoff," I mumble, rubbing the sore spot on the back of my head. He ignores me, choosing instead to stand beside … whoever or whatever it is in my apartment.

"Hey Alex," says Serapion. "Meet my boss. Alex, human and low-life waste of skin, meet Michael, Archangel and General in command of the armies of God." Important people know my name – I've never liked when that happens. Always spells trouble for me.

He's impossibly tall, which makes me think that heaven must have an awesome basketball team. But, although his general shape is human, it's just … wrong. It is a caricature of humanity – shoulders too broad, chest too thin, limbs too long, fingers and neck way too long. The effect is more spidery and angular than ethereal. His skin is unlike the skin of any creature I've ever seen and the clothing, it's like something imagined by someone who's never worn any.

Plus I feel cheated that there's no halo or wings. Yeah, I know it's stupid, but that's what comes to mind. I don't want a science-fiction alien, I want an *angel*.

Michael looks way down at me. I can't tell what he's thinking, because his face is so damn weird – there's just not enough in common with humanity for any insight. The chin and cheekbones almost form a sharp triangle. No eyebrows to speak of, no lips, and human eyes just don't have a lustre like that.

In any event, I don't appear to be important enough to talk to, and the archangel turns away from me.

My cat, my talking cat is back, sitting on the end table next to the phone, in the middle of what looks like a staring contest with Michael. I feel an urge to tell him not to bother – you just can't win against a cat. I know that for a fact. Just when I'm about to open my mouth, I catch a glimpse of Serapion. He's shaking his head at me, telling me not to.

"You see the cat too?" I ask.

Serapion nods.

"That's good. I thought I was hallucinating."

"In a way, you are," he says. "That's not a cat."

Right then, keep my damn distance from the cat too. I keep my back against the wall as I edge my way to the couch. Do I want to sit on my couch? That puts me pretty close to Michael, and maybe it'd be better to be in a more mobile position.

The cat takes a break from staring, turning to fix me with its yellow eyes – "I see you still didn't take my advice."

I shrug. "Hey, you weren't the one who got me away from the cops, or saved me from being spitted by a sword."

"Again, Alex, you're thinking like a dog."

I still don't get it. Fine. Enough with the cat.

"So," I say to tall, light and unnatural. "What brings you into town?" He ignores me.

"Not the friendly type, I take it," I say.

"Don't talk to him. He's an archangel. You should be grateful he decided to manifest as something vaguely human."

"Emphasis on vague."

Serapion shrugs. "Could have been worse; could have been visited by the Angel of Death."

"Yeah? What's his name?"

"Cheryl."

I cough. "What?"

He rolls his eyes. "Alex, you astound me at how gullible you are."

I flip him the finger, and head to the writing room. They can stay in the living room. Michael and Serapion can get sore asses from my very lumpy couch. If they don't like it, they can get me a new one.

Sit at my desk and ignore the whole damned divine lot of them. Roll a fresh piece of paper into the typewriter, and start working. I wish the chair faced away from the door, so that they could all just kiss my ass.

Surprise, surprise, the words flow. Channel all the crap I'm dealing with into my writing, all the pain, the fear, all of that, and something amazing happens. One little word emerges from all of that, something that has been missing all this time – hope. This is almost over, the whole ordeal. The key will be gone, no longer driving me crazy. Serapion will be out of my life, and the cat, and Michael. Back to real life and sanity for me.

Hope is what has been missing, from my life, my attitude and my script. My characters, they all trudged through their roles, hopeless, goddamn cardboard cut-outs. Even Pandora still had hope left to her, after she had released all the evils onto the world.

I know I can't fix it all right now, but it's a good start. Yeah. Dig dig dig through the pages stacked up, looking for those little moments. Find it, cross it out with a pencil. Hell with it, crumple the page into a ball and retype from scratch. There's more, but that can wait. Yeah, inspiration hits like a bomb. Scramble to light a cigarette, suck back the smoke and away I go again. If my chair was a car, I'd be laying down rubber as I pull out at full speed.

The sound of the keys drowns out anything my uninvited visitors might be saying, which is fine by me. Another page done in record time, and a second sheet rolled in and ready to go. It's good this time, really good stuff, not just me being caught up in the moment again.

"Alex," says the cat. Sitting at the threshold of the door.

Turn and glare, don't say a word. Bad enough when somebody interrupts my train of thought when things aren't going well. Even worse when I'm having my best writing moment in months, years. Right off the scale of annoying when the interrupter isn't even human.

The cat is unfazed. "Last chance, Alex." I'm about to ask what it's talking about, but before I do, Serapion boots the cat sideways, and closes the door behind him as he enters the room. What the hell? I don't really like animals, but I'm not into just kicking them at random either.

"We need to talk."

"Just give me an hour or so to get everything on paper, and I'll be thrilled to talk with you about whatever you want."

Serapion shakes his head. "No, we don't have that luxury right now. Remember when I said it's easier for me to do my job if you know a little about what's happening? Well, this is another one of those times."

There's a level of seriousness on his face that I haven't seen before – yeah, okay, so he isn't exactly a bundle of laughs, but this is something else. Fine, let him say what he wants so I can get back to my work. Fish out another cigarette, light it and lean back. "Okay, what's on your mind?"

He just stands there for a second, silent, motionless. From the living room comes an explosion and a shockwave that ripples through the floor. I can see a brilliant flash of light through the transom window over the door.

My hands are frozen to the arms of my chair, and the cigarette is dangling loosely from the edge of my lip. All I can do is stammer. The door opens and Michael comes in, the smell of burnt cat hair drifting in with him. Serapion pushes the door closed behind him.

"What the hell? Just what the hell was that? Did your friend just kill a cat in my living room?"

Serapion certainly doesn't look apologetic, and Michael, well, who knows what his face means. Nobody seems perturbed about it, except for me.

"Yeah," he says. "About that. We couldn't come to an agreement on certain issues."

"So you fried it? What the hell happened out there? What's going on?" I would try and sound casual if I could, but they aren't making it easy. The way they're standing, it's like I'm facing a giant wall. Neither looks particularly friendly ... or, I should say, they look more unfriendly than previously so.

"It's the end of the line, Alex. We are swiftly approaching the point where the key needs to be used."

"That's great. Thanks for telling me. Now you can just go back to my living room and maybe not shoot lightning bolts at anything. Couldn't we wait out the deadline like that? Like counting down to the New Year? Everybody could have party hats and champagne."

Serapion shrugs. "We're not going to be doing that, Alex. We need the key."

I can't even speak, nothing but a little cough escapes.

He continues. "Nothing personal, you understand. Strategically, this is an important place. God has had an okay run for the last six thousand years, but things aren't so good these days. We suspect we're going to lose our access to this reality soon – used to be He did miracles, and now the best you see is images of Jesus in a grilled cheese sandwich. If we want to dominate here for the next few thousand years, we're going to need to pour in troops like never before."

"But what about protecting me?" I sputter.

"My duty was to the key. Keeping you alive was just a side effect, to your benefit."

157

"What's going to happen to me?" I'm having visions of a key in a car ignition, or something. Maybe it'll do all sorts of things to me, turning me inside out or burning its way free. Unpleasant things.

"You're going to die, so that we can have the key."

My mouth gapes open wider, and the cigarette falls. Burns my hand as it bounces, but it barely registers with me. "My God, why?

"Because we need it, and that's how we get it. Why do you care, Alex? What possible reason could you have to give a damn about what happens?"

"You're talking about killing me. You told me yourself that you can't just use it without killing me."

Serapion snorts. "What's the big deal? You won't feel a thing - dead before you know it. And then, oblivion, nothing. No pain, no want, no fear. You've been hunting for that for so long that I don't understand why you're fighting it now. You won't be missed and you won't be noticed."

"And after I'm gone, what happens? You've got the key, and then what?"

Serapion shrugs again. "Right here, it's going to be Ground Zero for a battle of truly godly proportion. Earth is going to be gutted – not right away, although there's going to be a very hefty decline in the standard of living coming up as troops start massing and the skirmishes start. We're determined to keep ahold of this place, no matter the cost."

I'm gulping like a fish pulled from the water.

It's a good thing I'm sitting, because I'd have fallen to the floor otherwise. All this time, I've been trotting around with someone whose job was to make sure that the *right* people killed me. I'm the butcher's pet lamb, avoiding the wolves while following him to the chopping block.

So, I'm going to die. Sure, I would eventually, and most probably from something I inhaled, injected or contracted. By contrast, perhaps dying quietly in my apartment isn't such a bad thing. Less ignominious. Michael grasps and draws on the hilt of a sword. It ain't like he's wearing a scabbard on a belt – he just reaches out, and there it is.

I recognize it. Oh God, I've seen it before, in my dreams. Same sword, same flames licking up the length of the blade and for damn sure the same spidery hand on the hilt.

Just like in my dream, it scares the crap out of me on sight.

Run, my instincts scream, and my body obeys, leaping out of the chair and sprinting for the door. Serapion sidesteps, a goddamn monolith blocking my path. I try to dodge around, he sidesteps again. I'm sure my calf is hurting, but I don't feel it.

I spin around, looking for another way out in my panic. There isn't, of course. There's the door I came in through, and the window with a sheer drop below, and that's it. Oh God, my heart is beating so hard, it hurts. Everything hurts. Oh my God.

The transom over the door, maybe I could climb … The thought doesn't have a chance to finish before I shoot it down. Serapion would yank me back before I was half-way through.

"Just sit down, Alex," says Serapion. "You're not going anywhere."

"No!" I yell, and seize my typewriter. It's big, it's metal, and built like a tank. With a grunt, I throw it at Michael.

The archangel doesn't flinch, barely seems to notice what's happening, until he pops the tip of his sword up and parries it out of the air. His motion is diffident, almost negligent, but bats the typewriter aside like it was a cardboard box.

It skitters across the floor, in a half-dozen pieces, coming to rest against the wall. Man, I'm going to miss it. That typewriter was as close as I've had to a constant friend for a decade or more. Small tendrils of smoke drift off the parts.

Michael casually props his sword against the bedroom door. Even if I could make it past the two of them, I'd have to haul a piece of flaming metal out of the way with my bare hands. I'm trapped. There's a line from the Book of Genesis that pops into my head unbidden, of Michael using his flaming sword to bar Adam and Eve from the Garden of Eden. I find myself empathizing with them in a way that nobody else could ever match.

"We're almost there, Alex," says Serapion. "There's a right time and a wrong time to do this, and it's very close."

"So what's going to happen?" I ask, though I'm pretty sure what he means.

Michael opens his mouth and speaks and it's the sound of a hundred singers, all in exultation. It is beautiful, incredibly beautiful, so much that I'm almost knocked to my knees by it. "We will free the key from its prison, and take it for ourselves."

That's me then, the prison.

Stagger back to my chair and grope for it like a blind man. Half sit, half collapse into it. Most of my script is scattered on the floor. I want to pick it up, protect it like it was my baby, but my legs are still wobbly. If I made it down to the floor, I wouldn't be getting up again for a while, and time is in very short supply all of a sudden.

It hits me again – I'm about to die, and I'm staring face-to-face with my murderers. I want to cry for all the things I haven't done, but the tears don't come. Who am I kidding? This is a fucked up life I live, and there wasn't much I was going to do with it anyway. There's no tears, because there's nothing worth crying about.

"Okay, Alex, it's just about time. Do you want to go out like a man, or will I have to hold you down?"

He and I both know it wouldn't be a struggle. Even in what passed for my prime, well fed and dried out, how the hell do I win a wrestling match with an angel? Really now.

"Yeah," I say. "Just make it quick. No farting around, okay?"

Serapion nods.

Beaudry, I think, *Wherever the hell you are, a hearty fuck you from me. Was there nothing else you could've done?*

I shrug to myself. He was desperate, and more than just a little crazy. No big surprise that I got screwed over. Why should that have been any different from everything else in my life?

Michael says "it is time." He steps past the wreckage that used to be my beloved typewriter, and picks up his sword.

"Okay, Alex, stand up," says Serapion. He's between the door and me and even without the sword in the way, making a break for it would end quickly and badly. Doesn't matter, I'm not going to try it. Least I can do is die with a shred of dignity.

So I stand. My legs hold me, but just barely.

I can see through the window now, not that there's much to see. It looks out onto the alley, and a blank wall directly across the way, seen through grimy glass. The sunlight is shining through the dirt as best it can – probably the first sunny day I've seen in a month.

And the last one I'll see in my life. My God, it's a beautiful day to die.

A shudder runs up my spine, and my breath catches in my throat for a second. Swallowing hard, and taking a moment to regain whatever composure I can hang onto, I let the air out of my lungs in a rush.

"Okay, let's do this thing then." My voice is, thankfully, steady. I wasn't sure it would be, afraid that it would crack like I was going through puberty again. If they're going to be my last words, they can at least not embarrass me.

Serapion nods, and Michael moves near me. His feet still don't make a sound – it's the rising heat at my back that tells me.

"It's been good working with you," says Serapion.

"Just shut the fuck up," I say.

"Yeah," he says. "Sorry." I'm surprised - he sounds genuinely chastened.

The heat rises another couple of notches, I guess as Michael raises his sword for the killing blow. I can see my shadow on the wall ahead of me, made orange by the blue flames.

This is the world ends, and not just for me. I figure I'll feel a brief pain and then, what? Oblivion, hopefully? Better not be an afterlife, because I don't think that would be an improvement on the present one.

Definitely I'm not praying, not for forgiveness, not for absolution, not for a goddamn thing from a betraying god worshipped by generations of my family.

The rest of the world, though, has no idea what is about to hit it. What I've been going through is about to be reflected in the lives of every man, woman and child on Earth. All the pain, the misery, fear and panic. All of that and more, before finally the planet is destroyed, along with everybody on it.

And then, I realize something. Just like the sunlight that popped out through the clouds, it hits me: Serapion was lying to me. Again. He can't hold me down. He can't stop me. He can't interfere with the stupid decisions I make, any of them. I have free will.

I have free will.

I can do whatever I want to.

So I run, straight ahead, yelling like a berserker. Yeah.

"Stop him," commands Michael, in that beautiful voice.

"I can't," answers Serapion.

My outstretched hands hit the window and smash through, jagged points ripping the skin. A fraction of a second behind it is my face blasting out whatever is left of the glass.

There's pain, and blood, but I don't care. Wouldn't matter if I did anyway. I'm airborne now – nothing left to do but fall.

My arms and legs windmill like a pantomime of swimming. Below me are four storeys of empty space, and then an alleyway strewn with garbage and snow – not enough to break my fall, hopefully.

Shards of glass hang in the air around me as I fall. Looks like Galileo was right about that. Funny what goes through your mind.

I'm tumbling, head over heels. Michael and Serapion come into view briefly. I think Serapion is calling me an asshole, but it's hard to tell. I would laugh at him if I had enough time.

I see the pavement rushing up to catch me. God, I don't want to linger. I don't want to lie there with my back broken, unable to move.

I don't want Michael to stand over me with his sword, my sacrifice in vain.

Don't think I will, though. It's a long way down, and I'm not that healthy. I hope my sexy paramedic isn't the one who has to deal with me. I'd rather that if she ever thinks of me again, it's as some funny, cute guy she helped one morning.

There's sudden regret. Nobody will know. Life will go on. My body will be discovered eventually, and when they open my apartment, they'll find a broken typewriter, an unfinished script and a shattered window.

"Failed playwright commits suicide in fit of depression" – the headline will read, assuming my death is considered noteworthy enough to make it into the newspaper that day.

Claire will blame herself for not saving me, or my soul, but that's about it. Saves the world, and all he'll get is his sister at his funeral. But, I saved the world. Lots of people do nothing with their lives, or like me, totally screw them up. I fucked up everything else but in the end, how many people can honestly say they did what I did?

I saved the world.